The Custodians

Library of Congress Control Number: 2023946264

ISBN (paperback): 978-1-956450-87-3
ISBN (Ebook): 978-1-956450-88-0

Thousand Acres is an imprint of Armin Lear Press, Inc.
215 W Riverside Drive, #4362
Estes Park, CO 80517

The
Custodians

Jacalyn S. Burke

This book is dedicated to my mother Vincente Martinez

Acknowledgments

I would like to thank my family for their continued support throughout the writing of this book, and in particular, my wife Kate Fitzgerald for her tireless proof-reading, endless patience and artfully articulated plot suggestions. Integral to this project is Seth Parks, the book's excellent editor who lived vicariously through the characters and helped me to shape them further. I thank Ann Aptaker, Todd Komarnicki and the late Marie Morreale for teaching me how authors ought to act. In addition, I thank the team at Small Agency Pete and Maggie Savage for their vision and artistic wizardry.

I wish to thank Maryann Karinch my wonderful publisher, agent and mentor who has opened every door and kept my feet firmly planted on the ground. I thank Creator God for everything I have achieved and the countless kind and gracious people who have eased my path, as part of his plan. I must give high praise and gratitude to Kaya Usher, my friend, fellow traveler and teacher in this journey called Life. And finally, dear reader, I want to thank you for choosing to read this book and for spending a little time in my world.

Her (1)

Somewhere in Southwest France, time unknown

It was blackout dark.

She preferred the darkness.

Every now and then, candle light fingered along the walls towards her. But that light brought a horror beyond words. Something that could not be seen and survived.

So she had learned from the beginning to close her eyes, and to think of a moment from her past. Until the pain and the stench made her pass out.

How could it have come to this?

Just a short time ago she had been on holiday with …

Her husband. Yes, she has a husband.

Had a husband.

Dead.

She had wiped the details of his death from her mind but one image remained. Imprinted on the backs of her eyelids. A bloodied corpse strung up like a pig gutted in an abattoir. Entrails and shattered rib bones, quivering muscles but nothing that spoke to the man that she had loved.

A carcass that was bled and devoured.

Nearby

A small village in Rousinac, Southwest France 2019

Midnight.

It was an old church, ten a penny and in ruins; closed due to costly repairs. But on this night four cars occupied its curb. Inside the chapel room sat a small group: three men and a woman. An elderly man spoke, gesturing with a book. Holding it up. Eyeing it.

Everyone listened besides one man. He kept looking at the exit wanting to run. Only he couldn't. Like the others, there was nothing he could do but listen.

Finally the old man stopped talking.

Running his eyes over each face until he got an affirmative nod, he reached Didier Perodeau. For a few hard seconds Didier avoided the old man's stare. Then one by one he felt the room pressing in on him.

"I know what needs to be done," was all he said.

Across from the church, same time.

A local, Suzanne Prevat had seen the lights in the church but it hadn't struck her as odd. Freemasons sometimes used the chapel as a meeting place.

She'd been at a cousin's birthday dinner that had strayed a little too late.

"Let me give you a ride home … please," her cousin begged as he trailed her out into the night.

"I'll be home before you get that old car started."

"But it's late."

"I know, but look at that moon. It's as bright as day out here and …" She'd almost mentioned the lights. But he was already looking at the church, then to the cars. She knew what he was thinking.

"Suzanne, wait …"

"No. You've had too much to drink. Go to bed."

Louie Menard stumbled back inside to grab his car keys then searched for his cousin in the yard. But she had already disappeared through the bushes and beyond into hidden fields. He frowned, and spat on the ground.

"Merde!"

The trail that cut through a farmer's field of sunflowers was the type only a villager would know. Suzanne had walked this path since childhood. It had once led to her grandmother's cottage.

Above her, the moon shone so bright the grass glowed. It would have been a beautiful night for anyone other than a local of Rousinac.

Suzanne could see nothing but an illuminated lane ahead, on the other side of the field.

Get there.

Fast.

Quietly.

She was halfway across the field when something made her slow. Someone else was in the field, watching her. But where? The field fell silent. Suzanne strained to catch a sound, anything that could point to where they were.

Nothing.

Then.

Crack!

A sunflower stalk snapped.

She turned in its direction and saw ...

Shadows.

Run!

NOW!

She bolted.

They came crashing after her through the sunflowers, from all directions. The air stunk like carrion.

Them.

She ran so fast, her feet barely touched the ground. Her head thundering with condemnation.

Idiot – idiot!

Why did I offer to clean up?

She was a local. She knew the rules. The party had gone on and on. Too much booze.

Stupid.

It was late.

You never cut through the fields at night. You stuck to the roads where the mauve lights shone.

Putain!

"Help! HELP!"

She exploded through the hedgerow, into the lane. A light popped on ahead. A neighbor was on his porch.

"Jean-Pierre!"

She made it to his door and he pulled her inside.

"Who is it, Jean-Pierre?"

Someone called from upstairs.

Ignoring his wife, the man picked up his rifle and a flashlight.

It shone the same mauve as the street lamps.

"Let's go."

They walked to Suzanne's home in silence. It was understood.

They were locals.

The Tourists (1)
Rousinac, Southwest France 2019

A vintage Mercedes ripped down a highway, carrying a British couple in their early forties. He was handsome and dark. She was blonde and beautiful.

The driver's shirt hung loosely at the waist, unbuttoned at his neck. Casual slacks and loafers gave him the appearance of someone content and relaxed, but neither was true.

Tom Grayston was in fact burdened by a terrible secret.

Every now and then he looked at his wife, asleep, and his mind drifted back to the week before when she'd proposed this trip.

The week before.

"Oh Tom, Tom!"

"Yes?"

"I think I've found it. Listen to this. Large house. Holiday rental. Rousinac, Southwest France available August. Three bedrooms; all amenities; beautiful views, remote location.' The price is ridiculously low. What do you think?"

"How low?"

"What do you think?"

"Tell me more."

"Rousinac is a medieval town with a castle. Look!" She snatched up her device, running a finger across the screen. Two photographs loaded and a map.

"They're all black and white." Tom noted.

"Let me try again." She added "2019" to the search criteria but the results were the same.

"Huh."

"Bring up a map."

"Okay."

"Wow, look at that forest. That's a lot of trees."

"That's what makes it remote."

"Do you want to go somewhere that remote?" He countered.

"Why not? Off the beaten track. That's good, isn't it?"

"Would explain the low price I suppose."

Now, as he drove with his sleeping wife beside him, he wondered if he had made the right decision.

Do I tell her here?

The thought jackhammered until he exited the motorway, and the main road thinned into a web of twisting lanes.

Hours passed.

He took a few wrong turns. The thought faded, blistered by a need to focus on their route. Eventually Tom found Rousinac.

It hadn't been easy.

Once he'd entered an enormous forest that walled in the town, he'd lost all Wi-Fi. The Sat-Nav kept trying to turn him around, but all the road signs pointed in the opposite direction.

ROUSINAC.

He reached the town just after 4pm.

It was a pretty little town, but utterly deserted.

Odd for a sunny day.

There were signs of a population, cars parked bumper to bumper, rows of well-kept shops, a couple of bars and restaurants off the promenade, shutters open but he didn't see a soul.

Tom turned to the castle.

Rousinac was a fortified town dominated by a massive castle. It was breathtaking, towering over the surrounding buildings. He glanced at a plaque dedicated to the castle's history and deciphered the French.

"Installed upon a rocky mount, Rousinac castle's foundation was constructed in 1111 AD on Roman temple ruins. The site had been occupied for ceremonial use since prehistoric times. The rock contains a network of naturally-occurring tunnels that run deep into the surrounding forest, once a part of Queen Eleanor's estate. The castle was transformed in the 14th century to its present glory to house the Merovingian royal dynasty. Rousinac has withstood centuries of war and invasion, and prevailed. Our motto is *Sanguis, Sanguis. Totus est* (Blood is Blood. That is All)."

The last sentence struck him as bizarre.

There was nothing much about the town online but apparently it had been the seat of one of the most powerful royal families in European history?

Seriously?

Perplexed, Tom drove around the one road that circled the castle until he spied a sign for his holiday home's hamlet: Chemin de Perodeau. Out of curiosity he drove around the town again. All nine roads out of Rousinac pointed to a single destination, a village he presumed.

He eyed a street map, and noticed that the nine roads were perfectly aligned equi-distant to one another forming what appeared to be rays out of a sphere. The castle was situated at the dead center of the sphere, the rock mount.

He looked in his rear mirror and saw a man striding towards the car.

His eyes fixed on Tom.

He suddenly felt uneasy.

Where were all the tourists?

Tom pulled away with such force that Catherine stirred but she didn't wake, until they'd reached their destination.

"We're here, sweetheart."

Catherine Grayston stretched awake,

"Huh?"

"Chemin de Perodeau."

She looked about. They were on a dirt road lined by thick, black woodland. Ahead in the clearing stood a large gray house.

"What's the guy's name again; the owner?" Tom asked.

"Didier Perodeau." She replied.

"It's weird."

"What is?"

"That he's not here to take the money. He just mailed the keys?"

Catherine nodded.

"Don't you think that's weird?"

"Maybe they're more trusting in this country? He did say that his neighbor, Patrick Clayburn was close by if we needed anything."

"So where is this elusive Didier Perodeau?" Tom pressed.

"He's out of the country. I told you that already. Honestly sometimes I wonder if you listen to a word I say." Catherine snapped.

Tom shrugged, "Still weird."

As they climbed out of the Mercedes, the car's air conditioning evaporated. The late afternoon heat closed in, and a smell of damp earth filled the air. Catherine looked back up the lane, now hidden by a clutch of trees.

She turned to the house.

Her eyes fixed on its windows.

They were black, as though the whole house was black inside. The setting sun was picking out the trees, but not the windows. And there were no birds. No sounds of nature. Everything was eerily silent.

It was a strange thought.

Tom looked from her eyes to the house, then back again. She held his gaze.

Did he feel it too?

"It's cold. Maybe it will rain tonight." He said as he turned away.

"You get the door. I'll bring in the cases."

She felt the key in her hand but couldn't move.

"Catherine?"

His voice broke the spell and she moved towards the front door.

He stood and watched her. She looked magnificent in this light.

When do I tell her what I've done?

The Tourists (2)
Rousinac, Southwest France 2019

Bleach.

The house stunk of bleach but it barely masked another smell.

What was it?

Drains?

No, that wasn't it.

Something else, musty like an old church.

Graveyard.

She opened a couple of the windows.

"Shit!" Tom almost fell over.

"You okay?" Catherine called out.

"Tripped on the rug. It's so dark in here."

"I'll put on some lights."

Catherine fumbled for a switch.

Tom explored the downstairs rooms.

"There's an open fireplace in the living room. It's seen better days but it's still nice."

Catherine made it to the base of the stairs, at the far end of the hallway. She was relieved he hadn't noticed the smell.

She turned on the upstairs lights and climbed to the second floor. Tom followed, carrying their luggage.

"Wow, wooden floors. Everything's immaculate."

Tom was drawn toward a bay window that overlooked the garden. Catherine peered over his shoulder.

"Look at that. The forest completely encircles the house." He said in a whisper.

"Let's check out the bedrooms." Catherine suggested but Tom continued to gaze into the garden.

It's just forest. Miles of … forest.

"Two bedrooms en suite and a master bedroom here at the end."

She lingered in a doorway, "The bed's enormous."

Tom hesitated before turning to her. "Shall I take one of the smaller rooms?"

Catherine blinked in disbelief.

"What?"

Tom shrugged.

"It's just that I've slept in the spare room for … and I didn't want to presume."

"That's always been your decision. It was never what *I wanted.*"

Her insistence surprised him. Nothing more was said as Tom put his case silently down next to hers in the master bedroom.

Sleep escaped them both on that first night. They were city-dwellers used to the constant hum of traffic. Here, it was so still, it felt as though the world had been paused.

Then there was the intimacy of sharing a bed. Tom tossed and turned, trying to avoid an accidental touch of his wife. Catherine lay motionless as she chased random thoughts.

Around them, the house creaked like an old barge. The captured heat of the day crept out of its timbers, releasing odd noises. Catherine longed to hear people talking, a car alarm, anything that would normalize this primordial darkness. Instead, she heard fluttering wings, rustling in the skirting boards, and the padding of paws on the roof.

Could Tom hear these noises too?

She turned toward her husband, but he lay motionless. Catherine checked her phone. Dawn was just a few hours away.

The bedroom's windows and shutters had been left open to let in the night air. As she closed her eyes a noise startled her. Something was moving around on the stone drive below.

She reached for her husband. "T–"

But she stopped herself midway. He broke into a snore, then fell silent again.

Did we lock everything up? Catherine thought about the car.

She turned to her side of the bed. Feet planted on the floor she swung upright, listening. Whatever was out there had stopped moving.

Had it heard her?

A mosquito buzzed around her head. Swatting it shook the bed. Her husband mumbled something in his sleep.

Should I wake him?

She thought better of it and stood up. Her knees cracked. Tom slept on.

Her attention was drawn to another sound but it was not as close. It came from the forest to the left of the house. Something was moving in the undergrowth.

Was there more than one?

Catherine crept nearer the window. Something rustled below the bedroom window. She peered out.

Silence.

There was nothing out there, just a mass of blackness. Catherine closed the window and went back to bed, eventually drifting off. But the sounds from the garden penetrated her dreams. Something watched her from afar. Shadows chased her through the trees. Her sleep was fitful, hollowed out by nightmares.

Morning eventually arrived and with it an aroma of bacon. She leaned out of bed and pushed open the shutters. The garden was an eruption of greenery, covered in morning dew. It was beautiful but her body was still jittery from the nightmare.

Hot shower.

She made for the bathroom.

The house was still cool from the night air, and her feet tingled on the bathroom tiles. She caught a quick glance of herself in the mirror.

Her eyes looked dull.

Am I sad?

Ignoring the questions, she took a shower.

"Good morning lazy bones, one egg or two?" Tom asked as Catherine walked into the kitchen. A good night's sleep had transformed her husband. He already looked more relaxed, younger.

"Well?" he added more forcefully.

"Just the one," she said, yawning. "Do you need some help?"

"No, go and sit down and I'll bring it over," he ordered. "Do you want tea or coffee?"

"Tea, I think. Have you been up long?"

"About an hour. You were out for the count when I left," he winked.

"I think it was almost daylight before I nodded off." She added, loitering by the door, but her husband didn't respond.

Catherine went to the dining room and slumped into one of the tapestry woven chairs. Tom's bustle in the kitchen reminded her of when they were first married. He loved cooking in those days. She missed those evenings when he would wine and dine her.

He hasn't touched me in months.

There it was.

The truth.

Tom's voice rang out above the blare of a boiling kettle. It shook her out of the thought.

"What shall we do today?"

Without waiting for an answer, he continued, "how about a nice walk?"

"Maybe."

"Well, what would you like to do then?"

There was an unnatural pause.

"A walk sounds nice."

She's sad.

He thought, turning back to the stove. The heaviness was back. Reaching for a plate, he began thinking about his life and what it had become. He peered at his wife through the opening. She had barely changed over the years. Her blue eyes, blonde hair, and white skin continued to call something forth in him.

But the chasm between them seemed unfathomable and Tom knew that the root of the problem lay with him. He had put off his confession for months, postponing the inevitability of Catherine's pain.

But now …

They ate breakfast almost in silence.

Tom pretended to check his work emails and Catherine mindlessly thumbed through a holiday guide. He asked her a few times how the eggs were. The eggs were good. The toast was good. The tea was hot enough. He felt like he was slowly going mad. There was so much to say and no way of saying it.

After breakfast they took a walk into the forest that bordered the rental. They followed one of the dirt trails left by hunters. The brush throbbed with grasshoppers and an odd musk pervaded the woods. It reminded her of the smell in the house.

"What do you think that smell is?" She asked.

"What, here?"

"Yes."

"Probably a dead animal or something marking its territory."

"It's in the house too. Did you notice?"

"I think the plumbing's old, although ..."

"What?"

"I poked about in the garden this morning and at the back of the house are some old sewers. They jut right out of the ground, big as tunnels. The gates are open. It could be that. I could close them later."

"Tunnels?"

"Sewers, tunnels."

"Where do you think they lead?"

"No idea. Probably to some communal drain. But they reek, so I wouldn't want to find out."

They walked quietly for a while. Catherine was struggling to find things to say. For Tom it was agonizing.

"Did you hear any strange noises last night?" She asked.

"What do you mean?"

"Out of the ordinary?"

"An owl. Yes, I heard an owl. An owl." His answer sounded unnatural, and he caught himself.

"Why, what did you hear?"

"I'm not sure."

"Maybe it was a dream? You probably sleep deeper here."

"Maybe," she said under her breath.

He declined to mention the smashed terracotta planter he had cleaned up from the porch that morning. Whatever had tipped it over must have been big. He didn't want to worry her.

"I can't believe how quiet it is," Tom observed. Then a crow squawked above them and he jumped. Catherine giggled. He watched as she transformed into the girl he had fallen in love with.

In the old days he would have slipped his arm casually around her waist and pulled her in for a kiss. It was natural to be that assertive. Catherine loved that aspect of him. Now he stood impotent, watching her as she walked on ahead.

The Graystons followed a shaft of sunlight until it led to a clearing. At the wood's edge was a field of sunflowers.

"They look so beautiful on postcards but close up, they're quite …. creepy."

"How can flowers be creepy?" Tom smirked.

"They look like . . . dried corpses."

Without warning, Tom darted into the field and disappeared. Catherine traced his movements as the flower heads wobbled. Undergrowth crackled beneath his feet.

Then there was stillness. After a few seconds Catherine called out.

"Where are you?"

Tom's face appeared between two flowers.

"Boo!"

"Stop it for God's sake!"

"What's going on? You're a bag of nerves." Tom reached out to her.

"That wasn't funny." She shrank back.

"Okay. Let's go."

They trekked along a calcaire track through patchwork fields. Many of them were fallow, a mess of wild flowers. Tom wondered about that. It captured his focus.

Why aren't they growing things?

Every now and then they would pass a dead tree thrust up out of the ground like a witch's hand, or the ruins of a cottage or barn. Mostly though, the landscape was empty as though a plague had rolled through.

"Perodeau doesn't seem to have many neighbors, does he?"Tom said after a prolonged silence.

"You spoke too soon."

Catherine pointed to a building to their right framed by birch trees.

"Great. I hope it's a boulangerie."

Halfway across the field he slowed to a stop. "Oh wow! It's a café, and it's open. I can see people eating. Fancy a drink?" It wasn't quite noon, but he desperately needed a beer.

"Sounds good."

Picking up speed they came to a path that led into a courtyard. A few tables and benches were scattered about. The café's backdoor was open. Catherine pressed in close behind Tom. The din of diners halted immediately as the couple entered. All eyes were on them.

"Maybe this is where everyone is."Tom whispered.

"Bonjour," he offered awkwardly. Nobody replied and the majority of patrons resumed eating.

A woman dashed out from behind the bar.

"Bonjour Monsieur, Madame, are you lost?" she asked in English.

The woman was tall and slender. Her raven hair, long and silky, was dragged back into a braid but strands flopped down seductively over her large hazel eyes.

"No."

Tom pointed to a menu board.

"Uh… can we get two beers?"

"Yes. We have Stella Artois."

"Perfect."

The woman returned to the bar. Catherine watched her husband's eyes trail the hostess. He checked himself.

"Nice girl. Helpful."

Catherine rolled her eyes.

"Very helpful …"

The woman returned, and lingered after she had poured their beers.

"Laetitia Dupre. I'm the owner. Let me know if you need anything else."

"Thank you."

As they drank outside in the courtyard Catherine watched her husband relax. He had faced the sun and was groaning under its rising heat. Tom's dark hair now threaded with gray still had a boyish tendency to curl with perspiration. His face was a map of laughter. Deep lines fingered out from his brown eyes.

"We should have done this sooner," Tom said, breaking into her thoughts.

"You're right."

"Catherine, I've been so stupid," he suddenly blurted.

Oh God. This is it, Catherine thought as she watched some wildflowers dancing in the breeze. *This is when he tells me it's over.*

Tom waited for her to look at him, but she didn't. He took a deep breath.

"Catherine, first I want you to know that I love you very much."

Here it comes.

Laetitia approached the table, interrupting them.

"Would you like something else?"

"No, no thank you," Catherine said. Her eyes never leaving the flowers in the distance. The French woman continued to hover.

Silence.

"Are you passing through Rousinac?"

"No, we're staying here. It's the first time we've visited this part of France, isn't it darling?" Tom asked, looking directly at his wife.

Catherine sensed his desperation. She just nodded.

"Are you staying in town?" Laetitia pushed as she wiped down a nearby table.

"No, not too far from here actually. Do you know Monsieur Perodeau?"

Laetitia struggled to recover.

"You're staying at Didier Perodeau's house?"

"Yes," Tom confirmed.

"H-how long have you been there?"

"We arrived yesterday. Why? Is there a problem?"

Tom studied Laetitia's face.

"No, no, no. It's just that I have never known him to rent his house before."

"He told us that he rents it every year." Catherine countered.

"Was Monsieur Perodeau there when you arrived?"

"No." Tom replied.

"How did you hear about his house?"

"I saw it advertised online, why?"

"In *England*?"

"Yes." Tom frowned. "Why are you asking?"

"It isn't a good idea for you to be here."

"Why?" Catherine asked.

"Monsieur Perodeau's house is in the forest, where the sangliers are. This time of the year they have their young, and can be danger-ous. You should consider staying somewhere else immediately."

Catherine started to speak but Tom interrupted.

"What are sangliers?"

"A pig that lives in the woods."

"A wild boar?" Catherine asked.

"Yes, that's it, a boar."

Tom sighed.

"Phew. Thanks for the warning. We'll be sure to keep out of the forest at night," he said, winking at his wife.

Laetitia bristled.

"This is not a joking matter Monsieur. In the past they have killed people. You have no choice but to move. I will speak to our Mayor in the morning. But for tonight, be inside before dark and lock all your doors and shutters, okay?"

"Yes, got it." Tom agreed, winking at Catherine.

The café owner's words had disrupted the strain between the couple, postponing Tom's disclosure. They had left after one order to avoid more of her questions.

But neither one of them wanted to revisit the subject of Tom's revelation so soon and they occupied themselves with mundane things for the rest of the afternoon. The way British people avoid things.

That evening Tom cooked while Catherine lit a fire in the lounge. After dinner they watched as the logs burned in silence. They were both on edge, and for more than one reason.

Laetitia's warning about the sanglier had jarred Catherine. *Was it an omen?* Tom downed a third glass of wine. Catherine caught his eye. He flushed.

"I need to tell you."

"We need to lock the back door."

"Oh, come on, you're not still worrying about some wild pigs, are you?"

Catherine drew her knees up beneath her chin.

"She was serious."

"Did you see the look on her face when she found out we were staying here? Cafe Napoleon is probably a Bed and Breakfast. Maybe she doesn't like the competition?"

"Just lock the doors please."

He crossed through the kitchen, opened the back door, and gasped.

"CATHERINE! Come, quick!"

She ran to her husband.

"What is it?"

Tom did not reply.

The Locals (1)
Rousinac, Southwest France 2019

"Bonsoir Uncle, sorry to call you so late, but we have a problem."

"You sound upset. What's wrong?" An old man answered.

"Two British people came into the restaurant today."

Laetitia hesitated.

"What?"

"And they're staying at Didier's house."

Silence.

"That was never supposed to happen." She added.

"The idiot! Where is he?" Her uncle snapped.

"I don't know. I've tried ringing his cell, but I think it's switched off which means he's hiding somewhere. What are we going to do?"

"Right now, I don't know. I'll call you back. Stay calm."

As Pierre Malraux hung up the phone, his ulcer began to ache. He knew that he was in for a painful night.

Laetitia Dupre could not relax.

Her uncle had done little to allay her fears. She smoked pensively in the yard, scouring the black-knotted woods beyond.

Did they have enough time?

Gulping some wine, she noticed that the wind had begun to pick up. It carried the sound of dogs barking madly in the next village. They wouldn't stop.

She crushed her cigarette into a flowerpot and thundered back into the cafe.

"Merde!"

The Tourists (3)
Rousinac, Southwest France 2019

The back garden was beetle black and moonless. The sky was full of stars. Tom drew Catherine to him and this time she did not resist.

"See the Plough darling? And that's the Milky Way!" Tom glowed. "Look! A shooting star. Make a wish, go on."

"Tom, just tell me what you tried to tell me before, at the cafe. Just get it over with." Catherine said, leaning away from him.

"Now?"

"Yes, *now*."

"Okay," he resigned. "Let's go inside."

"Just lock the doors."

They wandered back to the fire that Catherine had kindled an hour before. Now it was a pile of red embers.

"I'm really sorry Catherine," Tom kneeled in front of his wife.

"Just tell me."

"We've lost everything," he blurted.

Catherine felt a pinch in her stomach.

"What?"

"We're ... on the verge of bankruptcy."

"I don't know what you're saying."

"Remember a couple of years back when we bought that development plot? We borrowed heavily from the bank to build on it. Everything was going to plan until the economy tanked. The firms that had promised to invest suddenly pulled out, one by one. I tried to sell some of our smaller holdings, but nobody was buying; contracts dried up; word got out that I was struggling. Then the creditors came out of the woodwork. The bank was the worst."

He buried his head in his hands.

"I'm the biggest loser."

Catherine twisted the edge of her skirt.

"You've lost *everything*?"

"Yes." he murmured.

"Why didn't you just tell me?"

"I should have! I know,"

"I don't get it! We're supposed to be partners."

"I know and I'm sorry. I feel so stupid."

"Why didn't you tell me?"

"Because I knew you would offer to bail me out and I was too stupid or pigheaded to let you. I kept hoping something would come up, a big contract, anything that would keep the bank off my back."

"But it didn't - did it?"

"No."

"So, all we have left is the house?"

"No."

"What?"

"I put the house up as collateral when I took out the loan."

There was a horrible pause and Tom braced himself. He knew that she had every right to leave him, to extricate herself from his incompetence. Catherine turned to him.

"That's everything?"

"Yes."

"Nothing else?"

"No."

She began to laugh uncontrollably.

"Catherine?"

"I thought you were having an affair."

"What?"

"Seriously?" Tom was shocked. "What on earth would make you think that?"

"Everything. You were never home! You'd become so..." Catherine choked on her words.

He took her hands and kissed them tenderly.

"Oh, Catherine, oh my God. I had no idea. I'm so sorry. I was just trying to find a way out. But nothing was working. And I just couldn't face you. I thought if I told you, you'd leave."

"You locked me out Tom. You left me thinking all kinds of things. I've been to hell and back wondering what I'd done wrong."

"Catherine, I'm so sorry. I'll do anything to put this right," Tom begged. "Being here with you for just these few days has been wonderful. I feel brand new. Can we put this right? Please? We could stay here."

"In France?"

"I could get a job."

"You don't even speak French."

"I could learn, I'll do anything. Maybe this is a blessing in disguise? We could start over again. What do you think, Catherine?"

He reached for her.

This time, she did not move.

The Tourists (4)
Rousinac, Southwest France 2019

Later, when the house lights went out, the strange sounds from the garden returned. They moved through the trees, but neither Catherine or Tom heard them.

Sex had come unexpectedly, and its release left them exhausted. Their bodies had twisted together like vines, and they'd drifted into a deep sleep.

Catherine had made the first move.

Tom welcomed it, offering himself with a vulnerability that left him sobbing. It was atonement and he swore he would never let her down again.

At 2 a.m. there were movements at the front door though the couple never stirred. Had they heard it, they might have thought it was a large animal that had picked up the scent of their garbage or possibly one of Laetitia's sangliers.

After lunch, Tom and Catherine decided to drive into town to do some grocery shopping. Had they not been lost in their reconnection they might have noticed a few odd things.

The p olice c ar t hat t railed t hem t hroughout t heir t rip. Rousinac's empty stores and streets. Hard stares that followed their every move. An air of coldness in the eyes of the locals. But none of this registered. Intimacy had changed everything. It had sealed Tom's confession and forged a new bond.

They both felt at peace for the first time in a long while. Catherine was back in love with her husband. Tom was utterly relieved. He felt lighter, eager to make it up to his wife.

It was just after five o'clock by the time they'd arrived back at Pero-deau's house. It sat baked like a brick in the fierce August sun. After they'd shared a light supper, Tom decided to explore the outhouses and grounds. Catherine lay on their bed.

She was thinking of ways to ease their financial situation and save their home. *What can we cut back on? What could we do without?* Her eagerness to forgive Tom had taken her by surprise. Was the faith she had in their marriage warranted?

Time would tell.

She heard Tom moving about in the garden and her mind drifted back to the sounds she'd heard the first night. She didn't hear Tom approaching.

"Got you!"

"Tom!"

"What's the matter?"

"You scared the life out of me."

"Look what I've found?" he said, pulling a rifle out from behind him.

"It's a 410."

He clutched it lovingly across his chest. "It's got an adjustable rear sight, and a tapered barrel. Philip at the rifle club owns one. He's a real collector. I've always wanted to fire one of these babies."

"Tom, it's not yours! You should put it back."

"No one will find out. Guess what else I found? It was in the small shed at the back of the house."

Tom produced a small pistol from his pocket.

"Look …"

"Don't point that thing at me." Catherine lurched upright.

"Sorry. It looks American, probably from World War II."

Tom slid open the small barrel which was empty.

"I'm going to buy some bullets and keep it right here," he placed it under the bed.

Catherine raised her eyebrows.

"Why?"

"In case a giant wild boar comes calling," he smiled reassuringly.

Catherine laughed as her husband paraded around the bedroom with the rifle pretending to shoot at imaginary beasts.

"Impressed, aren't you?"

He jumped onto the bed. She shrieked.

"Relax, it's not loaded."

He fell onto his back.

"I think Perodeau hunts. Perhaps he goes after the infamous sanglier. I might have a go myself tomorrow. Do you think he'd mind? Oh, who cares? He should have hidden this beauty better."

Catherine eyed him. "Do you think that's why Perodeau doesn't allow children here because of the guns?" Tom never heard her. He was up at the window taking aim and planning his next hunting trip.

That night they found a passion that had escaped them for years. It began impetuously with intimate touches that slowly gratified and aroused. Catherine tasted the wine on Tom's tongue as it found hers.

She rocked rhythmically above him resting her hands above his thick shoulders. Her full pale breasts brushed his face. She arched her back and fully accepted the movement beneath her and then inside of her. Tom felt a bolt of energy pass between them. His eyes rolled shut.

An hour later, Tom was holding his wife against his chest. He felt her drop heavier into sleep. Catherine's breathing lulled him. All at once his eyes flicked open. He hadn't locked the back door. He was glad that Catherine hadn't noticed.

Hours later, Catherine woke in darkness. The wine she had drunk earlier had left a bitter thirst. She reached for water and realized that she'd forgotten to re-fill her glass. A night light flickered in the hallway. She slipped from Tom's arms and tip-toed out of the bedroom.

Everything was quiet. She navigated the darkness in silence, mindful not to wake her husband. The stairs had been painstaking, but she had managed to descend a floor without creaking. Reaching the kitchen, she opened the fridge and got a pitcher of water. Leaning against the sink she poured herself a glass.

Catherine thought about Tom and the events of the past few days. It was strange that their impending bankruptcy was something she didn't fear. It had been an unexpected gift. A peace had returned to her heart. She was happy again.

A storm raged in the distance and the wind picked up. Lightning flushed out the silhouette of a nearby tree. Its branch began tap-tap-tapping at the window. Ticking from the dining room clock battled against the wind and claps of thunder. Tom had left the downstairs hallway light on, an old habit from home. The hall instinctively drew her. The floorboards moaned but the clock's ticking was a comfort.

But then.

Something moved in the corner of Catherine's eyes. Spinning

around she caught her own shadow on the wall. Her eyes shot to the back door.

Unlocked!

Pumped with adrenaline, Catherine rammed the two bolts shut. She leaned against the door, relieved. Then her legs began to tingle.

As a child, Catherine had been trapped in her bedroom by a rat. Her legs had tingled before she even saw it. She had been unable to move even as the rat crawled over her bare feet. A similar feeling now swept over her. Blood thudded through her head.

The door has been left open for hours.

Was someone already inside?

Catherine searched for signs of an intruder: dusty footprints, something moved out of place. The heavy velvet curtains in the hall's corner would be a good place for them to hide.

There was movement in the garden.

She strained her ears to listen. It didn't sound like a foraging animal. Something was moving about the calcaire driveway with determination.

The noise stopped directly outside of the dining room window. Catherine ducked down onto the floor. Other noises began at the front door. A peculiar sound like a hissing boiler or ... *whispers?*

Tom.

No sound left her lips.

A thwack followed by scratching at the kitchen window drew her attention. Someone was trying to pry open the shutters. A terrible smell wafted into the hallway.

Catherine watched as the back door handle turned downward. Force was applied. The bolts held the door and the movement stopped. Shadows were forming around the door.

CRACK!!!

Something had walloped the back door's reinforced glass. Catherine stormed the stairs.

"What the hell's going on down there?" Tom called out as they collided on the landing. Catherine stared down at the shadowed floor below. It took a couple of seconds to regain her composure.

"Th-there's someone down there, *outside,*" Catherine panted.

"And … they're trying to get in!"

"Where?"

"Down there – *there!*"

"Okay, listen, just take a couple of deep breaths," Tom said, trying to calm her.

"What did you see? A mouse?"

"NO! Someone just tried to open the fucking back door!"

Shit.

He hadn't locked it, but he didn't want to complicate matters.

"What were you doing down there anyway? It's the middle of the night."

"I-I wanted a drink of water,"

"Why didn't you wake me?"

"Tom, did you hear what I just said? Someone is out there, and they're trying to get in!"

Tom grabbed the rifle.

"It's probably just one of those wild pigs. I'll go down and take a look, okay?"

"Not by yourself."

"You've had a shock."

They heard something tip over in the garden. Tom struggled to stay calm.

"Okay. Okay. There's a storm coming so the wind's blowing things about. That's all it is, I'm sure."

He went to the top of the landing and leaned over, straining his ears. Catherine followed. Tom drew a finger to his lips. They heard the back door rattle. Then there was a click as though someone was trying to pick the lock.

"I locked the door. It wasn't …"

"I know."

"Okay, I'm going down there."

"No!" Catherine clung to Tom. "You're not opening that door!"

"I've got a gun."

"No! Stay here with me."

"Okay, but tomorrow, in the daylight I'm going to look for tracks."

Without warning Tom banged on a close-by window with his fist.

"Allez!" he shouted.

There was some heavy thumping about the drive, then some rustling in the bushes.

"Okay, whatever was out there just ran into the woods. They're gone." He said gently.

"Go back to bed. I'm going to spray the hallway. That's got to be the worst stink ever."

"No, I'll wait for you," Catherine said sitting on the stairs.

"Okay."

Neither Tom nor Catherine could go back to sleep. The storm eventually came. It broke through the trees rattling the house like a bag of bones. Rain whipped the shutters and pearled musty in the corners like sweat.

The couple held one another tightly. Catherine mentally resolved to pay the Cafe owner another visit, and Tom plotted a thorough examination of the surrounding woods. Only when the dawn bled the room's darkness gray, did they finally doze.

The Tourists (5)
Rousinac, Southwest France 2019

"Bonjour ….?"

Catherine had entered Café Napoleon, happy that she was the only customer. Laetitia looked up, startled to see that the English-woman was alone.

Laetitia. "Catherine, isn't it?"

Catherine nodded. The French woman was tense.

"Can I have a coffee please?"

"Certainly, a croissant also?"

Laetitia gestured for her to sit.

"No, just a coffee. Thanks."

"Sit down. I have some freshly made."

Catherine dropped into the nearest chair and took in the views.

"Do you take it black or with milk?" Laetitia asked, placing a tray on the table.

"Black is good, thank you. Will you join me?" Catherine tapped the chair next to her.

"Well, I'm …" Laetitia dithered.

"I just need to ask you something. It won't take more than a couple of minutes I promise."

"Okay, but I cannot sit for long."

"No problem." Catherine took a sip of coffee. She could feel Laetitia's eyes on her.

"I hope you thought about what I said yesterday."

Catherine didn't reply.

"Catherine?"

"Do the sanglier … ?" Catherine hesitated for a moment. "Do they ever try to get into the house?"

She met Laetitia's eyes dead on.

"Sometimes. If it's hot they come in search of water."

" I think, maybe, that's what happened last night. Some of them came right up to the back door and I swear they tried to open it."

Laetitia played with the crucifix around her neck.

"Well, I'm afraid you being there a-attracts them," she stammered.

"But to try to open a door, that's not possible for pigs, is it?" Catherine pressed.

"They are intelligent. The males can be large. Maybe a male pushed against the door and with its weight …"

"Yes, I guess that does seem more likely. And boy do they stink!" Catherine exhaled a sigh of relief.

"What do you mean?"

"Last night there was a terrible smell. It's gone now but it was awful. It's the same smell that comes from the sewers." Catherine noticed a vein in Laetitia's neck pulsing.

"Sewers?"

"Yes, there are some sewers, tunnels really, open on the land."

"I don't think Monsieur Perodeau was wise in renting his house to you. I have plenty of friends who rent properties closer in. Let me move you somewhere less inconvenient, perhaps a quiet house on the edge of town with a garden? You could sit out all night without a care. It wouldn't cost you anything extra. You can move today, and I would be happy to arrange it all myself."

Laetitia touched Catherine's hand. It felt too intimate, and she quickly withdrew. There was an awkward pause.

"Thank you, you're too kind. I know that I would feel better if we stayed somewhere else, but I need to talk to my husband first."

Laetitia hardened her approach.

"You must make him understand! It's for everyone's benefit that you move out of the woods immediately."

The front doorbell jangled. A local sauntered in. Laetitia reached into her apron for a pen. She scribbled something on a napkin. "Here's my number. Please call me as soon as you both decide. The move would be very quick, I can assure you."

Laetitia kissed the English woman lightly on both cheeks. Catherine forced a smile.

"Thank you, Laetitia, and please don't think that I'm being ungrateful but why would you do this? You barely know us." Catherine asked, holding the French woman's dark eyes.

"I don't normally interfere in Monsieur Perodeau's business. But…" Laetitia hesitated. "I don't want anything to happen to you. It's bad for everyone. If the sangliers came to the house once, they *will* come again."

Catherine returned to Perodeau's house, eager to discuss Laetitia's proposal with her husband. His reaction was explosive.

"We're NOT moving because of pigs Catherine! That's a ridiculous idea! You said yourself that we could simply lock the doors at night. Plus, I like it here."

Tom angrily wiped the sweat from his brow. Catherine looked at the gun tucked under his arm.

"Did you find anything in the woods?"

"No. A couple of grass snakes, nothing else. And certainly, no pig tracks."

Catherine was pleased. Tom sat down on the patio and downed a cold beer.

"But I did notice that horrible smell again, just behind the house. I had a good look around to see if anything had died. Didn't find anything besides the sewers, which are probably the culprits."

"Gross."

Her gaze drifted to the dining room shutter behind him.

"Well, something's been at that," she pointed.

"It's probably just storm damage."

"Look at those grooves."

Tom examined the dents more closely.

"Yeah, but maybe we hadn't noticed before."

"What if it's a petty thief or a local, knowing that the owner is away?" Catherine chewed her lip.

"At any rate we should let Monsieur Perodeau know," she said.

"Wait." Tom leaned closer to the shutter. "It doesn't look like a screwdriver made these marks. Look, a screwdriver would have made just one gash, but here…" he pointed to the other ridges, "…there are several almost as if…" he paused. "No, a boar wouldn't be able to get up that high. That's really weird."

"I don't like it," Catherine replied.

"Okay so do you want to just pack up and go home?"

"No! I love this part of France, but Laetitia offered us somewhere else to stay, a little closer to town."

"Yes, but again ....why, Catherine? Why would she do that?" Tom countered.

"Perhaps she's just concerned for us?"

"I doubt that very much. More like she has a grudge against Perodeau, and this is her handiwork?" He offered.

"Oh, don't be so ridiculous!"

"That's exactly my point. I don't want to move closer to town. It would be exactly like England. We came here for peace and quiet. *Please*, let's try to make the best of it darling," Tom implored.

Catherine was torn. Tom wound his arms around her.

"Listen, I'll keep the rifle by the bed tonight and if that animal or whatever, comes sniffing around again I'll give it the fright of its life from the upstairs window? Okay?"

"You bought bullets?"

"Yes, I thought I would go after a boar,"

She didn't respond.

Tom continued. "Let's give it one more night and if you're still unhappy, we'll call Laetitia tomorrow first thing."

She shrugged as Tom pressed her further.

"Okay, I'll even take that damned castle tour with you this afternoon." He offered.

Reluctantly, Catherine agreed to Tom's plan, although everything in her body was urging her to pack up and leave.

The Tourists (6)
Rousinac, Southwest France 2019

The castle tour proved a perfect distraction from the earlier discussions of the day.

Tom and Catherine had learned about Rousinac through the eyes of a local historian. Far from being a backwater, Rousinac was once the principality of an old European dynasty called the Merovingians.

English and French Kings had fought a hundred year war over its Duchy and natural resources. It had always been thickly wooded with primordial forest. In more recent times it had witnessed a lengthy Nazi occupation.

Tom was fascinated to discover that tunnels led from the castle into the surrounding woods. The tunnels formed a honeycomb of catacombs that had been sealed long ago and no one was permitted to go into them.

They were reportedly haunted by former prisoners, tortured to death. It was also rumored that over the years, smugglers had gained access to a few of the tunnels but that they had been driven out by strange looking occupants. Or so the tour guide had joked.

As they approached the entrance of one dungeon, Catherine was hit by a sulfurous scent. It somehow struck her as familiar. Tom assured her that all sewers smelled the same.

They had been the only people on the tour.

Weird.

Afterwards, Tom and Catherine dined outside in a hotel restaurant directly opposite the Château castle. Sipping champagne as night fell, they gasped when the castle lights came on.

The restaurant was empty apart from two other families. A couple with two small children sat at the table next to them and Tom played "peek-a-boo" with the baby. Catherine reveled in the simplicity of the moment.

"We would have made good parents," she said.

"I know."

Tom looked down at his food and mindlessly prodded the fish with a fork.

"It wasn't anybody's fault," he volunteered.

"Yeah, I'd say it was mine."

Tom touched her arm.

"The doctors said it was 50-50. We were just not meant to be parents."

She paused for a second.

"Not biological parents, but we could have had children. We talked about adoption, remember?"

"Yes, but your career was just taking off and ..." he trailed off.

"We could have arranged our lives better."

Catherine suddenly felt the weight of that statement. Tears erupted in her pale blue eyes. Tom impulsively squeezed her hand.

"We may not have had a family but think of all the kids you've helped in your life through your volunteer work and your job."

Catherine frowned.

"I didn't think it through. We could have had everything."

Tom looked back up at the castle.

"We can't change the past, Catherine. We just need to accept things, all things, as they are."

Tom poured them both another glass of red wine and smiled tenderly. *I love you*, he mouthed.

The Grayston's evening had strayed later than anticipated. The flow of conversation between them came like a torrent after months of silence. Eventually however they became aware of the fact that they were completely alone. There was no one in the streets. No one was in the restaurant.

Catherine's heart lurched when Tom sauntered inside to pay their bill. Fortunately, he returned unflustered, but it irked Catherine that Tom seemed cavalier by their insolvency. It was already beginning to eat away at her.

Had she simply switched one fear out for another.

How much they had left.

How many accounts had been frozen?

His debt would ruin her credit score. Their beautiful home would get repossessed as well as the car. They'd have to move to a cheaper part of town. What would her colleagues think? The worries were beginning to pile up like a mass of dead bodies.

What other secrets had he kept?

It was nearly midnight by the time the couple arrived back at Perodeau's house. By now the unlit drive was clotted in darkness. Even though it was a short walk from the car, the house seemed invisible. Sensing his wife's discomfort, Tom ran to turn on the outside lights. Bats fluttered noiselessly overhead.

"It's so quiet tonight," Catherine said as they entered the house.

The Tourists (7)
Rousinac, Southwest France 2019

The heaviness of their earlier conversations consumed Catherine and she was the first to go to bed. Tom hadn't heard her crying. He had remained downstairs staring at a dying fire wondering how their life would have been with children.

His own father had been adopted through a Catholic charity during the Second World War. It had left him with bitter scars of abandonment and shame. But times had changed, and Tom silently reproached himself for not pushing harder for adoption.

He had hoped that she would just fall pregnant, but that announcement never came. Then his mind settled briefly on their impending bankruptcy, and he muttered half-aloud,

"I would've just ruined more lives …"

Tom sensed that the honeymoon of their reconciliation had begun to dim and something new jack-hammered at his heart. Catherine feverishly checked their bank balances. He knew his business account had already been closed.

At some point he would run out of money and what would happen then? The car would get repossessed, then the house. He'd have to depend on her money.

Maybe we could bail on Monsieur Perodeau? After all, he hadn't told them about the wild boar. They didn't owe him anything. He could sell the pistol.

Desperate ideas swirled about his mind.

Tom didn't want to give in to depression, but his prospects were not looking good. He wasn't a young man, and the economy was still bad.

Where would they move to? What if she lost her job?

Perhaps in time Catherine would come to despise him, or even worse, pity him. He downed more Cognac.

When he finally made it to bed, he found Catherine so silent that he had to check her breathing. As he lay down beside her in the darkness he suddenly felt very alone. It would take him longer to fall asleep but fortunately at some point he did.

He wouldn't sleep for long.

Tom was the first to hear it.

"Catherine, wake up. I can hear something outside." He gently nudged his wife.

Catherine mumbled incoherently as she clung to a dream.

"Wake up!"

Tom shook her again with a little more force. By the time Catherine opened her eyes; Tom was already out of bed and dressed. A piercing screech from outside the house electrified her.

Within seconds she was fully alert.

"What was that?"

"Is that what you heard the other night at the door? Catherine.

Listen." Tom was insistent. Another screech sounded. It made them both jump.

"No, that's not it at all."

"That doesn't sound like a pig I've ever heard. I think someone's outside. I think it's a teenage prank." Tom ventured.

Laetitia?

Catherine glanced at the bedside clock: 3:12 a.m. She noticed her husband's jaw clench when the high-pitched noise sounded again.

"You're going to have to help me flush them out." Tom handed Catherine a pair of leggings.

"Get dressed."

"Did you lock up downstairs? Did you?" She repeated.

"Yes."

Tom picked up the rifle.

Catherine crept around the bed towards him. She grabbed a heavy flashlight positioned on the windowsill and gestured to him but there was no response. He stood transfixed; head cocked in disbelief as the bizarre sounds continued outside.

"Tom?" Catherine whispered louder.

Something inside of him clicked. He eyed the flashlight.

"Yes. When I indicate, shine the torch over my shoulder directly down into the garden. Okay?" His hand now edged toward the window's handle.

Before she could reply, they heard something else. It was coming from downstairs. It sounded as though someone was scraping or chipping away at the front door.

"What the hell's that?" Tom looked to his wife for an answer.

"I think this is a bad idea. Please don't open the window." Her face appeared unnatural to him for a second or two. He just stared at her.

"Tom?"

"I've got to. I've got to scare whoever's doing this. The fucking car's outside." Catherine shook her head.

"Don't worry everything's going to be okay. It's probably just a couple of kids like you said. Just don't shoot. You're a good marksman and ..."

Tom turned the window's handle and creaked it open. He pushed out one of the shutters. Everything outside became silent. Tom poked the gun barrel between the window ledge and the shutter. Catherine noticed a twitch on his forehead.

"Now!" he mouthed.

Catherine raised the flashlight over his shoulder. Her thumb fumbled for the switch. It was stuck. It wouldn't budge. She could hear Tom's labored breathing. The seconds stretched as she struggled to slide ON. The noise at the front door stopped. In the void below Tom could see grainy figures milling about.

ON!

The garden lit up like a stadium.

Catherine watched her husband's face paralyze. His bottom lip quivered. A swollen river of sweat ran into his ear.

"W-w-what the ..." he squeaked like a child.

Below in the garden, shadows were swarming. Tom could hear a collective murmur rising. The night air carried in an odor like carrion. He gagged.

"Fuck!"

Catherine steeled herself and peered over Tom's shoulder. She watched as black figures gathered at the edges of the flashlight. When the light moved, they moved, backing into the trees. Tom noticed that one of them had darted closer to the house.

There was a blind spot between the bush and the wall. It looked like the intruders were inching towards a lower exterior wall using shrub as cover.

They're trying to climb the wall. Catherine's sudden intake of breath jarred Tom's reflexes. The gun exploded.

A heart-stopping scream pierced the night. The couple lurched back.

Tom dropped the rifle and fumbled to close the shutters and window. Catherine turned on all of the lights. The gun smoked from the floor.

"W-what the hell? How could ... they...?" Tom gulped.

"...C-c-climb a wall?" she exclaimed. "Do you think they've gone?"

Tom backed away from the window.

"I hope so."

They listened from the top of the stairs. It was disconcertingly quiet.

Tom and Catherine edged back to the bedroom and locked the door. Catherine checked her cell phone. But it was pointless. One of the things that they had liked about the grounds was a lack of Wi-Fi. Tom caught her disappointment.

He darted a fearful look at her.

"No Wi-Fi?"

"None."

"It'll be light soon," she encouraged.

The strain was unbearable. After twenty minutes, Tom snatched Cognac from the bedside cabinet and gulped a mouthful.

"Here have some. It'll help steady your nerves."

He dragged a heavy linen chest and lodged it against their bedroom door. They withdrew to the bed, eyes racing from window to bedroom door and back again. There was nothing. No sound, or breeze, absolutely nothing. The silence felt unbearable.

"Did you see them trying to climb the bloody wall?"

"I don't know what I …" Her voice trailed off.

"I do and it definitely wasn't fucking pigs!"

"She knows something."

"Who?"

"Laetitia. She must. Perodeau knows too."

"You think?"

"I think we were set up Tom."

"What?" He was getting manic. He owed some unsavory types money back home but surely, they wouldn't have sent people after them out here – *would they?*

"Maybe they saw the car and thought …" Catherine interrupted his thoughts.

"That we're rich? What a joke that is!" Tom laughed.

"We need to stay awake tonight." Catherine said.

Tom grabbed the cognac bottle back and drank hard. Then he checked the rifle.

"Let's pack now and leave as soon as the sun comes up."

"Yes, of course. It will be light soon." Tom said quietly.

Catherine felt calmer knowing that the dawn was coming.

"We will go to the police first thing in the morning."

Tom double-checked the pistol under the bed. He did not respond.

"We'll go to the police as soon as we can," she repeated.

"Catherine, I took a shot at someone. Remember? What if they're wounded or …?"

"Then we will say it was self-defense, which is true." She replied. "I'm not going near any police here. Fuck that."

The couple hurriedly organized their departure, throwing clothes and other personals into cases.

"Wait. Did you hear that?"

Catherine tilted her head and motioned for silence.

"Hear what?" Tom asked as he leaned forward to listen.

"I thought I heard a man's voice."

The Tourists (8)
Rousinac, Southwest France 2019

Dawn finally broke. After several cups of strong coffee, Tom cocked the rifle and moved slowly towards the front door. He turned to his wife.

"Perhaps it'd be safer if you went to the bedroom and watched from upstairs."

"No, we stay together."

Tom kissed her lightly on the forehead and mouthed.

"I love you."

He took care not to make any noise. He teased the handle of the front door and patiently opened it. The smell had gone. Sunlight now rendered everything knowable. The couple stepped out into it.

Circling the house, they meticulously secured each corner.

"It's okay. They've gone," Catherine announced. "It feels different."

They wandered back to the patio.

"Look at this."

Tom pointed to some congealed dark red fluid. It ran like sap along the base of the wall splattering onto the shingle below.

"It's right underneath where I think …" he struggled for the right words, "they …fell."

Catherine bent over to take a closer look.

"Don't touch it. We don't know what it is," Tom cautioned.

"It's not blood. It's too dark," Catherine said as she prodded the substance with a stick. "It's like glue."

Tom leaned in.

"We need to get a sample before it degrades."

"I have a spare contact lens case."

"Good."

They looked at one another for a moment. Tom smiled.

"It's okay Catherine, like you said. They've gone."

Catherine knew that her husband was right. The everyday sounds of country life had returned. Birds fluttered above their heads in the trees, faraway cows mooed, and bees buzzed methodically over the patio's flower pots. She re-entered the house.

Tom stood up against the wall scouting the bushes beyond the patio, his rifle readied. Straining his ears, he tracked Catherine as she located the case. A few minutes later Tom had scraped the strange substance into it.

"Just be careful, don't let it touch your skin," Catherine warned.

Tom groaned. "It's disgusting."

"What do we do with it?"

"I have a friend from the rifle club. You don't know him, nice guy. His name's David … David Frankel. He joined the club six months ago. He's a medical examiner for New Scotland Yard. They deal with all sorts of forensic evidence, don't they?"

"Yes, but we don't even know what this is?"

"Which is why we should send it to him." Tom pushed.

"But why not take it back with us in the car? You could give it to him at the club?"

"No, I prefer posting it. It's a boundary thing. The club's well …. it's a club." Catherine suddenly realized that Tom probably hadn't been going to the rifle club, that his membership had expired months ago.

Or maybe it was a cover for some affair?

She immediately dashed the idea away, but he had noticed it.

"I couldn't afford the membership. I defaulted on payments … I can't just show up."

"I'll look up New Scotland Yard's address."

He flung the butter knife far into the garden brush.

"We'll go to the post office and send it express then follow up once he gets in touch."

"What about Laetitia and Perodeau?"

"What about them? We're not paying him that's for sure."

Catherine absent-mindedly kicked aside some shrubbery.

"Oh my God, Tom!"

"What?" He looked down into the bush.

"That looks like–"

"Blood. Oh, Jesus, Catherine!" Tom fell back against the wall.

She looked about. There were a few more splashes on Perodeau's back wall too.

"Catherine, what if I've killed someone?"

She thought for a moment.

"No. They'd still be lying here. You clipped them and they deserved it as far as I'm concerned." She tried to convince herself.

"I just want to get out of here." He shuddered.

"I think we should tell Laetitia."

"Are you fucking insane?"

"No, not about this. About the intruders. I want to see her face. I think she knows something"

"No way!" Tom shot back.

"She needs to understand that this cannot happen ever again."

"I just want to go home!"

"One quick visit."

"Catherine …. no."

"I promise Tom, then we'll go."

The Tourists (9)
Rousinac, Southwest France 2019

Catherine and Tom felt an immense relief after mailing the sample to David Frankel at New Scotland Yard. They had taken a step toward understanding what they had encountered; next stop was the Cafe Napoleon to confront Laetitia before they journeyed back home to England.

Laetitia Dupre was lost in the preparations of the day. The café's floor had been washed and a fresh pot of coffee was brewing behind the bar. She was setting the tables when a car ground to a halt outside. *Too early for the post.*

She peered toward the door. The man's voice was indistinguishable, but another's made her stomach lurch. *The English woman.* Footsteps advanced. Someone rapped the door. She heard the man's voice clearly this time.

"Laetitia, open up! It's the Graystons. We need to talk to you."

"Bonjour Monsieur, Madame. I'm sorry we're not open yet."

"We're not here to eat," Tom Grayston replied.

"Then how can I help you?"

She unlocked the door.

"You know why we're here Laetitia, stop pretending," Catherine pushed past her husband.

"What are you talking about?"

"A large group, we think a gang of teenagers, came to the house last night and *please* don't test our patience by saying they were wild pigs." Catherine blurted.

"Who are they, thugs sent by you?" Tom pressed.

Laetitia was speechless.

"You look shocked." Catherine noted.

"You actually *saw* them?" Laetitia replied.

"Yes!" Tom lied.

The French woman covered her mouth.

"Sit down."

Laetitia began.

"I warned you about the sanglier …"

"Pigs don't try to climb walls!" Catherine yelled.

Laetitia sank back into her chair. She had to think fast. *Smugglers*. Yes, they'd buy that story.

"Did you take a tour of the castle?"

"Yes," the couple said in unison.

"Then you heard about the tunnels under the city, leading out from the Château castle?"

"We saw them but …" Catherine offered.

"You didn't see the *real tunnels*," Laetitia replied.

"What are you talking about?!"

"There are other tunnels. That smugglers have used for hundreds of years. The truth is, some of those tunnels lead onto your garden, Didier Perodeau's land. He should never have rented his house to you."

"So, we've been dealing with smugglers?" Tom said.

"Yes." Laetitia confirmed.

"Well, we haven't left any money for Perodeau."

"Of course not, he's entirely to blame. So, you're leaving?"

"Yes, but we will be lodging a complaint with the authorities once we get back home. We don't want this happening to anyone else."

Panic hit Laetitia's stomach.

"Look I understand that it's ruined your vacation but please, I beg of you, leave the British police out of this. It's bad for Rousinac. It's bad for everyone. And I assure you we will deal with these people. It won't happen to anyone else." She pleaded. There was a pause.

She had been too insistent.

It now occurred to Tom and Catherine that Laetitia was directly involved.

"This isn't going away Laetitia. This will end with us." Tom said.

Laetitia got up and walked toward the bar. She placed three glasses on a small wooden tray.

It needn't have come to this.

"I'm asking you both for the last time. Go home. Leave this problem with us. I promise you I will personally take care of it. It will never happen to anyone else again."

She watched their faces harden. Tom crossed his arms and Catherine mumbled *absolutely not*. Laetitia sighed and looked up at the ceiling.

Well then, you've sealed your fate.

As the Graystons continued to talk under their breath, Laetitia reached inside a concealed drawer under the counter. She felt for two sachets.

"You will need to leave a report with Rousinac Police. I will come and help you with the language. Otherwise, nobody will understand. I just need to calm my nerves before we go. This is down to Perodeau, not me. I've been worried about you. I'm not the criminal here."

The couple did not reply. They eyed her from their table as she pulled down a bottle of cognac. She poured the first glass in front of them - her glass.

Smash!

Laetitia had deliberately rolled an empty glass off of the counter. The distraction allowed her enough time to tip some white powder into the open cognac bottle and then into a coffee pot. She swallowed a mouthful of the cognac that she'd already poured for herself and looked down at the shattered glass on the floor.

"You see? I've been a nervous wreck!" she jabbered on.

"We all rely on tourism here and these, these locals well … They are bad news."

"What tourists? We've been the only visitors here."Tom returned.

"Look, we're not here for coffee and we are not going to the police either. For all we know you're all in on something really bad."

Laetitia had to think fast. The gun in her cashier draw would be a last resort.

"The truth is. Perodeau is a drug dealer. No one likes him. He has made many enemies. I can give you the full story for your British police. I am sick of him. It's true we have no tourists here … yet, but our mayor is young, forward thinking. We want to open up to visitors. There's no money here, just farming and drugs."

The initial fizz from the powder subsided and the liquid cleared. Laetitia returned to the table carrying the coffee pot and balancing glasses, cups, and the bottle of cognac on a tray.

Her story had reeled the couple in.

"Yes but why would he rent out his house to us?"

"It's deliberate, of course. There's a large cache of drugs hidden on his property."

"In the tunnels?"

"No, in the house."

"Oh my God!" Tom gasped.

Catherine and Tom watched as Laetitia continued to gulp down her own cognac. She poured a glass for them both, and pushed it forward.

"He had some urgent business in Bordeaux and he left you at his house to keep people away. He figured they wouldn't risk breaking into an occupied house."

"Who?"

"Rivals. People he had screwed. He has a lot of enemies."

"And you knew this all along?" Catherine said, pushing her cognac away.

Tom drank his.

"Your suspicions were correct all along Madame. I'm sorry to say that I know the families involved: local people, no good. You have been incredibly unlucky to come across them," Laetitia poured Catherine a coffee.

Catherine sighed and took a sip.

"If you knew about these smugglers you should have said something from day one. This has completely ruined our vacation."

"I warned you not to stay there!" Laetitia shot back.

"Oh right, the pigs." Tom hissed sarcastically.

"She's been bullshitting us this whole time, Tom. Come on, let's just go." Catherine said.

"No not yet. I want to get to the bottom of this," Tom said

uneasily. Laetitia was relieved. The woman couldn't leave without drinking her coffee. She had to give them a show.

"I'm not bullshitting you! The smugglers are related to Perodeau, and they've used the tunnels on his land for years. It isn't what you think. It's not drugs. It's just a few crates of cognac or whisky here and there, nothing terrible. Anyway, they would cut Perodeau in on the deals but then he got greedy. All I know is that he closed the tunnels, and this led to bad blood. I can only think that they were just trying to pay Perodeau back by harassing you."

Laetitia gestured for Catherine to drink a cognac.

"I don't drink this early in the day," Catherine bristled. But she took up the coffee.

"You are a truly awful woman."

It was uncharacteristic of Catherine to say something like that, and it jarred the others. Laetitia's bottom lip trembled. The couple exchanged looks.

Maybe Laetitia had been a victim of the smugglers too?

Tom drained his second glass of Cognac.

"You're driving, remember?" Catherine said in a hush.

"I needed that." He suddenly felt exhausted.

"Laetitia, I'm finding it difficult … to believe … that you are not somehow … involved in this … thing … with Perodeau? My wife and I were … frightened half to death by these … criminals. Why wouldn't you just tell us … the truth - *the truth*?" Tom mumbled.

Catherine had finished her coffee.

"Tom?" Something was up.

"Just tired. I'm feeling incredibly tired." Tom rubbed his eyes.

"This will help. It's strong." Laetitia poured Tom a cup of coffee. He gulped it.

He was having a hard time focusing. Laetitia and her words

seemed to be moving away from him as if they were at different ends of a corridor. He looked to his wife for reassurance, but she just stared ahead, vacantly.

Catherine gazed at Laetitia. A halo had materialized around the French woman's head. It was mesmerizing. Laetitia avoided Catherine's wide and watery blue eyes. She knew that Catherine had suspected something all along.

"Women always know," Laetitia muttered under her breath.

"W-what was that Lae-Laetitia?" Tom slurred.

She waved her hand dismissively. *The husband is a fool. Any man worth his honor would have demanded to know the absolute truth, not this bullshit story.*

Tom was suddenly gripped with panic. He swallowed hard.

"Catherine?" He mouthed but his tongue wouldn't move.

Laetitia stood up and rocked Catherine backwards into a soft chair. She kissed her tenderly on the forehead.

"Je suis désolé Madame."

Tom was now completely paralyzed. Everything had slowed to a halt. He looked at his wife now soundly asleep on the chair. He was unconscious before he hit the table.

Tom's nose split open over Laetitia's porcelain coffee set: a thick, round spurt of blood pooled around his head.

"Merde!" Laetitia cursed as she leapt over him. "Merde!" She dashed into the kitchen in search of a mop and bucket.

There can be no trace of them.

The Tourists (10)
Rousinac, Southwest France 2019

Tom's dream withered under the pain. It slid through his head like a skewer. He groaned and tried to roll over. No good. A mouse sniffing at her wrist stirred Catherine. But like Tom, she wasn't able to move.

Laetitia had used a powerful tranquilizer on the couple. For hours it had rendered them as helpless as newborns. It was now almost midnight. In the darkness, Tom and Catherine slowly regained movement.

"Tom?"

Silence.

"Are you okay?"

Catherine flopped upright.

"I think I m-might have a s-slight concussion," Tom struggled to get the words out.

"W-where are w-we?"

She struggled to adjust to the darkness.

"I think we're back at Perodeau's house!"

This revelation jolted them.

"We need to wake up," Tom said. "They're probably coming back soon. Laetitia, Perodeau, the whole lot of them." They made their way towards the front door.

Tom and Catherine staggered outside trying to hold one another up.

"They left all of the doors open. Why would they do that?"

Tom raged. "They want us to make a run for it."

"Tom, let's take our chances and get to the main road. Maybe the car …"

"It's gone."

"We could try and hitch a ride out of Rousinac?" Catherine peered up the lane.

Tom looked at his watch.

"No. It's nearly midnight and the main road is at least a mile away. If this is some bizarre game, then they're waiting out there somewhere in the woods with guns. They'd pick us off in no time. We have to go back inside and barricade ourselves in and hide somewhere until the morning. It's our only hope!"

Catherine followed the outline of trees and began to cry.

"Stop it, Catherine! I need your help. We need to secure the house, now!"

"Maybe we can talk to them? We can tell them we won't go to the police if they let us go. After all, we didn't see anyone's face."

Tom pulled her back inside the house. He secured the main doors, bolted the shutters and locked all of the windows.

"We'll be safer upstairs. Help me pull this cupboard over. It will stop them from getting up the stairs."

"No lights, right Tom?"

"That's right sweetheart. Use your keyring flashlight. They won't be able to see where we are through the shutters."

They worked quickly in unison, speaking in hushed tones. Occasionally Tom would motion "stop'" as he listened to a new sound. *What was that?* For a few jagged seconds they held their breath. The welcome culprits, a barn owl or a fox, drew nervous smiles.

The Graystons checked their fortifications one last time before climbing over makeshift barricades and withdrawing to their bedroom, where there was a small closet. At a pinch it would be big enough for the two of them.

We will reason with them. We will pay them off. Tom plotted.

They marshaled simple weapons: an aerosol can, a cigarette lighter, carving knives and the rusted World War II pistol Tom had hidden earlier under the bed. The rifle was missing. *Taken,* Tom surmised. But he did have some bullets left. Some that would fit the pistol.

At long last, they took their positions and waited. Their agony intensified with each passing hour. They battled fatigue. Tom did fractions in his head. Catherine conjured up elaborate conspiracies. In her last attempt to stave off exhaustion, she whispered.

"What if they're all in on it?"

"Who?" Tom replied.

"The whole town?"

"I don't think so," Tom exhaled loudly, rubbing his eyes so hard, he saw stars.

"What if we've stumbled across something big. Something they're willing to come back and kill us for and make it look like the sanglier." Catherine rambled.

"Catherine, you're not thinking right!" Tom snapped. Her eyes suddenly flooded.

He cupped her face.

"I'm sorry sweetheart. I think this might just be a warning to keep us quiet. Think about it. They had an opportunity to kill us when we were unconscious. It took more than Laetitia to move us both here. No, this is a warning. They took Perodeau's drugs and they want us to keep our mouths shut and never come back." His reasoning soothed her.

As Tom listened to Catherine's breathing slow into sleep, he suddenly felt very alone. His reasoning hadn't convinced himself.

Tom knew that they - whoever they were - had likely taken Perodeau's drugs, their car, their luggage and papers. And that this dumping them back at Perodeau's drugged and helpless was a plot to disappear them and finger Perodeau.

They had walked right into their trap.

He had made some big mistakes. He thought about everything that had happened. He had ignored his wife's gut instincts. A big mistake. There had been early signs of criminal activity. He shouldn't have ignored that.

The criminals worked at night, generally a few hours short of dawn. And that, just before their arrival, everything stopped, in essence, total stillness. The animals heard them coming. There were more than a few of them, possibly as many as twelve. They knew the woods. They were locals.

On the first night of their stay Catherine had heard strange noises in the garden, a scout? On the second night, nothing happened, or at least nothing that they had detected. On their third night Catherine had gone downstairs for water and startled a few of them snooping around: a small party?

On the fourth night they had seen a bunch of them. A larger group had returned. Gunfire had repelled them. So, he doubted that they were armed although everyone here had access to hunting rifles.

But surely smugglers would carry guns? Maybe even semi-automatics?
And why hadn't they just broken in when we'd been out?

Then Tom remembered that he might have injured one of them.

Was that it? Was this revenge? None of it makes any sense.

Why would smugglers attack tourists? Why would they want to draw attention to themselves? And why would Laetitia implicate herself by drugging two innocent people? Was it a family business? Were these people inbred psychopaths?

Why had they been placed back in Perodeau's house? What did the locals want to do with them? There was an anomaly at play. Something they were missing: the X factor. Think Tom! Come on!

The Tourists (11)
Rousinac, Southwest France 2019

At 3am a crushing hush enveloped the house, so quiet that Tom's ears hummed. He lay frozen on the bed afraid even to breathe. Perspiration seeped around his eyebrows. His throat dried. When he swallowed, it clicked. The pistol felt light in his hands.

Then he heard a sound. Catherine had heard it too. Her eyes flew open. She grabbed his arm.

"Oh God, Tom, no."

"They're here."

"Where? The garden?"

"I don't know. Maybe closer."

"How close?"

"The roof or," Tom gestured towards their bedroom window.

He quietly slipped off the bed.

"What should I do now?" she whispered. "I don't know what to do Tom."

"Don't make noise."

"I want to hide now. Can't we just hide?"

He heard the panic in her voice.

"Listen, we have a gun, remember?"

Tom knelt back on the bed and pulled Catherine closer.

"We'll get through this."

A few minutes passed ... and then nothing. Tom and Catherine ached in anticipation. The silence was unbearable.

Then, all at once there was an onslaught downstairs: smashing, crunching, cracking, grinding. Movement everywhere, like an army attacking a fort.

A high-pitched sound rang out.

"What the fuck was that?"

"A battle cry?" Catherine replied.

The noise that had sounded was bizarre. For a moment, Catherine thought of her neighbor's cats back home, how they would cry and fight, and make horrible sounds. But this? This didn't sound natural.

The couple stood rigid. Tom's hand shook uncontrollably, rattling the pistol against an iron bed knob. The odor had returned. It was seeping through the vents.

They come through the sewers. Tom thought.

Catherine grabbed the aerosol can.

"What should we do now?"

"I don't know."

His chin quivered. She watched as he folded. The gun dropped from his hand.

The entire house was under siege. Doors, shutters, shingles, locks, everything shook violently. Something deep inside of Catherine snapped. She pulled the chest of drawers out of the way.

"What are you doing?"

Catherine unlocked the bedroom door and ran out onto the

landing. There was more movement coming from outside: dull, rhythmic thuds that scraped up against the exterior walls.

"They're climbing again," Tom said as he followed her to the top of the stairs.

"We have two options Tom. We can wait for them in that coffin of a room, or we can take our chances here."

Tom's face stiffened with resolve.

"Let's go!"

When they drowned the hallway in light the noises outside immediately ceased.

"They don't like the light," Tom said with relief.

"They don't want us to see their faces." Catherine replied.

"Wait. Listen."

"What …?"

"Why would they make animal sounds?" He almost laughed aloud.

All of the house lights went out. For a few terrible seconds they were in total darkness.

"They cut the power lines." Tom whispered.

"Why?" Catherine replied.

Because they're sick fucks and this is a game.

They had had the same thought at the exact same time. Neither of them spoke it out loud. Tom flicked on the flashlight. He pulled her away from the landing window.

"If they get in, use the lighter and aerosol. Aim for the face. The heat will repel them. Just keep out of my way. I'll need the light to shoot straight."

It was soundless below. Tom laid his arm on the banister, the gun aimed down the stairs. His trigger finger twitched.

"What's that?"

Catherine looked up towards the ceiling.

Someone was crawling across the roof. They heard the crash of roof tiles moving, thrown to the ground.

"Above."

Catherine clung to Tom's shirt. He tilted the pistol upwards. Desperate for breath, they vigilantly waited and watched. The noise above them stopped. Tom flicked back the gun's safety cap.

"J'ai un pistolet!" he yelled.

Silence. *Had he frightened them off?*

The lull was short-lived. From outside of the landing window, Tom recognized a sound he had heard before.

He had once watched a neighbor's dog corner a mouse under a dresser. It couldn't reach the rodent directly, but it had spent an hour circling the furniture, sniffing out the mouse's exact location. This sound was the same.

Do they have dogs? How could they get them on the roof?

"What...?"

Catherine was stopped mid-sentence by an explosive crash. It came from a bedroom window to their right. The wood appeared to be twisting under assault. Neither Tom nor Catherine made a sound as they ran along the landing and flooded the room with the flashlight. Whatever was on the other side swung backwards. The excitement outside escalated.

Chimpanzees... Catherine thought. *That's what they sound like, chimpanzees.* The howls drummed up again, rupturing a fragile peace.

"There must be dozens of them," Tom spit out.

Something broke through the front of the house. Instinctively Tom charged to the top of the stairs. Catherine snatched his sleeve.

"Tom, stop. We only have one flashlight. We need to stay together."

They could hear them downstairs filling the lounge with smashing and shredding. Thankfully, the couple had locked and nailed every interior door shut. It would at least delay them.

"Shit!" Tom cursed as something above them dropped into the attic with a heavy thud. *They're looking for an entry point.* Tom felt Catherine jump. The intruders were now everywhere on the ground floor of the house.

Tom surveyed their position. They were too vulnerable on the landing. And the closet in their master bedroom would be a coffin if set alight.

"Quick! Bathroom – NOW!" Tom commanded.

The bathroom was a good refuge: three stone walls and a solid oak door, Tom reasoned. He would shout a warning in schoolboy French. He would beg for their lives, offer them cash. No one would volunteer to burst through the door knowing the risk.

"Get in the bathtub and stand behind me," Tom said as he locked the bathroom door.

Then they waited.

It was quiet for what felt like the longest time.

They felt the vibrations on the floorboards first. Movement crept toward them from every corner of the house. The stairs creaked. Doors groaned open.

Tom listened to the pattern of the advancement. After each room was probed, the silence would resume. Then a kind of whispering would start.

Regrouping? Tom felt Catherine's knees buckle. Her heart banged against his back like a sledgehammer.

A revolting stench permeated the bathroom, like roadkill. Tom retched. His finger hovered on the trigger. He could now hear shuffling along their end of the landing. The bathroom door was tested. A cautious pressure was applied. The lock jangled in small, measured thrusts.

Each time this happened, Tom pointed the flashlight forward and shouted a warning that he had a gun. He said it in English. By this point he couldn't remember any French. This would cause the footsteps to retreat a few paces.

Please let the dawn come.

The flashlight was steadily dimming. Surely at first light they would leave them alone. *They had had their sport, right?*

All that stood between them, and the invaders was a flashlight battery. Catherine clasped the aerosol can, but the lighter lay rooted in her pocket. When the flashlight at last extinguished, the door's hinges whinnied under a new force.

Crack!

"Catherine, I love you. I'm so sorry for everything." Tom's voice was barely audible.

The door snapped in two like a wafer. Tom raised his pistol and aimed it at the shadows behind it. He didn't hear his wife clawing at the bath tiles behind her. One half of the door hit the side of the tub, the other remained suspended by a single sturdy hinge.

Tom fired once as the blackness enveloped them.

The Maquis* (1)

Rousinac, Southwest France 1944

*French resistance movement during WWII

Gerard Dupre sprinted through the sodden fields towards a country lane. It was a bitter cold dawn with frost dusting the back roads. He followed the lane until it forked.

One way led to the village of St. Sebastian, the other snaked up a gated muddy track. Gerard stopped at the crossroad and wiped his boots on the fence. Then he made an owl's call.

Silence.

He made it again.

Squinting up at a derelict farmhouse smothered by trees, he waited for a signal. A candle flickered in the window for a brief moment. Gerard carefully scanned the road behind him and ahead. Nothing stirred. Jumping the gate, he made for the house.

As Gerard entered, he saw a group of men warming themselves around a kerosene lamp. They turned to welcome the tall broad, black haired man, their Maquis leader and fellow townsman. Gerard returned the chorus of "bonjours."

A slender man stood up, Daniel Malraux, Gerard's second lieutenant.

"The drop didn't happen yesterday," he announced.

The others looked at their feet. Gerard turned to a sullen man sitting in the shadows. His ginger beard glowed in the lamplight.

"Merde!" Gerard spat. "What went wrong, Frederic?"

The man sighed.

"It's bad news."

Gerard took a seat.

"Tell me."

Frederic Arriver motioned for the wine jug. He took a long hard drink. The men huddled in as he began.

"Just a few hours ago, a man arrived in the forest. His eyes were wild, and he was covered in blood. He gave me this letter, took some water then left." Gerard grabbed the letter and read it aloud.

"Notice to all Maquis brothers in arms. Due to betrayal by a member of the Libourne Maquis, a British agent has been captured. The S.S. took him and after many days, he gave them everything. After that, knocks on the door at night. Maquis rounded up, tortured, killed. Our network is now compromised. All scheduled drops and operations are canceled. For now, do nothing. Lay low. Stay vigilant. Be patient. Keep strong. Vive la France."

Gerard groaned.

Daniel rested a hand on his shoulder.

"Farmers have been shot in their fields for wearing the Basque beret. Nothing is safe anymore. No one must stand out." He said softly.

"I've heard, for every German wounded or killed, they will kill ten ..." Charles Perodeau added.

"They're just desperate. They know they're losing." Daniel replied.

"Yes, but desperate men are dangerous. They are driving a wedge between us and the people. Anyone could snitch. The nights used to be ours but now …" Charles argued.

"Some say the war will be over in months." Charles Perodeau's brother, Phillipe, offered.

"They're burning every village they pass through, and *worse*, crucifying babies, violating our women, burning down churches. That's what he told me." Frederic Arriver suddenly blurted. The room fell horribly silent.

"They are not human. Their judgment can only come from God himself." Gerard declared.

"There will be another drop. We must be patient." Daniel countered.

The Maquis men drank wine and resigned themselves to the quiet of their own thoughts.

Gerard Dupre stared at the lamp until his eyes blurred. Many French men had lost a father, an uncle or a brother to the Germans in the Great War of 1914-18. Few had lost a mother. In 1916, Gerard's mother had been blown apart in an accident at a munitions factory. His father would fall under machine gun fire on the Western Front seven months later.

Raised by impoverished grandparents in the Rousinac country-side, Gerard would be subject to countless privations. When World War Two broke out, he had enthusiastically signed up to fight. But as a master butcher, he was denied. His work was categorized as an essential occupation. So, when dispatches warned of advancing German Forces, Gerard immediately formed a resistance group.

Daniel Malraux had no compelling motive to join the Maquis. His daily life and work hadn't changed with German occupation. He hadn't lost a relative to either war. For Daniel, none of that mattered. Joining the resistance was simply the right thing to do.

A regular patron of Gerard's butcher's shop in town, he'd let slip where his sympathies lay. As a Notaire (minor official) in Rousinac, he would prove invaluable for the Maquis. So, after some discreet enquiries he was recruited.

For brothers Phillipe and Charles Perodeau, the motive for resisting the Nazis was simple. They were now classified as "Jews" under the Second French Jewish Statute, Act of 2 June 1941 signed into law by Marshall Pétain. The fact that their French father Henri Perodeau had been killed in the Great War serving his country no longer counted.

There were two young men among the Maquis. At eighteen years of age, Alain Boussuet's and Jean-Baptist Fauvert's childhoods had ended upon invasion. The curfews, the food shortages, the lack of social events had fostered an intense hatred of the Germans in both boys. They were determined to do their part.

Then there was the strange one, Frederic Arriver. He had volunteered to be a scout in the woods as soon as the Germans rolled into Rousinac. It hadn't been a tough decision. Frederic didn't like most people, least of all Germans, preferring the natural world and the solitude it offered him from the war.

His only point of reference with the outside world came from Gerard Dupre. Someone he had known since school. A person he trusted like a dog its shepherd. For his part, Gerard knew how to handle the red-whiskered man.

Each man ruminated in the damp room, and silently vowed to keep fighting on. There would be another opportunity to deal their enemies a blow. It would come. They must fight on.

Finally, Gerard broke the silence.

"We'll regroup in a few days. Perhaps by then, we will have more news."

One by one the men dejectedly started toward the door.

"Quiet, there's movement outside." Frederic Arriver gestured for the men to get down.

A blast of light pierced the windows. The men dropped to the floor.

All at once the farmhouse was illuminated.

"You are surrounded. Come out with your hands above your heads and you will be spared!"

Gerard Dupre peered through the window. A German army company dotted the hedgerow.

One of them must have been followed somehow.

"Quick, to the back of the house," he shouted. "Back! Back!"

The Germans scuttled alongside the farmhouse to gain an advantage as the Maquis made a frantic dash to the rear. Daniel led the charge and kicked through the back door.

"No!" Gerard shouted.

He tackled the younger man to the ground as a shower of gunfire ripped into the rear's facade. Two German snipers were positioned behind a tumbled barn wall. Gerard's men shrank back into the house.

"We're trapped!" Charles Perodeau yelped.

The sinewy, mustached man looked to his leader in desperation. Gerard lowered his head and indicated for the men to gather around.

"I have an idea. Daniel, locate and distribute the weapons. I need two volunteers to join me on the roof to provide covering fire while the rest of you retreat into the woods."

One of the teen lads fell forward.

"I'll join you commander," Alain Boussuet offered.

Gerard patted the young man's shoulder as another, Jean-Baptist Fauvert, also volunteered.

"No, I will go with you Gerard." Daniel Malraux countered.

"Let these boys go home to their families."

Though they were young the lads were good shots with keen, fresh eyes. Daniel was near-sighted and next to useless with a rifle. War was no time for sentiment. He must take their sacrifice Gerard concluded.

"No."

"Come out, you French pigs!" the German commander roared from outside. "You have thirty seconds to surrender!"

The men cowered from the imposing silhouettes of Germans systematically preparing a firing squad. Gerard knew that they had little time left.

"Listen carefully, me and the boys will climb up and pin down the snipers at the back of the house. That is their weakest point. Run from here as soon as we open fire. Run as fast as you can. Use the outbuildings to shield you and slip into the woods. Split up and DO NOT go home. Not until you know the coast is clear. We'll keep you covered for as long as we can."

Gerard handed out pistols. The men hastily snatched them up, understanding his message.

If you get cornered, shoot the German bastards. Then shoot yourself.

He took Daniel's arm.

"If we don't get out, you're in command my friend. Good luck and Vive La France!"

Turning back to his two volunteers, Gerard winked reassuringly.

"Come my garçons, let's show Fritz some fireworks!"

Charging up a stairwell towards the loft, the three fighters edged their way toward a wooden flap. One by one they raised themselves onto the roof. Gerard searched the shadows for the man wearing an officer's insignia. That would be his first target.

Gerard's volunteers positioned themselves to take out the German soldiers at the rear. Gerard spotted his mark. The man had raised his head for just a second but that was all he needed. He killed the officer instantly. For a moment, a mist of blood hung in the air.

Alain and Jean-Baptist unleashed a spray of bullets, enabling most of their comrades to flee into the woods. While the Germans searched for cover, Gerard and his snipers tucked in against the chimney.

Gerard assessed the damage. A sound caught his ear. It was the slow, metallic creak of a machine gun being repositioned. Staying where they were would be suicide. He motioned for the boys to abandon the roof and fire randomly at the enemy.

The machine gun swiveled, aimed, then exploded. One side of the roof was obliterated. Gerard rolled and fell behind an old shutter, gashing his hand on a jagged tile. He retaliated with a hail of fire that dazed the gunner. The man clutched his chest and flopped forward like a rag doll.

The three remained pinned to the back of what was left of the farmhouse roof. Just as the Germans were about to surround the house and torch it, Daniel and the others began shooting from the forest. One soldier was killed instantly, a second was injured.

The German patrol was now leaderless, comprised mostly of inexperienced farmboys. The gunfire flushed them out, and they hurried into the woods in pursuit of Gerard's band.

The plan had worked.

Gerard could hear the thrashing of undergrowth and the distant *clap-clap-clap* of gunfire. He motioned for his young fighters not to shoot at the retreating rear. As tempting as it was. The boys hung onto the farmhouse chimney like bats. Their eyes glittered in the shadows.

"Down the chimney. Silence." Gerard mouthed pointing to the stumped, sooty stack in front of him. "Just like St Nicholas."

All three, inched along the roof's stone spine and dropped into the chimney's black mouth. They found a ledge and stood wedged against one another.

We can't stay. If they circle back they'll torch the place; we'll be baked alive like bread, Gerard thought.

"Let's go."

They jumped down into the house. Gerard peered from behind a ragged drape and inspected the muddy trail. It was empty. The machine gun smoked unattended.

They'd gone but they would come back.

The young men began to creep about the house.

"Stop! Split up. Go!" Gerard commanded, taking their guns. He watched as they disappeared into the hedgerows. Then he slid out of the house and ducked along a brook.

His gashed hand throbbed, and he cleaned the wound in the shallow waters, wrapping it in a handkerchief. He ached for normalcy: a warm simple breakfast; the touch of his children; a knowing smile from his wife.

But as he entered his home by the back door, Gerard found more than his family waiting for him.

The Maquis (2)
Rousinac, Southwest France 1944

"Good morning, Monsieur Dupre."

An SS officer greeted Gerard Dupre in perfect French.

The man continued to drink his coffee at Gerard's kitchen table. Upstairs, soldiers stomped and turned over furniture. Gerard glanced at his wife, Nicole, a buxom sandy-haired woman. The German noticed.

Nicole turned to fold laundry as Gerard crossed the kitchen and stood over a cracked enamel sink. One squeak from the tap sent ice-cold water running over the now-bloodied handkerchief. He stole a look down at his trousers and linen shirt, black with chimney soot.

"How can I help you today?" Gerard offered without turning.

Outside he could hear soldiers talking to his children. His eldest daughter was busy preventing her younger brother from entering the house. Gerard's middle children, two brown haired girls, sat solemnly on the cottage wall. The soldiers were offering them chocolate.

"Forgive our intrusion this morning," the officer sighed, pointing to the ceiling, "but we crushed a band of cowardly rebels a mile from here, at the Larousse farm."

Gerard knew this to be a lie, but he did not flinch.

"I see," he said gravely.

The German clucked his mouth with disgust.

"There was an ambush on one of our patrols, but the partisans were either killed or ran away of course. We expect to have all of the conspirator's names by this evening."

Nicole dropped a bar of soap, making the officer jump.

"Excuse me," she gasped.

"Not at all Madame, it must be difficult for you ..."

The officer eyed Gerard closely,

"... with your husband gone so often?"

Gerard approached the kitchen table. He dragged out a chair, sat down and looked the German square in the eyes. His wife poured him some coffee.

"The work is hard and the hours long, now that we have so few men available to help," Gerard finally said after sipping his brew.

The officer nodded, "Yes, yes."

His eyes rested on Gerard's gashed hand.

"So, you were at your butcher shop this morning Monsieur?"

Gerard gulped hard, straightening his neck. What had his children told the Germans? What had Nicole said? His bicycle remained against the wall. He could not have been at the shop; it was too far to walk. How could he explain the cut on his hand? The soot on his clothes?

Nicole had stooped to pick up a toy rabbit from the floor. She held it a little too long before folding it away with the laundry.

"No, Officer, uh ..." Gerard paused, peering deeply into the German's sterile gray eyes.

"Beck," the man replied. "Officer Beck."

Gerard smiled.

"Officer Beck, it's Sunday. On Sundays I rise at dawn and go into the fields to get a rabbit or two for supper."

At that, three soldiers tumbled down the stairs.

"Nothing, sir," they informed their superior.

The Officer motioned for them to leave. Nicole dashed Gerard a reassuring look, but he remained fixed upon the German. Officer Beck glanced at the rifle hanging over Gerard's kitchen mantle. His eyes narrowed.

"Hunting without a gun Monsieur? Returning without a rabbit?"

Gerard shrugged.

"In these parts we catch our rabbits with snares. I tried to catch one today, but as you can see, she had the better part of me."

He held up his injured hand. Officer Beck did not shift his stare from Gerard's eyes. The French man lowered his hand and resumed drinking. Officer Beck declined more coffee.

"If you were out hunting rabbits Monsieur, where did you go, *exactly?*" he pressed. Gerard's mind began to race. Fresh spots of perspiration popped over his forehead.

Nicole pointed to her husband's dirty clothing and was about to say something, but the German hushed her.

If I say I was near the Larousse farm he will ask if I heard any gunshots. But I know that's not where they were. If I say "yes" he will know I am lying. If I say I was on the other side of the woods he will know I was near our hideout. He will ask me if I heard anything there. Think! Think!

The leather in the German's boots squeaked as he stretched his toes. Gerard ran his finger over the cut. The kitchen clock ticked. There was a sudden peel of children's laughter from the yard.

Think. Think.

"Go on, tell him!" Nicole blurted.

Gerard blanched. *What?*

Officer Beck cocked his head towards her.

"Just tell him! Tell him who she is," Nicole hissed. "The children aren't here."

Gerard blinked madly. Nicole threw the linen basket onto the floor.

"Fine! Then I will. He was with some whore, Officer Beck, so please, if you would like to question my husband further feel free to take him from this house. In fact, I would be forever in your debt."

Officer Beck studied her face. It was flushed with anger. Gerard wiped his brow.

What was she talking about?

Nicole continued, "There are many women here without husbands, and the men who remain have little honor."

The German raised an eyebrow at Gerard. Gerard looked to the floor. *Mon Dieu, she is throwing me a lifeline. Which whore? Who was she thinking of? Who would I be condemning to this pig's interrogations?*

The Officer leaned forward impatiently.

"I must know who you were with this morning Monsieur. I must be able to verify this claim of your wife's. Who is the woman? You realize if she denies you, you will be arrested, and if she confirms you ..." he smirked, "... you'll be in even more trouble."

The couple's toddler started to cry loudly. Officer Beck grew irritated.

"It's cold. It would be a shame to leave your children outside much longer. Just give me a name. Who? Where? I will not leave until I know," he shouted.

Nicole began to speak but the officer raised his hand.

"You will find it purgative to confess Monsieur, believe me."

He pushed back his chair and studied Gerard and Nicole closely.

Gerard squirmed. The German tapped his cup with a spoon. Nicole turned toward a cupboard. Abruptly the front door flew open, and their youngest daughter entered.

"Mama, we're cold."

Nicole mumbled "coming" and turned to Officer Beck for approval. He nodded. As she passed her husband, Nicole placed a vase on the table. Gerard read the words: *Gipsy Rose* on one side. He knew that she had positioned it for a reason but what?

He sighed loudly forcing his eyes to wander the room, searching for a clue.

Gipsy Rose, Gipsy Rose...

The door slammed behind his wife and child. Gerard listened as Nicole comforted their children in the frigid air. The vase stood directly between Gerard and the German. Officer Beck tossed a sideways glance at it, before sliding it to the edge of the table.

"We both know you're lying and when I find enough evidence you and your family will face a firing squad."

Then as the German motioned to pick up the vase, Gerard dashed it against the fireplace.

"Merde!" he raged.

The Officer drew his pistol and sprang back. Two soldiers barged in. Gerard slumped back into his chair. Officer Beck ushered his men to leave.

"I am sorry, you must have mistaken me for something else, Officer Beck. You see I am just a weak and sinful man." Gerard cleared his throat.

"The woman I met this morning is called Leah, a gypsy girl, part of a traveling troupe of actors, part performers, part tinkers.

You know these people, *Jews*. I think some of them. They were in Rousinac all last week. They performed near the castle. They come every year. They camp down by the river, next to the orchards. I gave her the rabbits and she..."

The Nazi frowned.

"Where are they now?"

Gerard sighed heavily.

"Pfff ... God only knows. They don't take the normal routes. They could be anywhere."

The Officer went to the door.

"Madame Dupre?" he called softly. "Would you please come in? Yes, and the children also. Send them upstairs."

Officer Beck turned back to Gerard as the children breezed in. Nicole entered, apprehensive.

The German faced Gerard resolutely.

"Wait outside. I'd like a moment with your wife."

Gerard Dupre snatched his coat and walked outside. A soldier offered him a cigarette and he took it. Inside, a conversation began but it rarely ventured above a mumble. Gerard wandered toward the garden wall, finally settling to a stop. He hungrily smoked.

Giddiness overtook him, a welcome diversion from the drama of the past few hours. Tobacco had been in such short supply recently, almost impossible to obtain except through smugglers or transient foreign agents. He hadn't smoked an authentic cigarette in months. He welcomed the exotic taste the tar left in his mouth.

It wasn't long before the front door opened. Officer Beck emerged grim faced and blinking in the bright morning light. He ordered his men into their truck and motorcar, before standing next to Gerard by the wall.

Tapping the French man's wounded hand with his glove he whispered.

"I used to hunt rabbits myself as a boy Monsieur. My father owned a farm deep in the Bavarian woods. Rabbits are very predictable creatures, easy to catch, yes?"

Gerard nodded as the officer continued.

"Not so a wolf. A wolf is cunning. He comes and goes almost like a phantom, or so it seems. But eventually, if one is patient, one can catch a wolf because the wolf needs to hunt. He must eat, you see. He cannot disobey his nature. All one needs is patience and to be in the right place at the right time. I'm sure you understand?"

Gerard exhaled loudly.

"I do."

"Your children are very pretty Monsieur."

Officer Beck stood up and examined his gloves.

"Beware the wolf."

Gerard watched the military entourage become a speck on the road ahead. He let out a slow, guttural moan. Inside, his youngest began to wail. Gerard rushed to the bushes and threw up.

The Maquis (3)
Rousinac, Southwest France 1944

The church was bitterly cold.

The priest's mouth was moving but Cecile Malraux didn't hear his words. Her stomach growled with hunger.

Would this sermon ever end?

Eventually it did, and the parishioners hurried out, their breath clouding in front of them.

Where's Daniel?

Cecile went straight home.

She was worried. He had left her sleeping alone this Sunday morning, his bed clothes folded neatly on the side of the bed, his bicycle gone. He hadn't told her where he was going or whom he was meeting. He never did.

I'm doing this to protect you.

"Is that you?" Daniel called from the bath.

He'd heard his wife enter the apartment. Cecile ran to him.

"Hello …" Her voice trailed off when she saw the wound. A bloody hole above his right collarbone.

"It's not as bad as it looks ma cherie. *Really*."

Dark shadows pooled in his once youthful eyes.

"The bullet missed but I caught some shrapnel." Daniel indicated to some tweezers at the sink.

"I got most of it out I think."

Cecile examined the wound.

"Perhaps we should send for …"

"No, no, it's fine. The less people that know the better."

She silently accepted his decision.

Thank you, Daniel thought as Cecile slowly undressed and sunk down into the bath with him. The water was pink with the blood of her beloved.

"I didn't know you were home," she said as she tended to his wound. "The bike wasn't in the hallway."

"I lost it," Daniel frowned.

Cecile did not press the matter. She allowed Daniel his secrets. But the bike weighed heavily on his mind.

The bike is generic enough. It shouldn't point back to me. I could try to go back and get it but… Why did I leave it so close to the farmhouse? Idiot!

He turned to Cecile, feeling a sudden impulse to talk.

"I need to tell you something," he leaned forward and took her hands in his. "I want you to know why, if I ever …"

"Sssshhhhh! I won't have it." She pressed a finger to his lips. "It's bad luck to speak of one's own …"

"It's getting serious Cecile. Today was close. Too close."

"You cannot continue like this Daniel. You're not like the other men. You're different."

"I'm not." Tears steamed his glasses. She took them off with a tenderness that stopped his breath.

"Yes, you are. You have a decent job. The Germans need good administrative workers like you in Rousinac. Our lives needn't change."

"Our lives have already changed. You don't know what I do when I leave at night."

"You think us women are stupid? You think we don't understand what happens in those woods?"

"Cecile, I can't sit idly by while my countrymen are herded off in trucks to work as slaves!"

He kicked the water angrily.

"Be sensible! You can wait this war out Daniel. The BBC is saying it will all be over in less than a year. You can be invisible my love. You can stay here with me, working at the notaire's office."

"It's too late for that."

"What do you mean?"

"A woman from the village is scheduled to take over my job. I'm to train her to replace me."

"I don't understand…"

"I got my compulsory national service call Cecile. The STO… the damn *Service du Travail Obligatoire*. It was only a matter of time."

"But they cannot force you to do this Daniel."

"Don't be naïve my sweetheart, they can, and they will. Hundreds of thousands of French workers have already been deported to Germany."

Cecile hung her head. He was right.

"When would you leave?" She finally asked.

"The orders came Thursday direct from Paris to the Rousinac office. I've been putting off telling you. I've got two weeks to make the arrangements."

"Where will they send you?" She cried.

"East."

"East – do you mean Germany?"

"Yes, a place I've heard of."

"What place?"

Daniel took in a long hard breath.

"Dachau."

Cecile's lips trembled.

"They say the Germans burn people alive there."

" I know."

"How will you cope?"

He lurched upright, eyes aglow.

"I won't go Cecile! I won't work for the Third Reich. I'm joining the Bordeaux Maquis. There's much to be done. The allies may win the war, but *we* will liberate France!"

He watched her face darken.

" I've saved a little money and made provisions for you. It will last at least for a while."

She had wanted to scream and hit him. Instead, she found herself saying, "What will I tell the Germans when they ask?"

"Tell them that your husband is a coward, and that he ran away to Spain." He feigned a smile.

Cecile Malraux touched her husband's thin wrist and felt his pulse racing. She found no words to fill the silence in his blank eyes. There was no way she could tell him about the child growing inside of her now.

Her husband already looked like a dead man.

The Americans (1)
Embankment, South London 2019

A blond handsome American man sat in a fancy rooftop restaurant. He gazed at the foreign City sprawled out below him, never quite believing his luck to live and work here. The pretty young server had circled back.

Did he need another drink?

No thanks.

He told her he was waiting for a friend. She glanced at his empty glass then to the lunch shift that had just piled in. She smiled with her eyes, and blushed.

Okay.

The restaurant swelled, adding to his discomfort. He was occupying one of the best tables. He did another sweep of the restaurant. No sign of his lunch guest. He picked up his cell. No messages. No missed calls. *Nothing.* He munched on a second breadstick.

"DAVID! HEY!" Someone yelled from the elevator. The entire restaurant stopped to gawk. A man waved frantically as he weaved around tables, almost kicking over a champagne bucket.

"Whoops!"

He straightened the bottle and offered to pour the diners a drink. It was awkward. A waiter intervened.

"That's okay, sir, thank you."

David Frankel felt his stomach clench.

"Hey, buddy." He stood up, arms outstretched.

"Yeah, David, I don't do ..." James Harrison backed into another server.

"Right. I always forget."

"Y-you're way too homo-tactile for me."

James sat down and re-arranged every item on the table until it formed a geometric pattern. David knew not to interrupt this ritual. James had been like this from Day 1 when they'd bumped into one another in the college canteen.

He leaned back and browsed the menu.

"God-damned traffic trying to cross this Roman city. Be quicker on a donkey I swear. So, get this, the cab driver ..." James burst out a ton of detail. David sucked it up. There was no apology for his tardiness, just a litany of observations.

"Yeah, no worries, man." David said, with the unconscious ease of an old friend.

His companion ordered a mineral water, *two* ice-cubes, *one* squirt of lemon *but no lemon floating. In a clean glass. Make sure it's clean, no smears.* Then he studied the menu like a crossword puzzle.

A trio sat diagonal, were mesmerized by the disheveled American.

James' thick, jet-black hair was oddly coiffed, either with grease or wax. He wore a trench coat despite the day's rising heat. His sneakers didn't match, and under his coat he sported a purple shirt and a pair of combat shorts.

Was he homeless or just a lunatic? One of them snickered.

David felt the tension mounting as other patrons slowly turned in their direction. He stiffened. None of them knew what this guy had gone through for his country, for their freedoms. James' combat shorts were a military issue. They represented what service had cost him, severe PTSD, battle scars and aggravated Aspergers.

He held their stares until one by one the other diners turned away. He loved his man like a brother.

"Help me make sense of this mediocre menu." James blurted.

"Sure."

It took a while to navigate the menu given James' various (imagined) food allergies. The men finally settled on an organic *Chicken Cesar* salad each, without dressing for James.

"You look good." David found himself saying.

"No, I don't. I look like shit. I know I do. I haven't slept in days. I probably stink like roadkill too." Again, David's stomach tightened.

Aw fuck he's off his meds again.

"How's the conference?"

"Predictable, banal, disappointing. Plus, you don't give a shit. Let's be real. I wouldn't give a shit if I didn't have to be there. If my psychotic superior wasn't on a mission to destroy my entire fucking career and …."

"How can a conference on serial killers be banal?" David quipped. His joke fell on deaf ears.

James had wiped his side of the table clean for the third time and rattled off a bunch of conference data. The wait staff were watching his every move. It wasn't idle curiosity, David knew. They were wondering if this kook was going to pull out a gun and murder everyone.

He shook his head. You couldn't meet a less violent guy. New York's Hudson River loomed into his mind's eye. A memory surfaced of a crowd of students leaning over a Pier fence. Splashing about in the river, was a gangly dark-haired man. One strong arm above the water, held a soaked puppy. The other paddled towards the Pier. An old lady was calling. *Oh, come to Mama baby, come to Mama!* That was James. If he saw someone in harm's way, he jumped straight in.

The food arrived fast, and James ate like a prisoner. In huge noisy gulps with a paranoid eye and a knife poised in defense. David knew they couldn't over-stay this lunch. They would have to eat and leave.

The Americans (2)

Metropolitan Police Forensic Science laboratory, South London 2019

A walk along the river Thames hadn't done anything to change James' mania.

Would he get sectioned again? David wondered.

What damage to his career as a brilliant forensic psychologist could he cause before then? It was such a waste.

No one could connect the dots like James Harrison.

He had a Sherlock Holmes knack of cracking codes and profiling the most diabolical characters. It had kept him alive on active combat duty in the Middle East and it had made him invaluable to the alphabet agencies that procured his services.

David had lost count of the monsters James had put behind bars. But his OCD was increasingly debilitating making work engagements problematic. As a consequence, John Jay college where James taught, had placed him on temporary leave, "to get his shit together," a mutual friend back in the States, had emailed.

David knew that James was being given his last chance. The serial killer conference in London was meant to put him back on track. Although, if anything, it looked like it would derail him.

There was only one thing left to do.

"Boy, this is an unbelievable shit hole." James said as they walked through the security gates at New Scotland Yard's forensics HQ. The place where David Frankel worked as senior forensics medical examiner.

He was relieved they were in the elevator alone. It took less than a minute to reach his lab. Unfortunately, when they entered the room, they found it occupied.

"I'm not talking to anyone." James barked, avoiding everyone's eyes.

"Hey gang!"

Two men and a woman stood staring at James.

"What's up?" David interrupted. The woman elbowed a nervous kid. The nervous kid shuffled toward David.

"Well, you got this package, sir and …"

David glanced at the post-mark.

"This arrived almost three weeks ago?"

"It kind of got lost in the mail room, sir."

"Kind of? Jesus, this is a forensics lab Owen! What if it's perishable evidence?"

"Sorry sir."

David examined the package more thoroughly. It had come direct from France, handwritten and personally addressed to him. The envelope, he noted, had been purchased locally. It didn't appear to be official business. Gently, he prized the package open. A letter fell out first. He pulled on forensic gloves and read it in silence.

Dear David,

I hope you are well. This is Tom Grayston from the Hadley Woods Rifle Club. I know this might sound odd, but could you look at the enclosed sample and confirm what it is?

My wife and I were recently on holiday in France: c/o Monsieur Perodeau, Chemin de Perodeau, Rousinac, France 17260 a rental property, and we came across something criminal, maybe a smuggling ring? We believe people tried to break in even when we were home. After one incident we found this substance splattered quite high up, on an exterior wall. (That's the sample you're looking at.) We're wondering if it's some type of climbing glue?

Anyway – a ton of strange things happened over several nights. We're thinking about pressing charges against Perodeau (the owner) so no one else goes through this. The sample could be used as evidence so please keep it somewhere safe. I know you're busy so no big rush. Just thought I'd ask.

cheers,

Tom Grayston

C: 1-555-478-304

tgrayston@buildermail.com

David smiled. He liked Tom. The guy had a dry sense of humor. Once in a while they'd grab a beer.

Curious.

Tom hadn't shown up at the rifle club in months, which was odd because he was an avid shooter.

Was he still on vacation?

"Fortunately for you Owen, it wasn't urgent." David turned to the woman. She handed him a pile of documents.

"I would *really* appreciate it if these could get back to me by Friday. As you know David, I'm now managing two departments and …"

"Sure." He cut her off. She made to leave.

"Oh Hannah, can you check out a place in France called Rousinac? See if anything unusual comes up?"

"How do you spell it?" Hannah pulled out her cell.

"R-O-U-S-I-N-A-C."

His secretary and the kid left the lab. One other person remained, aside from James, who scowled from the other side of the room.

David donned his green, forensic overalls and tipped out a small container wedged at the bottom of the package. He held it up to the light. It contained a sample of what looked like tar.

"Okay I'm intrigued."

"Why am I here and why's that guy staring at me?" James blurted.

"Oh my God, are you …?" David's lab assistant began to ask.

"Yes, he is." David confirmed.

The lab assistant, Michael Jones, stood googly-eyed.

"Who is this imbecile?" James snarled. It snapped Michael out of his trance.

"I'm a great admirer of your work Mr. Harrison. I based my PhD on …"

"Yeah, awesome, whatever. David tell me why I'm here."

"Don't stare at him, it makes him uncomfortable." David mumbled to his assistant. He pointed to a white board, where a map of London hung. Several photographs of young girls were pinned to it.

"Abduction occurred a few days ago but we think it's connected

to a string of murders spanning back two years. We've profiled every type of killer. Zilch. This guy snatches girls in broad daylight, sixteen-year-olds. Suffocates them, decorates them in flowers then dumps them in a river. Eight girls in two years. We've found seven."
He handed James a folder with polaroids taken from crime scenes.

There was silence. James traced the map with his finger, then leaned in to read every last scrap of data. The locations, the times, the dates of each girl's kidnap and discovery.

David observed his lab assistant in an act of reverence. His hands clasped, mouth slightly open.

"We think it's someone with working access to rivers as ..." Michael began.

"Don't interrupt." James shot back.

Silence.

After ten minutes, James bowed his head and took a deep breath. Then he stood back, his eyes tightly closed.

"Serial killer. Confirmed. Superb attention to detail. The flower arrangements are astonishingly accurate. Look there, the poppies are of a certain .... it doesn't matter. This is a disciplined, highly focused mind... hunts top specimens, well-bred socialites from the best finishing school in London."

"So, what's the fetish here, posh girls?" Michael interrupted. He was ignored.

"The eight are an homage to the Pre-Raphaelite painter John Everette Millais, and his painting Ophelia."

"Where's the eighth?" Michael asked without a flinch.

"Where do you think the only Pre-Raphaelite redhead of the collection would be?"

"Collection? Jesus, James." David suddenly felt queasy.

"She even has the same initials as Elizabeth Eleanor Siddall. The killer might as well as telegrammed you … Look. There's only one redhead. It's the center-piece. The dead giveaway, no pun intended. The others are all supporting pieces. I imagine the killer had those subjects photographed before leaving the scene."

"What?" David asked.

"It's art. This is all part of a private exhibition."

"So, she's dead?" He tapped the photo of the redhead.

James sighed.

"Maybe. Maybe not. There's something to the final piece that might preserve this girl's life."

"Keep her fresh?" Michael said.

"Shut the fuck up! We're talking about a young girl!" David snapped.

"He's not wrong though and that attention to detail buys us time." James said.

"My guess is that the redhead will eventually be suspended, in a vitrine of sorts, exactly as Millais had Siddall pose in a bathtub for hours on end."

David rubbed his face. "Oh, God."

"Will he stop at eight?" Michael piped in.

"I guess you're not an art lover." James shot back.

"Please answer him."

"History art lecture for Dummies. The pre-Raphaelite Brotherhood had seven members. Each girl has a name that's connected to a founding member. They all share the same initials. See. The central piece being a dedication to the model Elizabeth Siddall herself." James grabbed a marker and scribbled names on a whiteboard next to the map.

"James Collinson, painter, member, first victim Jane Chung, initials J and C. William Holman Hunt, painter, member, second victim Winifred H. Hubbard, and so on and so forth until we get to the eighth girl, Emma Edith Smith. E, E, S, the initials for Elizabeth Eleanor Siddall."

David and Michael Jones drew closer to the map. James continued, "This was real clever. I mean, to procure this type of model, stage this type of exhibition."

"Exhibition?" David looked at Michael, who was now beaming with admiration.

"Taking notes, I hope?" He growled.

"Who would do a thing like this?" David asked.

"Well, any unhinged psychopath could do this to order. The question is, who would want this type of Dark Art? Yes, it's a genre. And how would a person like that meet someone disturbed and talented enough to procure the piece? That's the most intriguing part to me."

He was met by blank faces.

"We're looking at a very private clique of art lovers who enjoy Dark Art."

"Look on the Dark Web?" Michael blurted.

"Not necessarily. These creeps love to flaunt their work."

Silence.

"I'll explain it in toddler talk. Look for someone who creates disturbing art and has a following online. My bet is it's a talentless shit somehow high-brow, somehow rich. This talentless shit could walk through the front door of a private, exclusive school. They could enter by invitation. A talentless shit who could disarm the girls quickly, gain access to their personal information. Someone they would recognize. Maybe someone who groomed them through an art chat room? Who have you been questioning?"

"School janitors with previous records, contractors, river workers …" Michael answered.

James groaned.

"No evidence of sexual tampering, no visible injuries? Look at these floral displays!" He pulled down one of the photographs. David shrugged.

How could they have missed this?

"Look at the detail, the lengths taken to perfect this pose. This was a macabre act of devotion." James pressed.

"He drowned them, decorated them with flowers and dumped them in the river. I see no art in that." David argued.

"Then you're missing the point entirely…"

"Just tell me who we're looking for?!" David bit.

"Not a guy."

"What?"

"Female. Young. Attractive. A fine artist. Trendy and controversial. She has an accomplice, accomplices. This feels like a cult. Look for a vintage car with a large trunk, and maybe some kind of decoy, a cute dog, to lure the girls to her car."

"How did she …?"

"She came across like an airhead, a flake. Look for a blonde. She acts lost, drops her groceries. Can't hold onto her dog. So, the girls offer to help her. After all, they know her. Plus, she's a woman. They walk to a remote parking spot, and she sprays something that smells like perfume and poof, they're out. Then she lovingly folds them into the trunk. No marks, no cuts, no bruises, as you can see. No signs of struggle or distress. Damn, they even look peaceful. Sleeping beauties, which was the intention. The trunk is padded, lined with plastic. She wraps them, like a spider spinning a fly. They did not drown."

"No, they were all dead before they were …" Michael added.

"I wasn't asking a question. It was painless. They were suffocated while unconscious. They were cleaned and dressed. Meticulously I might add. Almost as though they were dolls. Then she moved quickly to place them before any type of pre-exhibition degradation could set in."

"Why did she stop?" Michael asked.

"I already answered that question." James said.

"Wow….you're amazing …" Micheal grinned.

"Mike!" David shoved his assistant.

"Get a grip!"

Oblivious to the tension, James continued.

"I am but let's not crack open the champagne just yet. Right now, and I mean, right now this girl is being prepared." He pulled off the redhead's photo.

"How long do we …?"

"Hours … tops."

"Where do …"

"You need a large dedicated team. Web and Dark web. Look for this woman. Look for Dark Art. Cross reference with the school visitor logs, CCTV cameras. Special visits or projects with an artist. Check every girl's social media, their cellphones, their media accounts."

"But they were snatched in school holidays miles away …"

"All these girls would have been carefully selected during term time. Our killer's a connoisseur. She takes her time."

Five hours later, thirty-eight year old, Austrian fine artist Valerina Brahms was arrested in Pimlico, West London, for the abductions and first-degree murder of seven British schoolgirls.

Just as James had predicted, Brahms was blonde, had a lapdog and was a self-proclaimed "space cadet". In stark contrast to her public persona, her work was described as "Sick Art" and hailed as "edgy, dark and avant garde on steroids" by highbrow art journals.

A high-profile resident of London, Brahms was an artist made famous for staging crime scenes as public works of art. Her pieces were exhibited in reputable galleries all over the world. She had a massive international client network including many celebrities.

Police found the eighth victim naked but unharmed in a small, padded room of Brahms' City townhouse. Steel cords nailed into the cross beam were attached to a large glass tank. Vats containing various embalming chemicals were assembled in a corner.

David met James in a café in East London to deliver the news of Brahms' arrest. It was a real coup for New Scotland Yard. More importantly, it signaled closure for all the families.

There was no pain, no sexual violence, David had insisted the parents be told.

"They were so relieved. They all expressed their gratitude to you James, especially Emma's parents." David murmured.

"Great."

He snatched Brahms' mugshot.

"Prettier than I imagined."

"She's one sick..."

"...fulfilling a demand. Think about who buys this twisted shit? That redhead was going on exhibition somewhere remote. China, Russia. Middle East, hell, maybe even here. Possessed by some fucked up billionaire whose artistic tastes and appetite won't dampen I'm afraid."

"We're looking into all Brahms' transactions."

"You won't find much."

David knew he was right.

The Americans (3)
South London, U.K 2019

It hadn't been an easy week for David.

The case had tested his friendship. He knew the side of James that was pure genius. Everyone else saw a freak. He was glad that a serial killer had been caught but ... *how had his entire team missed such obvious clues?* He needed to shake off his resentment.

Word of Brahms' arrest had gotten back to John Jay College, New York.

"Now, I'm a fucking superstar. Can you believe it? They want me back, a different department, more money ... slimy sons of bitches. Just because The New York Times ran a story on Brahms and her celebrity pals in Hollywood. Watch some asshole turn it into a Netflix series. Wonder who will play me?" James had texted.

David hadn't replied.

Once more, his thoughts returned to Tom Grayston's letter. He'd tried calling the guy a few times, but Tom's mailbox was full.

Meanwhile, James was in London another couple of days, and he was bugging David for more cases to solve.

Why not get his opinion on Tom's sample? He would run Tom's sample past his junior lab assistant, first.

A few hours later, at the New Scotland Yard lab.

"What do you make of this?"

He passed Tom's letter to his assistant.

Michael read it.

"Hmmm …. trespass with criminal intent?"

"Yes, but climbing glue? Doesn't that seem a bit far-fetched to you?" David studied Michael's face.

"Well. If he's pressing charges against the guy who rented him the house, I mean, to get his money back, he'll need to show malice and negligence, on the part of the owner."

"Okay, take a look at this sample. See if you can trace it to a manufacturer."

Michael placed the sample under a microscope and examined the sample. He turned it several times to inspect it from various angles. After a couple of minutes, he sat upright.

"Pass me that cloth behind you."

"Is there a problem?" David asked.

"Not sure."

Michael wiped the lens and returned to the scope.

"I don't believe it."

He rubbed his eyes then continued with his analysis.

"What is it?" David nudged down beside his assistant

"It's not glue. It's organic, blood, although I've never seen blood like that before." Michael declared, scratching his head.

"It has an abnormal concentration of white T-cells," David sat back from the scope.

"Odd, right? So, what exactly are we looking at?"

David tapped his chin.

"I don't know. I've never seen anything like it. The white cells make me think that it's an infected blood sample ... it's defo not human," Michael shrugged.

"Okay, let's see if anything comes up about where this sample came from."

David walked back to his office. Entering, he found a sticky note.

David – checked that return address for you. Rousinac is in the Southwest region of France. I've sent you a few links. It's about a couple of hours north of Bordeaux but really remote, in the middle of nowhere. Nothing comes up.
Hannah

David pulled out his cell phone and called James. There were never any niceties.

"What is it?"

"James, remember that friend of mine, Tom Grayston who ..."

"What about him?"

"He sent in a specimen for analysis from France when you were first here. He thought it was some type of climbing glue..."

David waited for a response before continuing. It didn't come.

"It's organic."

No reply.

"Would you come take a look at it and give me your opinion?" he pressed.

"What type of sample is it?"

"It's blood but it's atypical..."

"Go on."

"First of all, it's almost black, and the T-cells outnumber the red by a substantial ratio, real substantial."

David hoped that James would offer a simple, logical explanation. Perhaps the sample belonged to a wild animal, an anomaly he had come across before.

"Weird. The T-cell ratio alone indicates that the immune system of whatever this sample belongs to, is way off the charts. I'd need to take a look myself, maybe run some tests." James said.

"Of course, are you at your hotel now?" David asked.

"Yup."

"Can I send a car over?"

"One hour."

"You got it and thanks James. I really appreciate this and ..."

The line was dead.

An hour later, James Harrison arrived back at New Scotland Yard's forensics lab and immediately set to work. The two men were alone. James had insisted the lab assistant go home.

The silence in the room was painful. While James examined the specimen, David padded up and down like an expectant father. Finally, pulling back from the microscope James arched his back. A frown creased his large forehead. He didn't say anything.

David couldn't believe it. James was stumped.

"The platelets are abnormally enlarged so this animal, whatever it is, has a clotting mechanism far superior to ours or to anything I'm aware of. There's also another agent present that is just ... fucking mysterious. I can't identify it. Give me everything you've got. The who, the what ... the where ..."

David briefly outlined the arrival of the package and what Tom Grayston had told him.

"That's it?" James moaned.

"Yup."

"So, this guy and his wife were on vacation in France, and they just found this stuff?"

"Yep. I told you, on the exterior wall of the house they were renting. Grayston said they'd experienced something criminal."

"What kind of criminal?"

"He thought smugglers."

"Got his number?" James asked as David nodded. "So, call him, get more information."

"I keep getting his mailbox."

"So, dig. This is New Scotland Yard for Christ's sakes." James said, sparking a cigarette.

"You can't smoke in here." But James was already out the door and running down the fire escape stairwell.

David spent that evening trying to reach the Graystons. All calls went unanswered. Over and over again he was greeted by Tom's cheery voice followed by a sterile beep.

Although it was possible that the Graystons were out for the evening and had forgotten to charge their phones, David felt unsettled.

Tom Grayston's curious letter brought him little sleep.

The Locals (2)
Rousinac, Southwest France 2019

An old man sat in a chapel running the rosary through his fingers.

Didier Perodeau's disobedience had proved costly. There was a procedure to follow, and he had ignored it. Bad enough.

But it was Laetitia's rash decision that had infuriated and burdened Pierre Malraux. It was a usurping of his authority.

Even Patrick Clayburn was a disappointment. He'd simply gone along with Laetitia without reporting back. Other locals were now implicated. *It needn't have gone this way*, Pierre lamented.

The English couple could have been spoken to let go. So what if there had been an investigation by the U.K authorities? Rousinac Police station would have buried it in paperwork. Now, they had two disappeared foreigners and innocent blood on their hands. For the first time in decades, Pierre Malraux hadn't a clue what he would do next.

On the other side of Rousinac, Didier Perodeau was driving home. His dog Pako perched on the car's dashboard, its body quivering with excitement. He hadn't been away that long but to Didier, his childhood home already felt foreign to him.

The damage to the shutters and exterior doors was alarming. He surveyed the unsettled grounds for clues. He hung his head. *They had to be dead, right?* Pako bolted off into the bushes to chase something. Didier suddenly felt uneasy being alone.

His eyes were drawn to the back bathroom window. The glass had been shattered. Its frame ripped from the stone. He looked into the woods. He had tunnels to seal.

Afterwards, Didier returned to the house and unlocked the main door. He hesitated for a moment, then pushed it open. A familiar smell wafted – a pungent odor – the coppery scent of blood mixed with sulfur. A cloud of blue bottles swarmed past him. Others buzzed inside the house.

His dog was back. It growled a low and steady gurgle before bolting past him to the foot of the stairs. Pako stopped and stared at the landing above. His tail dropped.

Didier smacked the side of his leg. The dog ran to him like a puppy.

"It's okay Pako, they've gone."

The formidable task of forensic removal lay ahead. Reluctantly, he made his way to the kitchen and dug out a bucket, mop and industrial strength bleach. *The rest of the house will have to wait. I will make a start on the bathroom window,* he thought. *It is easily visible from the outside.*

Didier was reaching for a ladder when his cell phone rang. He recognized the number. It was one he could not ignore.

"Pierre."

"You're back."

"Yes, I just got home today."

"Is that all you have to say?!"

"What do you want? I regret it very much but there was nothing else I could do."

"What about *The Plan*!" Pierre raged.

"I was running out of time. What was I to do? I panicked!" Didier babbled.

"You should have come straight to us! Do you realize the danger you have put all of us in?" Pierre snapped back.

"I – ah ..." Didier returned.

"Four this afternoon we are meeting at Clayburn's. Be there!"

The phone went dead. *Merde,* thought Perodeau. *I'm fed up with this. How much longer must I wait until I pass this on to my son. I was younger than he is now before my father placed the burden on me. I've never shirked my responsibilities, ever. I make one mistake and now they're all on my back. Well, I've had enough and if they start on me, I'll tell them all to go to hell!*

He'd simply rented out his house to foreign holiday-makers like *The Plan* says - *that's all.*

The Locals (3)
Rousinac, Southwest France 2019

At exactly four o'clock in the afternoon Didier Perodeau entered Patrick Clayburn's courtyard. He drove so slow his engine purred. The yard was strewn with vehicles parked haphazardly. Bouncing his eyes from car to car, Didier immediately knew who was there.

He shuffled towards a large front door framed by roses. As he reached for the bell, the door sprang opened and startled him, as it was no doubt intended. Madame Clayburn's commanding figure filled the doorway.

"They're in the dining room."

The coldness in her eyes irked him.

"Monique, please," he pleaded.

He slouched past her making his way down a narrow hallway toward a chorus of raised voices. All eyes fell on him as he entered the room.

"Sit down, Perodeau."

Patrick Clayburn pushed a chair towards Didier. Didier didn't like being called by his surname. It made him feel like a stranger in his own community.

A large coffee pot rested on the table. Patrick Clayburn, Pierre Malraux and Laetitia Dupre each held a cup, but nothing was offered to him. He looked down at his hands, unable to meet anyone's eyes.

"Okay, let's get this over with," Didier said.

Pierre Malraux leaned forward.

"You think it's that simple?"

"No, But what can I do about it now?"

"That's not good enough Perodeau," Patrick Clayburn pushed.

"We always follow *The Plan!*" Pierre snapped as he began to pace the room.

"You simply left your tunnels open. You couldn't even do the job yourself. You lazy bastard." Laetitia added.

"*The Plan* only permits the damned to be taken." Patrick pounded his fist on the table.

"I-I thought she was German. I swear. Look, I left it too late and panicked," Didier blubbered. "I'll admit it."

"Oh, I see," Pierre added. "So, although *The Plan* has worked flawlessly for over seventy-years you took it upon yourself to completely ignore it and bring in two innocent people from England? Then if that wasn't bad enough, you left us to clear up your mess! Laetitia in particular was put in a dangerous position. She tried her best to persuade the foreigners to leave your house, only they didn't, and they *saw them.*"

Didier's heart thundered. *Saw them?*

"Yes, but if I hadn't found a female it would have been disastrous!" Didier replied. He faced Laetitia hoping for a glimmer of empathy.

Pierre tossed a chair sideways and got in Didier's face.

"You dumb idiot! You should have come to us!"

His face was purple with anger.

"Calm down uncle, this will not help us now. You'll just make yourself ill," Laetitia tugged at his arm.

"They need women, and we all know what for. Nobody questions that part. It's like you're all saints. Yet I'm the villain here." Didier moaned.

Pierre hung over Didier as if stalking prey. Didier could smell the soured garlic and wine on his breath.

"Be quiet you fool! None of us chose this path. None of us question it either. But for now, we have already dealt with your visitors' car. You will go back and remove all other traces of them from your house," he yelled. "Do you hear?"

He jabbed Didier hard on his chest. Didier nodded.

"Yes – yes, I will, I will!"

"Did you actually meet them, the Graystons?" Patrick asked, dragging his chair closer to Didier.

He tried to shrug the question off.

"No-no everything was done over the phone."

"Your phone?"

"A pay as you go phone. I threw it away."

"No emails?"

"The phone I said, just the phone."

"The woman told me it was an online advert."

"Yes, a free site."

"You'd need an email then."

Putain!

"No, just a phone. They sent me a code."

"How did they pay you?"

"Cash. They agreed to leave cash in the house."

"So, no money trail."

Didier squirmed as he lied. He hadn't thought about that *one email.* It would connect them to him. His stomach lurched.

Didier began to sweat. He had placed the same advert all over Europe. There were at least twenty ads out there linked to his email address. Any decent cop would be able to find him.

Patrick snorted.

"Well, that's something in your favor. So, if anyone comes looking for them, you will simply say that the Graystons let you down and never arrived."

Didier shot Pierre a frightened glance.

"Okay – okay."

Pierre pulled out a pen and paper.

"So, let's start at the beginning. We will go over this very carefully and try to anticipate all possible problems. And, if you ever do anything like this again Didier, I swear I'll take you with my own bare hands and hurl you into the tunnels myself."

The Americans (4)
South London, U.K. 2019

Over the next 48-hours David Frankel discovered that Tom and Catherine Grayston had not returned to their Hertfordshire home from France; that their house was in foreclosure; and that a bunch of creditors were circling in on Tom's business assets.

In a visit to the Grayston's house David had run into a neighbor, who worked with Catherine as a teacher at the local secondary school.

The woman insisted that no matter what, "Catherine would have come back to her job. It was very unlike her not to return. She adored those kids. She was a total professional."

David had also discovered that no money had been withdrawn from the Grayston's bank accounts for weeks. In fact, the last debit made on Tom's credit card was a month prior at a gas station in Rousinac.

Worried family members were now contacting the authorities, however, the couple's disappearance, when placed within the context of debt and inevitable bankruptcy, and no bodies had made the police reluctant to open a criminal investigation.

But David wasn't convinced that the Graystons had simply taken off and disappeared themselves for financial reasons. Something in his gut told him that they were in trouble. He called James up and filled him in on everything. A long pause followed.

"That's one hell of a twist. I've got to admit." James finally said.

"I'm thinking of going over there," David declared.

"France?"

"Yep. I've got some time owed, and something about this is bugging me."

"You think some bad shit's gone down?"

"I do."

James sighed.

"I can't let you go alone. You'd totally screw it up. Plus, I'm bored with London and don't quote Samuel Johnson."

"There's no way. You're a complete liability off your meds."

"I'll take them. Promise. You can pop them in my mouth and check under my tongue like a psych nurse." James cackled.

"This is not a good idea."

"I'm going, with or without you. I need a distraction. I'll even shower and wear matching shoes." David knew that James was already obsessed with the missing Brits. He wouldn't just go away.

The Maquis (5)
Rousinac, Southwest France 1944

On the morning of the German ambush, Alain Boussuet and Jean-Baptist Fauvert had sprung home like rabbits.

The escapade on the farmhouse roof with their Maquis leader had been a baptism of fire. For Jean-Baptist and Alain Boussuet, it couldn't have been more timely. The following week both teens would receive an "invitation" to work in Germany through the STO* scheme.

*The *Service du Travail Obligatoire* (Compulsory Work Service) instituted by the law of Feb 16, 1943, requisitioned young French men born from 1920-22 and sent them to work in Germany for two years.

Alain could not go to Germany. He had proven far too useful to Rousinac's Maquis already. Unlike most locals he was tall and blond. To the Germans, he was a reminder of home, and they gave him deference over others.

Second, Alain had put his schoolboy German to good use and

conversed with the occupiers at every opportunity. He could also eavesdrop and pass information along.

Jean-Baptist Fauvert spoke next to little German, but he was an athletic lad and therefore useful in other ways. The Fauverts lived on a large farm located at the bottom of the Château de Rousinac.

The Fauverts had cultivated the surrounding fields for generations, providing the gentry fresh produce in exchange for protection within its fortified walls. Since occupation, they had set up a similar trade with the occupiers.

Jean-Baptist was tasked with running provisions to the Germans headquartered in the Chateau. As such, he got to know many of the sentries at the gates. They would trade cigarettes and cards of naked women for wine or a good cheese.

Once Maquis leader Gerard Dupre heard about the boys' STO summons he had ordered Jean-Baptist's father to get his son and Alain Boussuet work in town at the Rousinac munitions depot.

On the surface, it appeared a plausible request. Families naturally wanted to stay together in wartime. Plus, there were many other less-desirable candidates available for STO transfer.

Jean-Baptist knew Alain from school, and the Germans had observed them both goofing around and chatting up girls in the chateau's main square many times. They seemed like two ordinary eighteen-year-olds.

And although he'd sweated like a pig through-out his petition, Jean-Baptist's father had made his case well. In a matter of days, the two junior Maquis men were working in one of the largest munitions depots of the war.

This would prove to be instrumental just a few weeks later.

The Americans (5)
Rousinac, Southwest France 2019

David's secretary had arranged a direct flight to Bordeaux the following afternoon. The two Americans were to pick up a rental car at the airport then make their way to The Fromblier, the only hotel listed in Rousinac.

Normally, two alumni from John Jay College would have spent the entire flight reminiscing or going over what they wanted to accomplish in France. Instead, James immediately plugged into a podcast series and slugged cognac until he passed out.

It wasn't long before his snoring (David and James had shared a dorm together as students) set in. David occupied himself with thoughts of his own children, Nathan (13) and Amy (9) who lived back home in the States with his ex. He browsed photos of them on his phone and tried to call a couple of times. No one picked up.

It would be an early morning in New York. The frantic school run downtown was about to unfold. He could see, in his mind's eye, the kids running around the apartment, looking for this and that, trying to avoid trampling the dog.

He could see his beautiful ex-wife, Lisa Frankel. Her petite body erect at the breakfast counter, poised, watching everything like a cat. She was always quietly in control. Her slim hand wrapped around a cup of coffee. *The New York Times* online edition at her elbow, screen open to the editorial section.

Maybe, his son would pick up texts later in his day. *Kids these days never replied*, David checked Nathan's social media. Every account was private. *It was normal for a thirteen-year-old to want privacy*, he tried to convince himself. But he couldn't shift the ache in his heart, that sinking feeling, of slowly floating away from the two most important people in his life.

On paper, the divorce had been amicable. His marriage had been falling apart for years, in small, unconscious acts. Then, one day, they had both woken up and realized that they had absolutely nothing in common.

"I want more, more than *this*."

She'd told him.

There were no third parties. It was awful. He still felt sad about it.

A job offer from New Scotland Yard had come a month after her announcement. His parents had urged him not to go. It was a bad optic, bad for the kids. But he had packed his bags and gone anyway.

A day had not passed since, when he hadn't second-guessed that decision. He browsed more photographs of his kids, of his ex-wife and their time together.

Why do I keep these photos of us?

David suddenly felt sad. Tears stung his eyes. He turned to his unconscious partner. There would be no help from that quarter. He knocked back a couple of merlots and melted into a tipsy nap.

The Americans arrived at the small town of Rousinac much later than expected. Their baggage had been delayed and the paperwork for the car took forever. David had suggested that they settle in at their hotel and get a good night's sleep before making any immediate enquiries after the Graystons.

Their rooms were clean and spacious, and after a hot shower and some good local cuisine James fell quickly to sleep.

David waited for the inevitable guttural snore before checking whether James had packed his medications. They were there. A half-drunk glass of water and a bottle of meds in the bathroom suggested that he'd popped two before bed. One side effect was heavy sleep.

Relieved, David closed his eyes and wondered what the morning would bring. It wasn't long before he too was sound asleep.

The following day at the breakfast table, David and James traced country roads on a map, detailing the quickest route to Didier Perodeau's house.

They were the only patrons in the dining area.

A waitress hovered under the pretense of pouring more coffee. In reality, the map had caught her attention along with questions posed in bad French about an English couple.

An hour or so later after some exasperation at the proliferation of unmarked roads (les chemins) in Rousinac's rural outskirts, James and David finally located a small country lane that led to Chez Perodeau.

Grinding the car almost to a halt they rolled down Didier's driveway. David half expected to see an English car parked out front. Instead, a small Peugeot, with French number plates sat diagonal to the house. Before they had even alighted from their car, James and David saw the front door fly open. A plump man stuck out his head, one arm constraining a large, barking dog.

James wound down his window and muttered.

"Guilty as fuck, note the aggressive stance?"

David shouted, "Bonjour. Monsieur Perodeau?"

"Yes. What do you want?"

"Great, you speak English,"

"Wait."

The man waved his hand and pushed the dog inside.

Closing the front door Didier Perodeau approached the two foreigners occupying his driveway.

"Bonjour, my name is David, and this is my colleague, James. We're looking for our friend Tom Grayston?" David said as he stepped out of the car.

Didier's face reddened. "What makes you think I can help you?"

"Uhm, well, they gave us this address, and told us they were renting your house." James began. Didier eyeballed James.

"What are you saying?"

"Monsieur, our friend Tom Grayston hasn't returned from a vacation in France and …" David looked up at one of the shattered shutters before continuing.

"… and he gave this as his vacation address …"

"Yes, well, your friend, Monsieur, didn't show up and he still has the keys I sent. Perhaps when you see Monsieur Grayston, you can remind him of this. I lost a month's rental because of him."

Perodeau traced James' stare up at the tattered shutters.

"There's no work here for our young people and when I'm away, I'm afraid this is what happens."

He flapped his arm in disgust.

"Anyway, I am very disappointed your friends didn't honor their …"

"We have a letter from the Graystons giving this as a return address, *mailed* from

Rousinac," James interrupted. "How do you explain that?"

"You call me a liar?" Perodeau snapped.

"No, of course not," David intervened as James' moved to respond.

"My friend's simply stating the facts. Look, there's got to be a logical explanation. Maybe the Graystons changed their minds and stayed somewhere else in Rousinac and mistakenly put down this address? We're not questioning your honesty."

"I don't know anything. Please leave." Perodeau grumbled.

David glared at James as they both retreated to the car. Didier eyed the men suspiciously.

He rubbed his wiry beard.

"Wait, before you go."

James and David stopped.

"You're Americans, no?"

David nodded.

"So how do you know the Graystons, why are you here? Who are you?" Perodeau quizzed.

David glanced at his companion. *What do we say?*

James gave Didier a side-ways look.

"We told you already, we are colleagues Monsieur. Property developers. Tom was looking at some houses for us in this region, but he hasn't returned back to work."

"Yes, well maybe he's still looking."

Didier Perodeau mumbled under his breath as he shuffled back to the house. From an upstairs window he watched as the two Americans sped away.

Colleagues? Merde! This is a big fucking problem. Putain!

"He's lying," James rattled off a list of tell-tale signs, as they headed back to the center of Rousinac.

"Agreed, but if we hit him head on, we'll get nowhere fast. Plus, we've got zero evidence that the Graystons even stayed there and no theory on what happened to them if anything." David asserted.

"Did you check out the shutters, the smell of industrial disinfectant? That motherfucker was erasing something." There was a pause and then James added.

"We've got to go back."

"And do what?"

"Watch him,"

David searched his friend's face.

"You mean like a stakeout?"

"Exactly."

"Why?"

"Don't know, just a hunch. Maybe we'll catch him doing something suspicious like moving a body. We'll wait until he leaves the place and break in."

"Break in?"

"Notice the ladder at the side of the house? Propped up against a wall right under that broken window? It's the easiest entry point, right?"

"I'm not comfortable breaking and entering James, just so you know."

"Stop being a pussy. You came here to get answers, not improve your fucking French."

"Well, that guy's hiding something for sure … but what?"

"That's what we're here to find out Sherlock."

The Americans (6)
Rousinac, Southwest France 2019

David and James rushed lunch at their hotel, eager to make some headway in the British couple's disappearance. Egged on by James, David had reached out to a co-worker, Graham Wells, at New Scotland Yard.

Graham had access to the Interpol data-base, and he promised to call David back once he had something about the area. An hour had crawled past before the phone finally rang.

"David, Graham."

"Did you find anything?"

Light danced a grid across Graham's glasses as he gazed into a huge monitor.

"I contacted a mate in Lyon since they cover all of France. He did a sweep of Rousinac and surrounding areas. Okay, so apparently, there have been a cluster of unexplained disappearances of tourists over the last fifty-years or so in that general region. The weird part is that they were all mostly from Germany. One was from Austria. All young women. That's it. Interpol hasn't been able to determine why or even how they disappeared."

"Put him on speaker," James ordered.

"Can you give us an example?" David continued.

Graham tapped at the keyboard. A photograph popped up of a reflection of a smiling young woman wearing a backpack.

"Here's one: Tina Schuster, a twenty-six-year-old from Munich told her parents that she'd received an offer of au pair work in Bordeaux. This was back in the seventies. She sets off to France basically backpacking around down there. It looks like the last time her relatives heard from her she was heading towards St Emilion most likely through Rousinac. Then she disappeared. It says here that the local police and Interpol made a thorough search scouring rivers and campsites but found nothing."

"What about the families of the women? Did they follow up?"

David heard keys tapping.

"Well, some of the families did go to the police but nothing came of it. The verdicts were all the same: misadventure. Does any of this help?"

"Yes ..." David began. James grabbed the phone.

"No, I need to get an excel sheet detailing every disappearance over a fifty year period. All the info, don't leave anything out."

"Who is this?"

"Graham ..." David tried to get his phone from James.

"It's James Harrison. I'm kind of famous, or rather infamous for solving cases British cops can't." He jumped from bed to bed avoiding David's arms.

James tossed the phone onto the bed.

Asshole! David mouthed.

"Hi Graham, would you be able to send that to *me*? I totally appreciate it. Awesome, thanks!"

David heard the click of the telephone on the other side.

"Don't fuck with my work colleagues. I mean it James."

James cracked his knuckles.

"All young women. Could have been a trafficking ring. But what's the connection to Germany? Maybe a Sheik with a taste for the Teutonic?"

"Yes, but over a fifty-year period?"

"Think outside the box David. I know that's hard for you."

"You think there's a connection between these women and the Graystons?"

"I just want data."

"You'll get it when it's ready."

"You're not picking up any weird vibes?"

"Don't be an idiot."

"Is that why you took the precaution of reporting our location?" James belly-laughed.

"You hacked my phone again?"

"I feel safer already. Okay, what's next?"

"Well, we'll stay clear of Perodeau's for a bit. I think we spooked him. Maybe we just act like tourists and get a feel for Rousinac. Ask around about the Graystons, but *casually*, James. No Men In Black stuff. We have some facts to go on. We know for example they filled up on gas and bought groceries. One of the transactions is from a café not far from here. Someone must have seen them. Once we verify that ..." David realized that James wasn't listening.

"What are you doing?"

"I'm looking for Perodeau online."

"James!"

"I'm presuming you've got a good photograph of them?"

"Who?"

"John and Yoko!"

"Here." David opened an image of the British couple on his cellphone.

"Recent?"

"Yes. We'll show people the …"

"….good old-fashioned detective work. Wow …"

David grew irritated.

"What's your bright idea then?"

"I could hack the CCTV cameras?"

"Seen any?"

"Let's take a walk."

The Americans meandered through the empty streets of Rousinac.

"It's so quiet." David noted.

"Yeah, for August, prime tourist season …:weird."

They followed the half dozen locations that had shown up on Tom Grayston's credit card transactions: grocery stores, wine stores, gas stations.

The response each time was the same.

"Non."

No one had recalled seeing the British couple let alone interacting with them.

It was now 3pm and they decided to make a café their last stop for the day.

"This is a ten minute walk from Perodeau's house." James noted as they approached.

"We know they bought a couple of beers here." David added.

"Yeah, that hasn't exactly helped us now, has it?"

An elderly couple were the café's only occupants. A wizened man, farmer type, sat slouched over a newspaper with a carafe of house red. His dining companion stared vacantly out of the window.

A young waitress served James and David two chilled aperitifs. When they showed her a photograph of Tom and Catherine, she replied that she hadn't seen them. The men sat for a while in silence.

"I feel like a fucking squash ball." James blurted after downing his second drink.

"What?"

"Hitting fucking walls."

David doodled on a napkin.

"It's like the entire town is in on it." James mumbled.

"Don't be insane."

"Seriously, not one single person recalls seeing them? Don't you find that odd?"

"Not really. It's the tourist season. We're asking people to remember two people out of, say, thousands."

"Uhm, notice any tourists?" James quipped.

"I know, it's weird." David admitted.

"The answer lies at Perodeau's. There's something about him."

David reluctantly agreed and the men ordered another round.

"Tomorrow we'll go watch the house." James said.

Meanwhile, Laetitia Dupre had entered through the back door of the café. Spying the two foreigners, she immediately called the waitress over.

"Sylvie. Who are those two?"

The girl looked back toward the Americans.

"I think they're English."

"What are they doing here?"

"Drinking."

Sylvie eyed her employer.

"I can see that! Do they seem official?"

"You mean like Gendarmes?"

"Yes."

"Not sure … they showed me a photograph of an English couple and asked if I had seen them recently."

Laetitia's stomach tightened.

"What did you say?"

"That I hadn't, which is true. Why?"

"Nothing."

Laetitia sauntered through the café to observe the two men more closely. They were both handsome, in their mid-forties. One in a weird, Nick Cave way. The other guy looked like Brad Pitt, blond and toned.

"Bonjour Messieurs." She forced a smile.

"Mademoiselle." David straightened in his chair.

"Make these your last, eh? The Gendarme are strict with drivers here, even on the back roads. They issue heavy fines on the spot." She said flatly.

"Wow, your English is amazing." James noted.

"I studied it in school."

"Won't you join us?" David asked.

"No thank you Monsieur another time perhaps."

"Oh, come on, how many *Americans* walk in this place every day?" James jabbed. The other guests turned in the men's direction.

Laetitia began to perspire.

"No," was all she offered as she walked away.

Laetitia went back to the bar. The foreign men huddled to whisper. She wondered if she'd given anything away. Returning with their check Laetitia was surprised when the blond man drew up a chair behind her.

"Let me formally introduce ourselves. My name is David, this is my friend James. We're looking for our friends Tom and Catherine."

Laetitia reluctantly sat down.

"You are on holiday?" she asked, avoiding David's eyes.

"Well, a mix of business and … sorry, I didn't catch your name?"

"Laetitia."

"Beautiful name for a beautiful woman," James cracked.

Laetitia cleared her throat and peered absently out of the window behind them.

"So, what about your friends?" She asked.

James clumsily interjected.

"Do you get a lot of English here?"

"We're not a tourist destination."

"We heard something different. See, a lot of our friends are British…" James began.

"So?" Laetitia snapped.

The darker man's attitude annoyed her, and she rose from the chair.

"We met one of your neighbors today," James announced.

"We drove down a lane near here and spoke to Monsieur Perodeau, right David?"

David eyed his friend wearily. The alcohol had loosened his impulse control. He wondered how he could rescue the situation.

"Monsieur P-Perodeau?" Laetitia stammered. "Are you looking for a rental?"

David felt a shift in her tone. He began to say, "We're looking for prime real estate and …" but James interrupted him.

"We told you, we're looking for our British friends, Tom and

Catherine Grayston. They said they were staying at the Perodeau house …Show her the photo David." he blabbed.

"Excuse me, I have work to do."

Laetitia stood up so abruptly her chair toppled over.

"You okay?"

She hesitated for a moment.

"No, I have a headache. We are closing the café early today. Excuse me." She began to move away.

David took her aside, away from James and the table.

"Look, we didn't mean to make you feel uncomfortable."

"Tell her about the *beers* David." James said loudly. David shot his friend an exasperated glare.

"Go ahead." James added, folding his arms.

Laetitia's heart raced. *Beers!*

"Look, we're in real estate. Myself, my partner over there and a British man, Tom Grayston. He was here recently on vacation with his wife. He told us about this café and some of the properties in the area. He recommended us to come here; said you served good beers."

"Yes, well, lots of people come here. You expect me to remember everyone I serve?"

"No, of course not. See, the thing is, he's just disappeared, along with his wife Catherine. It's annoying. He had contracts to fulfill."

Laetitia's body suddenly flushed with adrenaline.

"Could I show you a photo of them? It might jog your memory." David held up his phone.

"No, I don't recognize them, sorry." She had barely looked at the screen.

Laetitia tried to move past David, but he wouldn't budge.

"I wondered." He paused and lowered his voice.

"Would you like to get a glass of wine with me, or lunch,

sometime? Like I said, we're in real estate and I bet you know some pretty neat places?"

Laetitia was completely taken aback. She found herself nodding.

"Maybe. My number's on our cards at the counter."

She brushed against him, taking in his scent. He felt the warmth from her body.

"David ..." he called out after her. "... the name's David."

James and David drove back to the hotel in silence. As they entered the hotel lobby, James stormed ahead without waiting for his friend.

"James, wait. What's up?" David probed.

"Look, I get she's hot. But what were you thinking of asking her out on a date?" James exploded.

"Didn't you notice how she reacted when we mentioned Perodeau and the Brits, which by the way you totally let out of the bag!" David protested.

"She would have found out anyway, small town like this." James shot back.

"Whatever my point is, she was totally freaked out."

"Just don't get too distracted. This has to do with Perodeau not some piece of ass."

David rolled his eyes.

"I know what I'm doing."

James waved his hand dismissively.

"I need to eat."

He made for the dining room. David stared after him.

"Wait..."

"Later!"

The Locals (4)
Rousinac, Southwest France 2019

"Uncle, we have another problem,"

"What is it?" Pierre Malraux had woken from a nap.

"I had two Americans sitting in my restaurant this afternoon. They went to see Perodeau, and they asked if I had seen that British couple, the Graystons."

"What!?"

"On top of that, one of them even had the nerve to ask me out on a date."

The line went quiet for a few seconds.

"Well, I already know about them," Pierre said.

"Monsieur Fromblier called me this morning, told me two Americans were staying at his hotel: one man blond, the other, odd looking."

"That's them!"

"And one of the waitresses saw them mapping a route somewhere local. I didn't want to alarm anyone."

"Mon Dieu!" Laetitia gasped.

"Maybe you should go with them. Keep your eyes and ears open. Find out what they know. Meanwhile I'll tell Fromblier to track their movements as best he can."

"What if?"

"Then we will deal with it."

The Maquis (6)
Rousinac, Southwest France 1944

Gerard Dupre sat thinking.

It was odd since the incident at the abandoned farmhouse, and SS Beck's visit that nothing else had happened. No mass arrests of the usual suspects: petty thieves, drunks, prostitutes and known informants. It was as though nothing had happened.

The death of a German Officer and the wounding of many others had yet to provoke any retaliation. Elsewhere, such an offense could have ended in a massacre.

There were rumors too. Foreign agents told stories of irregular interrogation methods conducted deep inside Rousinac's castle, and of mangled bodies dumped in the woods.

Gerard's mind returned to the black chambers that riddled the castle's foundation. The same dungeons that had witnessed a thousand years of evil delivered by degenerate dynasties.

Had the war come to Rousinac because of an evil that already existed here?

But something else would soon occupy his mind.

As communicated to Frederic Arriver (The Maquis look-out in the woods) the British had sent the Rousinac Maquis "a new asset" to replace the one that had been captured by the SS in Libourne.

Gerard had been instructed to bicycle to a chateau, situated twenty or so miles outside of Rousinac, under the pretense of delivering some sausages.

The cover story went like this.

A certain Madame Dubonnet was hosting a banquet for some Nazi bigwigs quartered at her chateau. During the event, an intelligence asset would be placed right under their noses: Madame Dubonnet's nephew Jean.

Jean Dubonnet would then pass on any useful intel to the Rousinac Maquis, who in turn, would pass it down the chain of a new intelligence network.

None of it sat right in Gerard's stomach.

Upon his approach he had stopped briefly at the large iron gates to gawk. The estate was impressive, intimidating in its grandeur and well-kept lawns. Given the depravations that even the local gentry were facing, it seemed odd. *Maybe that's the price of collaboration?* He wondered.

After he'd handed over the meat in the kitchen, Gerard was taken to a back garden ringed with towering rose bushes. Flowers perfumed the air, complimenting the opera music coming from a ground floor summer lounge. He had been left to stand there for a few minutes, feeling awkward.

Finally, a tall slim man dressed in a kimono popped his head out of an upstairs window and waved.

"Sit down Monsieur Dupre and pour yourself a cup of tea."

What were the British thinking putting this poof in charge of operations?

When he next appeared, Jean Dubonnet was dressed in a pale linen suit, beautifully tailored. Cologne wafted about him. There had been no handshake, just a grunt from Gerard, as Jean poured them both a cup of tea.

"My aunt is very excited about her dinner party. Are you able to fulfill this meat order?" A list of items lay on the table between the two men.

Gerard eyed it and added loudly.

"Beef, as you know, is in short supply. The garrison in Rousinac has requisitioned every prime animal we have." The comment roused a chuckle from Dubonnet.

"Come, come, we both know the peasants hide a good fat heifer in the woods. Our guests turn a blind eye, mostly."

He offered Gerard a German cigarette then lit his own.

"One cow will do. A fattened calf even. I've heard you're an expert at cuts."

A maid, bringing water for the tea, caught Gerard's eye.

"Such an animal would feed a family through the winter and ..." Gerard began but was cut off.

"I shall leave the particulars to you." Dubonnet whispered.

Once the maid had left, there followed an uncomfortable half hour of coded chit-chat, of substituted words and double entendres. Through-out their conversation, Gerard felt queasy. German soldiers were walking the grounds. A guard was positioned a few yards away.

But Dubonnet was nonchalant, even when he had broken out of code.

"The truth is the Allies are closing in. Germany will be defeated. But one small obstacle stands in their way." He suddenly blurted.

"What?"

"The munitions mine in Rousinac."

Gerard fidgeted in his chair. Surely this dandy had no idea that two Maquis men were already working in the depo.

What if they did blow the mine up? The Germans would surely wipe Rousinac off the face of the earth. The British were using France like a chessboard. Rousinac would be one more pawn.

"I'm afraid it's impossible." Gerard said.

"Not at all. You already have two fox cubs in the hen house."

Merde! How did he know? It seemed incredulous to Gerard. *Who was the mole?*

"It's too dangerous. They're just boys." His comment was ignored.

"My aunt's birthday is in four-weeks, Monsieur Dupre. I understand this is a tall order, but our guests are *most insistent* that it goes ahead. I suggest that you find a way to gather every item. Nothing can be overlooked. Do you understand? And of course, I will need to stay informed of all the *plans*. We will arrange another rendezvous soon, to go over the details."

There was an unnatural silence as Gerard deciphered the code.

The timeline is one month, and the first task is reconnaissance work. I will need a complete plan of the mine, each floor, each stockpile, everything.

"Is there no other way for you to obtain this meat, Monsieur Dubonnet?" Gerard pressed.

"Nothing by air these days, as you know, and we know of no other producer."

There is no other choice. The delay as Gerard decoded their conversation irritated Jean. He looked about then said.

"Destroying the mine through strategic aerial bombardment has already been taken off the table. The only option left is local sabotage."

"It's a suicidal order. It can't be done."

Jean leaned in.

"Either sabotage or Rousinac will be wiped from the map. And they're not bluffing."

The Maquis (7)
Le Dubonnet Château, Rousinac,
Southwest France 1944

The butcher, while handsome, had smelled bad.

By contrast, Jean Dubonnet (aka Edouard de Aureville) adored the German guests at the Le Dubonnet house. They wore cologne, were sophisticated, and were a welcome respite from the agonizing task his British handlers had given him.

The attraction was mutual. Jean spoke elegant German and knew many of the country's great writers and thinkers. More than that, Germany had been his cultural home for years. A war wouldn't change that about him.

Nor the fact that he was queer.

It was forbidden, and needless to say reckless, to combine an undercover mission with an illegal pleasure but Jean had never played by the rules.

When one of the German soldiers had given him a look of recognition, a longing had ignited. *Connection.* It was more than just sex. Jean simply craved touch, sharing an intimate joke ... queer humanity.

He had long learned to channel his emptiness into music. Playing the piano soothed him and every afternoon he would retire to the salon and play a medley of songs.

The music naturally drew in the chateau's foreign guests. After lunch, the Germans had fallen into the French custom of *siesta*. Although, they took it Aryan-style, back-rigid but dozing in armchairs.

One other welcome respite came for Jean, in the form of his aunt's afternoon nap. She was a long-term British asset from World War 1 and her constant micromanagement had become tiresome not to mention noticeable.

Peace.

The serenity of the airy salon with views of the rose garden left Jean heady. He would often close his eyes and melt into his own thoughts. Everything else would disappear. Besides, that is, the stare of one man.

A sentry had been posted by the door, to guard while his superiors slept. It was the one Jean had locked eyes with on day one. A beautiful, clean-shaven youth with bright green eyes.

"That's an impressive Steinway." The soldier finally said, mindful not to wake the officers. Jean nodded. *This could be dangerous.* He had to play it cool.

The man crossed the room.

"You play so beautifully."

"Thank you."

"Please, play on."

He wanted to tell this man that he'd perfected his playing in Berlin's queer clubs. In 1931 he took his post-graduate studies there.

The city had a well-established, Avant Garde society offering fertile ground to bohemians and sexual renegades alike.

Every place had a piano.

"Play some honky tonk French boy!"

The crowds would bay. And, if he were drunk enough, he'd play.

"I *love* Cole Porter." The German soldier whispered in French.

Silence.

Jean had played a Porter song a few days before when he'd thought no one was around. The sentry stroked the piano. His hand was trembling.

"It always reminds me of when I went to see Mädchen in Uniform."

There it was.

The code.

Jean's stomach tightened.

Leontine Sagan's 1931 art film had become a magnet for curious men to "queer it up", to fumble, and explore in the safety of cinematic darkness. The soldier leaned closer. Jean felt the heat from his thigh. Now, it was Jean's hands that shook.

"Would you mind playing …"

"Vogel?!"

The sound, sudden and voluminous, made both men jump. It roused everyone in the room. The soldier stepped away from the piano so awkwardly that he'd almost tripped. Eyes wide, the guilt was written all over his face.

It was a horrible moment.

All at once a fluster of Nazi uniforms and shouting encircled the piano. It transported Jean to the day Berlin fell. Homosexual clubs had gone up in smoke. The city had burned for days.

"Get outside you fucking faggot!" A gray-whiskered Officer

raged. The others, taking his meaning, grabbed the offender and kicked him all the way to the front door. It soon became apparent that the young man was being whipped outside.

FAGGOT!

FILTHY FUCKING FAGGOT!

DIRTY PERVERT!

Putain.

Jean had been so close to reciprocating the soldier's attention. But judging from the glares he'd received the cat was now out of the bag. Why had he been so stupid?

Ever since Hitler's Night of the Long Knives in 1934, when the dictator had decided to purge the Nazi party of "undesirables", no queer no matter how senior had been spared.

What would happen to the soft-spoken soldier? Jean wondered. He would be severely disciplined, that's for sure. Relocated. Absolutely. And now, these hawks would watch him. He banged the piano in frustration. *Damn this war!*

Ernst.

The fleshy face of the head of the Brown Shirts loomed in his mind's eye. *Lover.* Jean's relationship with Ernst Rohm had been known in certain circles. With the ransacking of Röhm's apartment and offices it hadn't taken long for letters to surface. What if these pigs started to poke around in his past?

So very, very long ago ...

Thud!

The whimpering had stopped. Something heavy fell to the ground. Laughter followed and jackboots in the hallway. Jean closed his eyes and took a deep breath.

He began to play Clair de Lune, a tear streaming down his cheek stopping only at his perfectly trimmed mustache.

The Maquis (8)
Le Dubonnet Château, Rousinac,
Southwest France 1944

As he played, Jean recalled the year 1934.

That's when the British had snatched him in Berlin. *Another war's coming*, he had been told, and he would be an invaluable asset behind enemy lines when France fell. His strategic expertise in reading complex maps and engineering plans, his experience with languages, notably German, made him invaluable.

It had been presented so matter of fact.

Mai, non … was his response.

Jean had needed some persuading in a dimly lit South London room. Oh, he'd been roughed up before, but these guys were experts. Two days of detainment at His Majesty's Pleasure and he was ready to sign up as a British asset.

"Glad you've come to your senses. We know all about your kraut bum boys. We've got it all down here." The grubby nailed intelligence agent had announced, flopping down a hefty brown folder. Inside was a dossier citing every "act of deviancy imaginable," accompanied by dozens of photographs. The agent rattled off a list of "obscenities."

"Says here you liked going to queer stews. Powdered boys in frocks …eh?"

"Non, non." Jean had playfully interrupted.

"I much prefer a man in uniform." This comment had won him a gloved thwack across the face.

The agent had then spread out photographs showing Jean in various forms of feminine dress.

"You don't seem too ashamed of yourself." He goaded. Jean shrugged. *What was there to say?*

"Disgusting pervert." The man mumbled as he bundled up the images. Jean's mouth motioned to form a question. *How many hookers have you violated and beaten?*

He'd consoled too many tarts in Berlin cafes to know the answer. *The police were animals*, in his opinion. Just like the Nazis.

"Now then, we can hand all this over to the relevant French authorities when the time comes, or you can work for us. Choice is yours."

No choice.

It had started then and there. Spying for the British. Specialist training at various stately homes in England, mostly surveillance operations. The Second World War erupted just a few years later and so it had begun. Back to back assignments all over occupied France.

Every one of them dangerous, every one of them a success.

But five years on, the man behind Jean Dubonnet had grown weary. Clandestine operations, assuming identities, and repeated interrogations by the S.S. were chipping away pieces of him. His nerves were shattered. Chain-smoking added to a decline in his health. Even his British handlers could see that the writing was on the wall.

"One more job." They'd told him.

"You said that the last time."

"Then you're retired. Canada, right?"

"I was promised New York, once it's safe to cross the Atlantic." No reply.

The British agent unfurled a large map. X marked a location.

"That's your target, right there."

Jean leaned in to study the map.

"Oh God. Rousinac? It's a back-water."

"Because of this …" The man tapped the "X."

"That is one of the most important munitions depots of the German army. If we can destroy this mine, we will effectively cut off all supplies for the defense of the Atlantic Wall. Which means we can push forward, and the jerries will be paralyzed."

"So, you want me to …"

"Get people inside. Blow the fucker up."

"It won't be easy. It'll be heavily fortified, patrolled."

"That's not our problem."

"It's mine."

"As an engineer you'll know where its weak spots are."

"It will be a delicate operation. It can't be done overnight."

"This ain't needlework sweetheart. It has to be quick. The war won't wait. You're going to figure out the weak spots and tell us what ammo you need."

"And what's my cover for being in Rousinac?"

"You're the nephew of some Duchess or whatever you frogs call them. Your name is Jean Dubonnet. We thought you'd like a nice girl's name. You've gone back to take care of her, as she's not been well. Play up the homo act because she's got Nazis top brass stationed with her. And you know how krauts like a bit of the queer other. Plus, it will divert them from what you're really up to."

"Which is."

"Listening to their conversations. Reporting back to us."

"Who's my contact in Rousinac?"

"A butcher called Gerard Dupre."

"I'm imagining that's a joke?" The agent's dead stare answered him.

"He leads the local Maquis."

Jean rolled his eyes – *bush men, peasants.* The agent grew irritated.

"It will be *his men* doing the dying, so have some respect." He handed Jean a small radio and a notebook.

"Memorize these codes and listen out for our broadcasts. It's set so don't move the dial."

Jean took it silently.

Merde, I'm that guy.

Every Maquis group had a radio man. It was one of the deadliest jobs of all. Radio operators were considered a prized asset. The S.S. had developed specific techniques for extracting every scrap of information from a suspect.

Was this a British retirement?

The Americans (7)
Rousinac, Southwest France 2019

Later that evening James and David decided to head back to Didier Perodeau's house after all. The encounter at the café with the French woman had stirred their suspicions.

Driving their rental car towards the dirt road that led to Perodeau's property, they parked in a nearby lane and proceeded on foot towards it. The woods led into a thick boscage that James dashed through with ease. But David got continually snagged on blackberry bushes.

Eventually they found an ideal spot to set up a lookout. It gave them plenty of cover and a clean view of the house.

"You sure no one can see the car from the main road?"

"Nope, way too many trees," James confirmed. They looked at Perodeau's house. The lights were on, and his car was there. David groaned.

"Let's stay put for an hour and see if he leaves. If he does, you'll go straight in. I'll be look-out." James said.

"Why me?"

"You're a forensics expert."

"You're assuming three things," David countered. "First, that he'll go out, second that he'll stay out a while and third that no one else is home. That's a lot of assuming."

"Wish we could just wire the place." James added.

They worked their way closer to the house.

"Not too close. The dog will smell us."

They huddled down and waited.

"Christ, what's that stink?" James winced.

"Something died around here recently."

"Well, you'd know, I guess."

Pulling out his binoculars, James focused on Perodeau's house.

"Damn, the ladder's gone. I hope he hasn't locked it away otherwise this will be a wasted trip."

"I guess we'll just have to wait and see."

For the next hour they took turns watching the house. Finally, the front door opened and Perodeau stepped out accompanied by his dog. David signaled to James to duck down, and they watched as the French man's car pulled out of the driveway and up the lane. He'd passed right by them as they cowered in the bushes.

"Glad he took that dog," James said.

"Okay, so I'm going straight over that wall?"

"Correct."

"James, any sign of him, call me. *Call me*," he stressed.

James patted David on the shoulder.

"Got it chief."

David donned latex gloves and sprinted toward Perodeau's wall. He vaulted neatly over the top, grateful that the terrace below was raised one level higher to avoid flooding. He found the ladder and placed it under the broken upstairs window. He was in the house within seconds, and in a few minutes, standing in a bathroom. Immediately, David began to take mental notes.

Bathroom door frame is completely shattered.

Door missing.

Smells like bathroom scrubbed rigorously in neat bleach.

Nothing.

He looked again at the condition of the door and doorframe. It perplexed him. *Why has it been ripped off like that? Why was Perodeau renovating?* He wandered toward the bedrooms.

He inspected the four bedrooms along the hallway for any signs of occupancy. Two were nicely furnished but did not appear to be in use. The other two were filled with antique furniture and storage boxes. One of them contained a large four-poster bed. Everything had been stripped and covered in plastic wrap, taped down.

Outside in the woods, James struggled to remain attentive. The smell near the lookout was becoming increasingly intolerable. *What kind of animal makes a stink like that?* Looking around he grew more curious.

He strained to listen for any unusual noises or movement. To his right he noticed a large broken branch, its end tapered off into a sharp point. He snatched it up. Wielding this new weapon, he began to probe the ground around him.

Upon first examination the ground resembled any other piece of bramble turf. But here and there James could detect man-made disturbances in the foliage. He patiently followed his hunch and prized aside a thorn branch. As he advanced the stench grew stronger.

Ahead was a thin bed of flattened grass. The way the blades had been crushed suggested bipedal movement, human. Several yards into thick bush and he came across a large mound. James cleared away some branches.

It was a tunnel opening, probably leading to an underground

cellar. Not unusual in rural areas, James concluded. The door was iron. *Shit.* A bolt lock sealed it shut. *Shit.* But its hinges could easily be screwed off. *Bingo.*

Eight thick screws held the door in place. He pulled out a large pair of pliers from his bag. Before long, he had successfully removed all eight. The door swung open. A foul odor overtook him, making him dry heave. He grasped for a handkerchief and made a mask around his face.

James peered into the tunnel. He guessed that it led to a system of sewers further along. In the distance he heard a rumble. His attention turned back to Perodeau's house.

David had explored the entire house but had found no evidence of the Graystons. Without getting a warrant for a team of forensics he knew there was little chance of being able to prove that the couple had stayed in Perodeau's house.

He spun about the downstairs rooms one more time desperately searching for any indication that the British couple had been there – a lost earring, any clue that would lead him to them.

His cell phone buzzed at the same time as Perodeau's car pulled around into the drive. Its headlights lit up the room David was standing in.

"Shit!"

He couldn't run out of the front door. The back door was locked. David mounted the hallway stairs. His footsteps hadn't registered with Didier, but the dog had heard them. It bolted through Didier's legs and scratched ferociously as he inserted his house key.

"Hear a mouse, eh Pako?" Didier smiled.

David had made it to the bathroom window as the front door flew open.

What if Perodeau had seen the ladder against the wall and moved it? What had James been doing?

The ladder was still there. *Thank God.*

David shimmied down as the dog lunged through the bathroom window at him.

"Who's there?" Didier called out as he climbed the staircase.

Scaling the wall, David sprinted to James' location in the woods and bolted past him. He made it back to the car in seconds. James tagged behind afraid his friend would leave without him.

"I nearly got caught by that fucking dog. What the hell were you thinking?" David yelled, as he pressed down hard on the car's accelerator.

James fumbled with his seat belt. His other hand gripped the dashboard.

"Slow down. You're grinding gravel!"

After a mile or so David pulled the car over onto a dirt track. He got out of the car, keeled over and tried to catch his breath.

James stood beside him.

"I'm sorry man. Perodeau must have come on a back road. I didn't see him, I swear."

David waved his hand. He knew that James had probably been distracted by something minutia. It wasn't his fault. The guy was on a spectrum.

"It's okay. It just sucks that I didn't find a God-damn thing to show that the Graystons were there."

"Listen, I found a tunnel. The perfect place to dump two bodies and it stunk worse than hell. We should check it out." James declared.

"Are you actually insane? Why would Perodeau kill the two people renting his house?"

"Why does anyone kill anyone? Desperation, risk of exposure, accident, lust, rage."

"Motive?"

"The Brits said something about criminal activity?"

"Smugglers."

"Maybe Perodeau runs some kind of contraband operation from ..."

"So why rent out the place?"

"Maybe it was petty criminals like Perodeau said. Remember the broken shutter?"

"The Graystons confronted petty criminals ...?"

"Kids, druggies, maybe they panicked and over-reacted. Killed the Brits. Then Perodeau shows up, finds the bodies, panics and ..."

"Decided to clean up?"

"Sounds dumb I know."

"A bit. Why not just report it to the police?"

"Don't know, I think that French chick at the café knows something."

"Why would she know anything?"

"Call her when we get back to the hotel."

Perodeau had heard the car pull away. Hurrying outside he looked up the lane that linked the main Rousinac road to his. Red brake lights had blinked in the distance, the smell of exhaust hung in the air. Rubbing his beard roughly he took a look in the yard.

"Mon Dieu! The ladder's been moved!"

It was now propped up directly beneath the shattered ledge. Perodeau squinted up at the broken bathroom window. A curtain flapped in the evening breeze. He spat on the floor.

"Damn those Americans came back." He cursed.

The Americans (8)
Rousinac, Southwest France 2019

A night and a morning had passed since the Americans' intrusion onto Perodeau's land. The men had driven straight back to the Fromblier hotel and stayed put. There were no repercussions from the Gendarme or Perodeau. Relieved by this, David had moved forward with his plan.

James watched as David shaved.

"So, you called Laetitia, asked her to go sightseeing with you and she just said yes?"

David admired his cleanly shaven face in the mirror.

"Yup."

"And you don't think that's weird?"

"Nope."

"It hasn't crossed your mind that she knows something and wants to know who we are."

"Don't worry I'm on a mission. I won't give anything away."

"Tell your dick that."

"And you're good with going through Graham's data?"

"Yes, that's my idea of hot. The answer lies in that data. I'm convinced."

"You're seriously weird." There was no reply. James pulled out his laptop and viewed a spreadsheet filled with unsolved cases.

"How many?" David asked.

"Ten, possibly fifteen and already, see that? Clusters around certain years. Patterns ..."

"Happy digging."

Half an hour later, David walked towards the front door of Laetitia's restaurant. He repeated a mantra in his head. *It's just a date. Be cool.*

"Bonjour David." Laetitia appeared suddenly in the doorway. David stifled a gasp.

Laetitia's sleek black hair was loosely tied up in folds framing her sparkling hazel eyes. She wore a flowing white dress that rested delicately at knee length revealing long, shapely legs. Her skin glowed a deep, brown. Her breasts, high and firm, nipples erect in the breeze.

"Bonjour Laetitia, wow you look amazing!" David gushed.

Laetitia smiled seductively.

"You can leave your car here David. I have a surprise."

She pulled out two helmets from the hallway. David spun around to see a small *Vespa* leaning against the garden wall.

"Yours?"

"Yes, they are the best way to get around my little town."

David's eyes fluttered uncontrollably as Laetitia hitched up her dress, threw her toned leg over the seat and mounted the bike. She inched it forward and handed him a black helmet.

"Okay let's go. Hop-on."

David straddled the moped and sidled up against Laetitia.

"Hold on tightly David."

With pleasure.

The moped groaned under their weight like a tin bicycle as it rimmed the country lanes. With each jolt and thud in the road, David found his arms pulling more tightly around her. Laetitia labored to ignore the heat of David's stiff groin against her buttocks.

She struggled to focus. *Who is he? What does he want?*

The main turret of Rousinac's medieval castle loomed high above a promenade of trees as the mid-day sun baked its pavements. Within minutes, the moped was whizzing through the ancient walled section of the town.

It effortlessly sped through paths once trod by donkeys. Laetitia drew the moped to a spluttering halt behind the castle and lingered for a moment in the clutch of David's arms.

"No visit is complete without a tour of our beautiful castle." She announced.

They slowly prized themselves apart and dismounted. David smoothed out the creases on his trousers. Avoiding Laetitia's eyes, he quickly glanced up at the main turret where a single, barred window caught his attention.

Laetitia indicated toward the entrance.

"Come on," she teased. "I can show you around, and if you misbehave I'll have to lock you up in the tower!"

She seems way too friendly. David caught himself thinking for a second or maybe two.

The Locals (5)
Rousinac, Southwest France 2019

Pierre Malraux locked his car and walked along a stone pathway edged with trim rose bushes. The afternoon sun penetrated his large straw hat and perspiration drooled over his brow.

"Ah, bonjour stranger, how nice to see you," Maria Dubonnet said with a smile as she opened her backdoor.

"Maria, looking as beautiful as ever," Pierre cooed.

They embraced in a delicate four-cheeked kiss while he peered behind her toward the garden.

"In the garden?" he asked.

"Where else?" Maria clucked. "I swear he gives more attention to those roses than he does to me!"

Pierre pulled a handkerchief from his flannel pants and dabbed his face.

"When are you going to come to your senses and move in with me, Mon Cherie?" He pursed his lips into a kiss.

"Go on you naughty man," Maria flapped as she sidestepped his embrace.

Pierre followed her along the hallway and through the patio doors out towards a landscaped garden.

"Francois, look who's here," Maria called out.

A man waved from a gazebo and beckoned Pierre to advance.

"Pierre, it's been a long time since we've seen you at the lodge," Francois Dubonnet said with slight apprehension.

"Would you like a cold drink?" Maria asked.

"Yes please," the men replied in unison.

"Come and sit down." Francois pointed to the ornate table and chairs adjacent.

"You look as if you have the weight of the world on your shoulders." He added.

"Not quite the world Francois. But I do need your help," Pierre said solemnly.

"Go on, I'm listening."

"It has to do with Perodeau," Pierre announced grimly.

"Just tell me what to do," Francois softly replied.

Pierre pulled out a folded paper.

"Fromblier has two Americans staying at his hotel." He retrieved his reading glasses from a jacket pocket. "They're booked under the name of David Long and they pay everything in cash. They say they are here as property developers but there are one or two things that make us think differently."

"You want me to find out who they really are?" Francois coaxed.

"Please," Pierre replied.

"I will call into the station this afternoon and see what I can find."

"Francois, you are a true brother."

"Always," Francoise nodded.

Pierre smiled. Francois as head of the gendarmerie in Rousinac had never let him down.

Maria waddled out with a tray laden with snacks and drinks.

"Have you two finished gossiping?"

They raised their glasses and clinked. The ice cubes fizzed.

"We would never put gossip before you," Pierre responded.

"Ever the charmer," Maria beamed.

The Americans (9)
Rousinac, Southwest France 2019

James had spent most of the afternoon analyzing the data Graham Wells had sent him from New Scotland Yard. His mind buzzed with theories about the young women who'd disappeared near Rousinac, but he had no one to share them with.

Growing restless, he wandered from his hotel room to the lobby and then back again. Glancing at his watch, James wondered if David would be successful. But he had his doubts the French woman would let anything slip. It was more likely David would.

At 6pm a maid knocked on the door requesting to clean his room. Reluctantly, James moved downstairs into the hotel's empty lounge and out onto the patio. Two cognacs later he was even more obsessed with Perodeau. But more than anything, he needed cigarettes. He sauntered out in search of a Tabac.

Suddenly he spied Perodeau.

The French man was unloading groceries from his car. An older woman waited on a nearby doorstep as Perodeau's dog darted back and forth. Perodeau kissed the woman and presented her with a colorful bouquet of flowers before returning to the vehicle. Then he abruptly stopped and turned around.

James ducked behind a stone pillar. After a moment, Didier Perodeau stepped back toward the trunk and slammed it shut. He locked the car doors, called for his dog and entered the woman's house.

Was Perodeau out for the night?

Although he trusted David's exploration of the house when they'd first arrived, James wanted to look for more evidence around the outside. Bodies were notoriously hard to get rid of. They always left a trace somewhere.

No car, fuck!

He made for the lobby and interrupted the concierge.

"Hey, I need a car."

James noticed that Monsieur Fromblier was across the room talking to an elderly man. Both men looked at James and nodded in acknowledgement.

"Oui, Monsieur. Let me see what I can do for you." The concierge replied.

"I'll be right back. I just need to get something from my room."

As he began to leave, Monsieur Fromblier approached him and grabbed him by the arm. The elderly man he had been talking to, took the opportunity to slip away.

"Just a minute, please …" Fromblier said.

James slid his arm free. *Don't touch me.*

"You can't go upstairs, Monsieur, there is a problem with your room."

While the hotel owner spoke, James' eyes trailed the elderly man as he hobbled up the lobby's main stairway. Fromblier reached for the American's arm again. Their eyes locked.

"You see the ... how do you call it ... the ... maid ... her ... uhm?" Fromblier motioned using a vacuum cleaner.

"Vacuum? You mean the vacuum cleaner?" James offered.

"Yes, yes - the maid's vacuum broke unexpectedly and has made quite a mess in your room so I'm afraid you will not be able to enter it for perhaps half an hour or so," Fromblier sighed. "May I offer you a complimentary cocktail or hors d'oeuvres?"

"I just wanted to grab a map. It won't interfere with the clean-up." James blurted. He instantly regretted his impulsivity.

Fromblier arched an eyebrow.

"Where did you plan to go? I was born here in Rousinac. I am happy to direct you anywhere."

I can't let on where I want to go.

"Oh, I don't know. I'm just going to take a drive, you know, check out the countryside before the sun goes down. It's a beautiful evening, don't you think?" James blabbed.

"So, what is preventing you?" Fromblier glanced at the car park.

"I don't have a car. My partner took it. The concierge is trying to get a rental car for me now."

"Ah, but there's no need."

Fromblier made toward the car park and gestured for James to follow.

The French man exuberantly pulled out a set of keys from his pocket.

"Please, take this one." He nodded toward a blue Renault.

Fromblier thrust the keys into his hand.

"It is the least I can do since we have *inconvenienced* you."

Fromblier twisted his mouth into a sneer, but James didn't notice. He wasn't adept at reading faces or body language. All he could think about was seeing Perodeau in the street and the golden opportunity that he now had to search his house.

Fromblier seized James' arm once again and tugged him toward the car.

Stop touching me.

Fromblier leaned in closer.

"There are many beautiful sites in Rousinac…"

The hotel owner's eyes held a deadly cold stare.

"You're not worried I'll steal it?" James giggled. Fromblier wasn't sure what the American had said.

"You know us Yanks, crazy sons of bitches," he went on.

"I have no idea of what you talk." Fromblier muttered.

"Ok then, I won't be long. Merci beaucoup." James cleared his throat and jumped into the car.

"Take as long as you wish Monsieur. You will find a detailed local map in the glove box."

James watched Fromblier in his rear view mirror as he pulled away. The proprietor stood with his arms crossed. Had he not been on a spectrum he would have noticed a slight grin on Fromblier's mouth. But as it was, all James could think about was driving to Didier Perodeau's house.

He sped out of the hotel's courtyard and followed signs for Perodeau's lane. Within fifteen minutes he had reached it.

James switched off the car's engine and rolled it downhill until he reached the thick perimeter of woods that ringed Perodeau's home. The house was barely visible through it.

He lowered his window to get some fresh air.

"Jesus, what the hell!" he spluttered. "That's some pig shit they use around here!"

A distinct smell of carrion invaded the car. He powered the window shut and gasped for breath.

He had originally intended to head toward the house, break in and search for clues, but he now thought better of it. *What the hell was I thinking? I need a lookout. Besides, who knows who's in there?*

James studied Perodeau's house from the safety of his car. It was eerily quiet: no breeze, no occupants, no sound.

The deafening silence of the woods created a faint buzzing in his ears. The lull had a tranquilizing effect on him as a mild headache began to creep over his temples. The two cognacs he had drunk that afternoon were starting to take their toll.

In the distance, the sky was an explosion of orange and wispy clouds. James' eyes grew heavy as he trailed the V of migrating geese. Within moments his head was resting on the steering wheel, his eyes closed.

Fuck! Wake up!

James knew he would have to do something definitive on this trip or else go back to the hotel. He couldn't waste this opportunity to find evidence of foul play. He pulled out a small flashlight and made his way to the tunnel he had discovered on his last visit.

The door had been screwed securely back on. James pulled out his pliers and prized it off again. It didn't take him long. The result was the same, a peculiar stench, the darkness of a deep tunnel and silence.

Weird.

If one waited long enough, one would hear rats scurrying in sewers like this. But in this tunnel, nothing. It didn't feel right. Rats avoided bigger predators. *What was down there?*

He shone a flashlight into the tunnel. It was wider than he had first thought. He could step in and stand upright. *Fuck it.* Water lapped around his ankles, leaching into his sneakers. The tunnel loomed ahead, straight, seemingly for miles. James turned back to the opening.

Always secure your location. His sergeant had drilled.

He pocketed the screws and peered back into the tunnel. Did he really need to do this? Then, something clicked, and he found himself moving forward. His arms felt light, no weapon. He went back to the opening a third time and grabbed a large, jagged stick.

He moved forward, quietly, slowly. Disturbing the water would sound an alarm further down the current. As would a bright light. He turned his flashlight off. He'd need to allow his eyes to adjust and venture in like an animal, half-blind, but with other senses sharp.

In response his body enlivened to the challenge. Information streamed in. The tunnel had occupants, not close, but somewhere deep inside. He concentrated on his breath, visualizing a cloak of invisibility around his body. He stifled a laugh. This type of *Zen Buddhist shit* had kept him alive on countless maneuvers in the desert.

Make your environment a weapon.

James leaned flat against the tunnel, guessing that at this angle no one peering in would spot him. He stopped and ran things over in his mind.

His car had been strategically parked. Perodeau wouldn't suspect the tunnel had been opened. From his position in the darkness, he would be alerted to intruders before they were aware of him. His muscles relaxed. Excitement crept in.

Curiosity consumed his thoughts. *What was being kept down here?* He crept further into the tunnel. And then, he stopped.

Whisperings. Murmurs.

Was that the water? He arched his head.

Echoes. Whispers. Footsteps?

Way ahead of him.

James froze.

He looked down at his feet. A tremor pimpled the water's surface. A pattern that suggested movement. Someone else was down here, maybe more than one. His ears got sharper. The sounds got clearer. There was a cadence, two distinct tones, suggesting a conversation.

They don't know I'm here.

He stared into the darkness beyond.

Should I go forward? What then? What if it's kids? What if it's junkies or smugglers?

The sounds stopped.

Silence.

A thick stench like rotting corpses wafted toward him. The water began to pulse, then wave around his ankles.

He tightened his grip around the stick.

His knuckle cracked.

FUCK!

The tunnel exploded into sound.

In panic James dropped his weapon and charged toward the opening. Once outside, he thrashed through the undergrowth toward his car. Behind him, he could hear feet charging through the water.

Whatever was in that tunnel was now pursuing him. Their movements fanned outside. They thundered through the bushes.

WHAT THE FUCK?!

A loud, high-pitched noise punctured the forest. It sounded like a banshee siren, feminine, menacing, animalistic. Other sounds followed as though in response, sharp, heightened like a pack of hyenas chasing prey.

He turned just once to catch a look.

A scream gargled in his throat as scores of hooded figures skidded up the lane toward him.

SLAP!

His hands alighted on the driver's door.

SLAM!

He yanked it shut.

Click!

All the doors got locked.

James turned the ignition so hard it stalled. Hands sweaty he tried again, painfully slower. All the while a swarm was closing in. As the engine choked into life, the headlights illuminated the trail in front of him.

"FUCK!"

A tall hooded form moved in and out of the light's oval periphery. He jammed the car into a steep three-point turn, determined not to stop no matter what. In the rear mirror he saw two more moving through the exhaust making toward the car.

Hooded.

Pales faces.

Black eyes.

He banged the gears, pumped the gas and sped off.

THUD!

Something had jumped onto the car's roof.

The metal above his head buckled. James bore down on the gas pedal and pressed forward. The car labored under the intruder's weight as it zigzagged up the country lane. Finally, blaring lights from the main road forced it off.

He sped toward Rousinac, not looking back. He remembered nothing of the journey home, intent only upon his destination. When he at last reached the hotel, his entire body was soaked in sweat. He took a piss in some nearby bushes and looked back at the car.

A huge dent had crinkled its roof. His eyes dropped to the sides and back where deep scratches had gashed the bodywork.

What would he tell Fromblier?

The Locals (6)
Rousinac, Southwest France 2019

"Bonjour Pierre. It's François."

"I didn't expect a call from you so soon."

"I am afraid it's not good news. The Americans are no more property developers than we are."

"Police?" Pierre Malraux asked.

"Well, yes and no. David Long's real name is David Frankel, and he works for New Scotland Yard as a medical examiner in the forensics department. His companion, James Harrison is a famous criminal psychologist."

"A what?"

"Someone who studies the behavior of killers."

Pierre sighed heavily.

"Then I'm afraid they can only be here for one reason."

"What will you do?" Francois asked.

"I'm not sure yet. I need to speak to the others." Pierre replied.

"If there's anything else you need from me, don't hesitate

– anything. As you know my nephew Claude is …" He added, but Pierre interjected.

"Laetitia is with one of the Americans now. I will let you know if she needs assistance. Thank you, my friend, once again you have come to the aid of the Order. This will not be forgotten."

The Maquis (9)
Rousinac, Southwest France 1944

Since his meeting with Jean Dubonnet, Gerard Dupre hadn't slept properly. While his men were well-positioned to execute Dubonnet's plan, that didn't mean they could pull it off.

First, there was their age. Alain and Jean-Baptist were rebellious and had been caught out numerous times after curfew. Would they get too cocky? Could they be trusted to stay calm, to act normal? Would they brag to a friend, or let something slip to a sweetheart?

Then there was the location itself. The munitions depot was in a series of caves. Humidity and a lack of good light could prove detrimental for lighting fuses.

Third, how would they get the explosives in? Every day they had to walk through machine-gun checkpoints surrounded by minefields and barbed wire. They could be stopped and searched at any time. Both boys would buckle under interrogation.

Despite these reservations, Alain Boussuet had been able to pass a plan of the depot, as well as an estimate of ammunition stock, back to Gerard Dupre. In turn, he had passed it back to Jean Dubonnet.

The Allies were quick to respond. As Jean had predicted, a small but strategic rucksack of explosives along with instructions and a map, were brought into Rousinac on a freight train three days later.

Everyone, especially the Germans had the jitters. But given that the munitions depot was underground, the soldiers there knew that they wouldn't be the target of the now daily bombing raids in the region.

They felt safer than their patrolling comrades, within a wall of machine guns and minefields, and so they naturally grew complacent. The night shift was often an opportunity to snooze, or drink and play cards.

Alain and Jean-Baptist had arranged to work a series of night shifts together. The timing was perfect. *Was it too perfect?* Gerard agonized.

Over several nights, Jean-Baptist wandered the chambers checking that the map Alain had given Gerard was still correct. Meanwhile, Alain spent his time as a look-out, distracting the Germans with small talk about local girls.

Getting the explosives in had been nerve-wracking. Jean Dubonnet had suggested that a female bring in a food basket. But neither man wanted to compromise a relative. After much thought, Alain hit upon the idea of repurposing a flask and smuggling the explosives in, a stick at a time. This process would eat up precious days, but eventually every stick of dynamite had found its home within the munitions depot.

After several detonator tests, where the wicks were checked for dampness, the young patriots waited for their orders. Allied troop disembarkation had already begun along the coast. A final push against the Third Reich was afoot.

Twenty-four hours later the order was finally given.

The Maquis (10)
Rousinac, Southwest France 1944

On June 11th, Jean Dubonnet received a message from "Ici Londres", a Free French radio service.

"Today's supper is goose with haricot vert."

It had come in, time coded at 5:22am. Jean knew that "vert" signified "go," whereas "supper" specified PM. When the numbers were combined, the value gave a time: 5 + 2 + 2 = 9pm.

Jean understood that Operation Blitz* had just been announced. He immediately sent word to Gerard. *An Allied Operation he had previously been briefed about.

"The goose will arrive at 9pm today. Assemble your men at the Bar Chateau at eight tonight. Everyone must be there."

Was this a trap? Was Jean a double agent? For a few moments Gerard panicked. *What was he leading his men into?* Then, he looked down at his son pushing a tin train along the floor.

Ultimately, there was no choice but to risk this. He had to trust in something higher than himself. His children would have no future until the Germans were wiped from their homeland.

This is for you, my son.

Gerard kissed the boy and steeled himself.

It's on.

He sent word to his men, "Tonight, 8pm, we meet at the Bar Chateau. We will play a game of cards."

The location was obvious. The Bar Chateau in Rousinac's central square at the foot of the castle, was popular with German officers. They would all be seen. Or as Jean put it, they would be "hidden in plain sight."

Man by man they had sauntered in, just a group of locals gathering to play a quiet game of cards.

Here we all are then, the brave and heroic Maquis, playing games while two boys decide the fate of France.

Gerard thought as he surveyed his men.

Phillipe Perodeau shuffled a deck of cards and stole a look at his leader.

Gerard Dupre was gray with fatigue, and he felt the same way. His wife was expecting their second and he longed for her, for his other child. Tonight, they were en route to relatives in the South of France, along with his mother.

Charles Perodeau reviewed his hand of cards then searched for his brother's eyes. Phillipe's words still rang in his head.

They will come for all of us Jews.

He knew this to be true. The Germans were unrelenting in their violence. Just a week before, his neighbor had been caught selling stolen German goods that he had pilfered from an idle supply truck.

He had committed this act randomly to feed his children. Soldiers had come quietly to the man's house while he was out at the market with his wife. They had inquired politely of the older children if they had any knowledge of their father's theft. In truth, the children had replied that they knew nothing.

The three boys and two toddler girls had been asked to line up beside a brick wall in order of age in return for chocolate. The children had eagerly complied thinking it was a game.

A soldier sketched their outline in chalk. And then, one by one the Germans had shot them dead. When the man came home with his wife, they had found their babies face down in pools of dry blood.

Charles Perodeau glanced at the German officers and hardened his gaze. *I would kill every one of you with my bare hands if I could.*

A stray card popped from the deck and brushed Gerard's hand. He locked eyes with Charles.

This is it then. Our time has come.

Charles nodded in salute. Gerard smiled. *We are in the lion's den now boys. No turning back.*

He peered into the bottom of his glass, Swallowing the remainder of Bar Chateau's cloudy red. His thoughts turned to his baby boy Remy.

Not even two years old, was it likely that Remy would even remember his father should he be killed tonight? Would Gerard miss his son's first words, his first beer, his first shave, his first everything? What about the girls? How could he protect them? Who would grow old with his wife?

Like the other men in the group, he had sent his family into hiding. But he worried about them traveling through the back villages. A hand landed on his shoulder and dragged him back into reality. It was Daniel Malraux – *Mon Dieu.*

"Bonsoir gentlemen." Daniel eyed his companions in turn and sat down. Phillipe Perodeau dealt Daniel a hand of cards. It was a bad hand. *An omen?*

Gerard turned to his lieutenant.

"Soon, mon ami, soon our goose will be cooked."

Daniel arched an eyebrow towards a German sitting to their immediate right. *Was he listening?* He lowered his voice.

"I don't like just sitting here doing …" Daniel trailed off. *Nothing*. Gerard put down a card and whispered.

"You have to be seen, all of us. Now play cards like you care."

As if in response, one of the German high commands strutted in and surveyed the bar. In the distance, the men could hear convoy after convoy roaring around under the distant din of planes. German anxiety was palpable.

Officers were pounding drinks and talking in low tones. There were rumors that a massive Allied bombing campaign was imminent, and that the skies would be black with planes.

Charles Perodeau exhaled his cigarette smoke with a dramatic puff, laying down a winning hand.

"Tonight, we turn the tide."

Gerard silently doubted that.

"Finally, …" Daniel Malraux whispered as Gerard Dupre felt his heart break.

The Americans (10)
Rousinac, Southwest France 2019

Throughout the day, both David and Laetitia had been preoccupied with following their own agenda: Laetitia was keen to know more about David's visit, and David was looking for any signs connecting Laetitia to the Graystons' disappearance.

Naturally, the conversation had strayed from time to time into personal details, family history, anecdotes, past relationships and careers. David had fabricated his surname as well as his occupation. As he compounded his tale, it suddenly occurred to him that Laetitia could easily find his true profile, if she dug deep enough.

His face was on a hundred sites and medical blogs. But Laetitia appeared convinced, perhaps even enchanted by David Long the property developer. More importantly, David strove to keep a more pressing matter at bay, a persistent urge that charged between him and Laetitia.

As he sipped cognac, he found himself succumbing to the evening's balmy air and Laetitia's allure.

"I cannot believe that such a small town could hold someone as remarkable as you." He found himself saying.

Laetitia leaned toward David defiantly.

"I hadn't always wanted to stay here, you know."

"No?"

"When I was younger, I applied to study history at the Madrid University."

"Oh really? What era?"

"Middle Ages. I'm fascinated by the royal families of France. They were so important to Europe. They were ferocious. They took their blood everywhere." She raised her arm. "It flows through my veins too, so beware." She watched as David processed her last statement. It felt odd to him, she'd guessed.

Who cared? What did these ignorant Americans know about anything other than killing the natives? Her mouth curled into a smile.

She was utterly bewitching to David. The way her eyelids fluttered when she wanted to make a point. The pensiveness of her mouth. He found himself simply gazing. Sensing his growing desire, she turned her body away from him.

"Anyway, it never happened. I went to Bordeaux instead and studied business. I'd rather not say why." That statement had closed his mouth.

My adoptive parents forbade it. She had wanted to say but that comment would have opened a can of worms. There was a pause as David pondered his next question.

"Do you mind me asking about …?" He looked away and shuffled in his seat.

"Husbands? Lovers?" She threw back. He sniggered with embarrassment.

She gave him a line or two about being too busy for romance

but sensed that he didn't buy it. She asked about him. The American talked about his ex-wife and kids, and how his business travel had ended his marriage.

Bla bla bla Americans give you their life story.

When he got up to use the restroom, Laetitia's mind wandered. *Andre Marchand.*

She had met him at University. His mother was from Senegal, his father from Marseilles. Andre had taken the best parts of both. His height of over six feet and his green eyes were entirely French. His full lips and tightly curled black hair were the gifts of his mother. Only his skin was unique. The tell-tale sign of two races merged into one. It was a deep golden brown and when he blushed his cheeks turned honey-colored.

Andre hadn't taken her virginity. That prize had belonged to some bungling local in the back of a car.

No, Andre had been the first man to make love to her. Even now, when she closed her eyes and recalled his touch, a powerful sensation pulsed inside of her. For three years they had been inseparable.

He had asked her to go to Paris with him and further their studies together. It was a case she powerfully presented to her relatives. Just a few years away from home, and afterwards, she would return with him. They would buy an old decaying chateau and convert it into a high-end hotel.

Laetitia's request had fallen on deaf ears. *Non, absolument!*

Andre hadn't been rejected on account of his color. He was denied because of his blood. He wasn't a local. It would never work. It was forbidden to bring in outsiders. The consequences of disobedience would be severe especially for Andre. There had been no choice other than to let him believe that she was related to a bunch of racists. Well, it wasn't too far from the truth.

After that she had refused to marry. There were lovers here and there. Usually, they were transient workers, rugged Portuguese grape-pickers, visiting officials, but never a local.

David had returned to the table.

"Do you want children?" He asked unexpectedly.

His question made her mouth rigid.

"Too busy." Laetitia mumbled.

Sensing her discomfort, David decided to change the subject. He glanced at a nearby war monument.

"It's almost as though the war is still raging here in Rousinac."

"What do you mean?"

"Was that an insensitive thing to say?"

"Of course not! W-why would you think that?" She snapped.

"It's just that … everywhere you look here there's some statue dedicated to what happened here in the war." He mused.

"And why not?" She wiped the table with her napkin.

"Well, it's like Rousinac seems determined never to forget. Am I right?"

David attempted a smile, but he felt too intimidated by Laetitia's stiffened demeanor to let it emerge. *Never mention the war in Europe – isn't that what they say? Idiot.*

"I'm sorry I didn't mean to bring up something so personal," he mumbled.

Laetitia's eyes widened.

"Personal? It was over seventy-five years ago," she smirked.

"Right – right. It's just that, I noticed."

"What?"

"That … some of the names of the …"

"Maquis?" Laetitia clarified.

"Maquis?"

"The French resistance." She explained.

The men who liberated France, not the other cowboys.

"Oh right. That their names are, like, everywhere, on businesses, street signs, it's like ..."

"It's a small town."

"Well, that's my point ... Perodeau, Malraux, Dubonnet ..."

"And Dupre?" She added.

"That's your name, right?" He pressed.

"Yes."

"So, was that Maquis Dupre a relative of yours?"

Her eyes darkened.

"I'd rather not discuss it if you don't mind."

David instantly felt embarrassed.

"I'm sorry."

Laetitia peered into the road as a police car rolled past and came to a halt. The officer inside the vehicle nodded to her.

"Bonjour Laetitia, everything okay?"

The man discreetly gestured towards David.

"Yes. Have a good night, Vincent," she smiled as the car pulled away.

"As I told you, Rousinac's a *very small town.*"

Laetitia waved to the waitress for the check.

"It's late." She said sternly.

David crumpled. *Mission aborted.*

Laetitia felt frustrated that she hadn't learned anything of significance about the American. In fact, she'd feared she'd given a few things away. *How did he know about the Maquis? It was impossible for him to know unless ... Was he a secret agent? Or was he just a handsome buffoon?* She was determined to find out. Perhaps in her bed David would let something slip.

It was almost midnight when they arrived back at Cafe Napoleon. David walked Laetitia to the door. She delayed for a few seconds before unlocking it. Torn between his agenda and libido, David harbored the hope that their day would not end here. When she turned and smiled seductively at him, he almost exploded with relief.

After a nightcap on the patio, Laetitia took David by the hand and led him up to her bedroom. David found himself lost in thoughts of sex.

Laetitia moved to undress him. She kissed him deeply, and unbuckled his belt. Her pleasure became audible as his tongue explored her mouth in return. David moaned when her nails found his buttocks. Her bare breasts now rubbed against his chest.

Laetitia stepped out of her panties and draped a leg around David's naked hips. They tumbled onto the bed, and she pulled him on top. He was already rock hard, and he thrust into her again and again.

As their bodies fell into a rhythmic tussle, David felt Laetitia's body writhe and shudder with each push until she groaned loudly. A few seconds later he came. He felt her body open as she relaxed after the tension of climax.

Body heat forced them apart and they basked in the cool night air. David watched Laetitia's glistening naked body, as she got back her breath. She rolled her eyes over his lean torso.

How easy you are David Long if that's even your real name?

He curled her up in his arms and didn't think once about the Graystons or James. She stroked his downy chest and listened to his breathing until it slowed into a deep sleep.

A few hours passed.

Noise penetrated the room. David woke. His hand felt for Laetitia but the bed was empty. Propping himself up onto his elbows, he was startled to see the French woman facing him as she rocked back and forth in a small chair.

"Can't sleep?"

"No," she yawned. "I am used to sleeping alone."

"You want me to leave?"

"No, I want you to tell me why you went to Didier Pero-deau's house?"

"Okay. But only if you come back to bed."

Crap!

He pulled the sheet back and moved to one side. She climbed into the warmth left by his body.

"Tell me."

"Okay. So, Tom Grayston, my colleague, had singled out Monsieur Perodeau's property as a prospective purchase for the company. The land alone would have been worth us developing. Tom had some vacation time owed and he and his wife decided to kill two birds with one stone."

"What?"

"They decided to combine business with a vacation here in Rousinac."

He said that he thought Tom and his wife were still in the region, maybe touring and that he wanted to catch up with them. But the story barely convinced him let alone Laetitia.

There was a pause then she asked.

"Why are *you* actually here?"

"I told you."

"You don't look like a real estate man to me."

David felt his body tense.

"Really? What do I look like?"

Was she beginning to suspect him?

Laetitia fell silent for a few seconds.

"How long do you intend to stay in Rousinac?" she finally asked.

"I'm not sure, it all depends on James. If he finds a property that catches his eye, we'll stay longer."

David noticed that his pants were crumpled beside the chair that Laetitia had been sitting in.

Had she checked his wallet?

His driver's license read David Frankel not David Long, the name he had given at the hotel. His New Scotland Yard access card was tucked directly behind it. It would take seconds to find his profile online. His heart began to race.

Laetitia could hear it thudding.

"You will find it difficult to buy in this area. The local people don't sell to outsiders." She whispered.

"Outsiders?"

Laetitia stiffened.

"You know what I mean. Someone who is not from here."

"Well I think it's because no one knows about Rousinac. I haven't met one other tourist, which is weird. Not much agriculture either. It's mostly woods. How does the town sustain its economy?"

"I need to sleep now David."

She crawled to the other side of the bed and David felt a chasm open up between them.

David Frankel. You dirty liar.

The Americans (11)
Rousinac, Southwest France 2019

It was nine o'clock in the morning when David finally arrived back at the hotel. He found James sitting outside on the patio smoking furiously. Laptop open. A coffee pot, two cups and fresh croissants to his right.

James pushed the tray towards David.

"Eat. I'm not hungry."

David sat down.

"You look awful."

"I didn't get much sleep last night, and neither did you by the looks of it," James snarled.

David ignored the comment.

"Why couldn't you sleep?"

"Coffee first. You'll need it." James said.

"What's going on?"

David held the coffee cup halfway to his mouth and paused as James began.

"Last night I got bored crunching cold cases, so..."

"Oh God, what did you do?"

James told David about his trip to Perodeau's house. He waited for David's response.

"Are you fucking nuts? Have you forgotten that two people have gone missing, and, who knows what else? And you go there ALONE?"

The waitress glared at them. David lowered his voice.

"What did Fromblier say?"

"Nothing. I told him a branch fell on the car in the storm last night. He didn't ask any questions. Said the insurance would cover it."

"You could have been …"

"It was fucked up."

"It was reckless."

"There's something else I found out about Rousinac last night," James said in a hush.

"But we can't talk about it here."

"Okay let's go."

They drove to the outskirts of Rousinac in silence. James pulled into a layby, then handed David his iPad.

"Check that out."

As David read, James fidgeted.

"Did you get anything out of Laetitia last night, besides a blow …"

"Stop. No."

He read the page.

"I don't get it."

James groaned.

"Well, we know that girls have gone missing over a fifty year period which suggests a smuggling enterprise and rules out a single serial killer."

"So?"

"The stats about missing girls end in the zeros."

"Zeros?"

"The year 2000, keep up!"

"Okay."

"No more German girls."

"So."

"So, the smugglers turned to something else, something more lucrative. Maybe narcotics, guns, kids."

"Here?"

"Don't be fooled by the rustic scenery David. I think there's some weird smuggling shit going on down here. Which makes sense when you look at how cloistered the place is, plus you've got a ton of tunnels leading out from an old castle, an isolated community tucked away in the forest, and a seemingly okay economy."

"Seemingly?"

"Look around. It's like a ghost town every place we go. No industry, nothing. How do people live? I think Rousinac is a smuggling hub."

"Smuggling what?"

"Drugs. People."

"Oh come on!"

"I told you, I saw some fucked up junkies on Perodeau's land."

"But what's this got to do with the Graystons?" David pushed.

"Ding dong, anyone home?"

"What?"

"Well, Einstein, what if the Brits inadvertently stumbled across something illegal on Perodeau's land?"

David rubbed his eyes.

"Jeez, this is far out even for you. I mean, let's just say there's a connection, chances are that the locals would know all about it, right?"

"Correct, which makes sense of no one seeing the Brits anywhere."

"You really think the whole town knows about it?"

James shrugged.

"Well take yesterday, the maid allegedly made a mess in my room with the vacuum cleaner. Fromblier wouldn't let me go back up there. He insisted I take his car. Probably to buy *them* some more time to search our rooms and by the way I think I was drugged by Fromblier yesterday because …"

"Stop! Who's them?" David shouted.

"Some other guy at the hotel, old, looked like a retired cop to me. That's when I went to Perodeau's land and got chased by a bunch of zombies in hoodies. I think it's connected to the tunnel system they got here. It's really old, like Roman and the tunnels run all over the place. I'm telling you, who-ever or whatever is hanging around Perodeau's pad ain't normal..." James trailed off.

"You know how insane this sounds, right?" David asked.

"If they killed the Brits over what's going on at Perodeau's then wouldn't they come after us?" James wondered aloud. David knew that he needed to calm his friend down.

"Let's just say you're right. All they need are two more dead bodies, especially Americans to deal with? Besides, they don't know we know anything."

"Okay stay with my theory that the entire town of Rousinac is in on it. Now ask yourself. What have *we* done?"

"What?"

"First, we head straight to Perodeau and let the cat out of the bag. Then, we go and tell Laetitia that we're looking for our vanished colleague Tom Grayston and *oh by the way have you seen him lately?*"

"Leaving our passports in our rooms." David added.

"It's like that movie Dumb and Dumber."

"Oh fuck."

"Like you said, they won't risk bumping us off. Think about it, two more unexplained disappearances, New Scotland Yard, John Jay guys? More questions? More eyeballs?" James jabbered on.

David ran his fingers through his hair.

"Okay but I still don't get how any of this relates to the Graystons? They were here for a vacation. Why would Perodeau risk two foreigners finding out about a smuggling operation? It sounds nutty. Are you taking your meds?"

James rolled his eyes.

"Were you even fucking listening David? I'm telling you, not for nothing, there's some fucked up shit going down on Perodeau's land. And we know the Brits stayed there. What if they stumbled across the whole damn thing? Think about it. Something freaked them out enough to mail you a sample. You said you knew the guy, how? That British guy!"

"We belonged to the same rifle association."

"Right, so the guy knows how to shoot. Maybe he carries a firearm. Then something goes horribly wrong one night. Maybe he saw what I saw, and he took a shot at one of them. He obviously didn't get close enough to get a good look at it or he would have mentioned it in his letter. But he had the smarts to take a sample and send it to you, a forensic specialist. So, I'm guessing the Brits knew that what they were dealing with wasn't kosher?"

"Sure." David reluctantly agreed.

"Although how the blood sample fits into this is still not clear." James tilted his head sideways and closed his eyes.

"But it's a big part of the puzzle."

Silence.

A police car passed them in the layby.

"They've spotted us. Let's go."

They drove a little further along the road.

"Okay so, what if, whatever this secret is, what if they came back and finished the Graystons off? Or the Graystons confronted Perodeau and threatened to blow the lid. And he killed them and buried them on his land?"

"It still sounds nutty."

"I know. But that's all we've got for now. I've got a hunch that the German girls are a missing link too. I just can't figure out why right now. If we're going to find out anything definitively, we'll need to get back to Perodeau's house. Pay him another visit and this time we bluff him into telling us whatever he knows."

"How?"

"We tell him what we have and what we know."

"What *we think* we know."

James watched the resignation building in David's face.

"I think you need to go home James."

"What?"

James pulled over to the curb.

"You're a liability."

"Fuck you!"

"This is exactly the reason John Jay's letting you go!"

David got out of the car and walked toward the main road.

"Where do you think you're going, asshole?"

"You're insane!"

"Come back David!"

David ignored him and carried on walking.

Rousinac was 10 km away, the route back was a busy road.

Not pleasant but doable.

He needed to put some distance and sanity between him and James.

Half an hour later, sweaty and irritated David arrived at Le Chateau Bar and Restaurant. It was the only place that kept a bar open all day. David needed a strong drink.

He took a seat outside and waited. After a few minutes he poked his head into the reception. It was completely empty. David called out.

Eventually, a tanned man appeared with a menu.

"Sorry, I didn't see you out there." He ushered David back outside, lit up a cigarette and arched his back, face up to the sun.

"How did you know I spoke English?" David asked.

"American right?" The guy added.

"Yeah."

"I'm usually right. You're not used to waiting. Even the Brits will wait. Americans, no."

David chuckled.

"I'll take a double cognac and an espresso. Thank you."

"Sure." He lingered, finishing his cigarette.

"Do you get many Brits here? In Rousinac?"

"No, most Brits head straight to the Dordogne."

David frowned.

"Have you seen this couple?" He showed a photograph of the Graystons.

The man paused, studying the faces.

"Yes. Not long ago, in fact. They came here for dinner one night. Are they friends of yours?"

"When exactly?" David pressed.

The man shrugged.

"Hard to say, a month ago?"

"Were they staying in Rousinac?"

"Are you a cop?"

The man dumped his cigarette, looked up and down the empty street.

"No-no. A friend. We were supposed to meet up and head further South, but I lost touch with him and his wife, and …"

"Let me get your drinks." The man went back inside. A few minutes later he returned carrying a tray. Two cognacs and a coffee.

"Mind?" He pulled over a chair.

"Please."

The man lit another cigarette and extended his hand.

"Alex."

"David."

"Pleasure. That is a forty-year old cognac. Enjoy."

"Boy, that's good."

"The best."

"So, you own …" David peered up at the hotel sign.

"Hell no. My wife and I manage it. But we're leaving tomorrow."

"Why?"

"Take a look around." Alex pointed to the abandoned street.

"Siesta?"

"No. Rousinac is a ghost town."

"Are you from around here?"

"Belgium. A damned foreigner like you and …"

"So, they came here to eat?"

Alex knocked back his cognac in one.

"Yes. We were unusually busy. Two other families plus your friends." He chuckled at his own joke.

"It was a hot night, so everyone was outside. Your friends included. I asked where they were staying. Hey, I run a hotel, so I am always curious. You know? The wife, well, she was pretty, right? I wanted to flirt with her. So, I took their order."

"Where did they say they were staying?"

"Some place on the outskirts."

"Didier Perodeau?"

"I don't remember. Then some late night drinkers came in and I had to manage the bar. But your friends stayed late. One of the last to go home. Then, when it came to the bill."

He paused.

"What?"

"Sorry to say but, your friend's card didn't work. He swiped every card, none worked. So, he starts pulling everything from his wallet. You know, notes, change. It was embarrassing."

"How short was he?"

"Fifty, sixty euros."

"Shit."

"He was sweating. I felt bad for him. He kept looking over his shoulder. Guess he didn't want his wife to know."

"You let him off?"

"I let him off."

"That's real nice of you."

"Hey, we've all been in that position, right? But I banned him. I had to. My wife would have divorced me if I hadn't."

On cue a pretty woman appeared at the hotel door.

"Coming baby!"

The woman eyed him knowingly and went back inside.

"She hates it here. We both do. Like I said, most people move through. It's a strange place." He got up to clear the table.

"Strange. *How?*" David asked.

"I can't say for sure. It's just … "

"Quiet?"

"Yes but more than that. It's …."

Pause.

"…. creepy."

Alex peered up at a window across the street.

"Take your time, enjoy your coffee in the sun." He said softly.

David noticed a shadow at that exact window. It made him feel uneasy. He went back into the hotel lobby and paid his check.

"Whoa! That's way too much." Alex pushed back the hundred euro bill.

"American tip." David insisted. Both men understood that he had covered Tom's bill.

"Thank you, David."

"Good luck Alex."

It was a five minute walk back to his hotel, but David decided to prolong his return. He took a walk along the pretty canal that ringed the castle town. Despite being a beautiful day, it was eerily quiet. David recalled Alex's words.

Creepy.

After his altercation with David, James had decided he would go back to their hotel and research Rousinac some more. There wasn't much to go on. For a quaint castle town, it was a digital desert. And yet, despite being a ghost town there was evidence of a bustling local economy.

The town's houses and main streets were well-maintained but most of the businesses were boarded up. Its parks and squares were immaculate and empty.

What was Rousinac's secret?

The Americans (12)
Rousinac, Southwest France 2019

David sat quietly staring into the canal.

What had happened to the Graystons? What was the town's secret? Were they in danger?

PING!

He got a text message.

"Come back now."

There was no ignoring James.

Reluctantly, he made his way back to the hotel.

James got straight into it, rapid fire.

"No tourists. No viable local economy. No poverty either. Missing girls. Weird blood sample. It has to be a smuggling hub."

Silence.

"Rousinac is perfectly situated." James finally said.

"What's Perodeau's role?"

"I think he's a major player."

"But I don't understand why he would let out his house to the Graystons?"

"Me neither. Makes no sense, unless …"

"What?"

"Unless Tom was somehow involved."

"What?"

"You said he had money worries. Maybe he was a crook."

"No way! Tom's a nice guy …"

"How else do you explain him being in the wrong place at the wrong time?"

"Tom, a drug smuggler?"

"Guy's a gun owner. That ain't normal for Brits unless he was ex-military. They took a ferry, drove in their car. No checkpoints. What if …"

"Oh this is nuts."

"You see it all the time, admit it. Crime scene, homicide, no motive then you dig a little. Find out about the husband's cheating, or the wife's got a drug problem. You dig and it gets dirty."

"You think …"

"Maybe the Graystons were dirty."

"And?"

"No idea but it all points back to Rousinac to Perodeau."

"I'm not crazy about going back, James. That place gives me the creeps. Are you sure about this?"

"As far as we know, it's where the Graystons spent their last known hours. Coupled with what I bumped into the other night. Anyway, I think we go back and surveille. If we hide well enough we could get some photos. Take them back as evidence."

David sighed. It was no use trying to talk James down. He resolved to check his friend's meds again that night. If James grew more erratic, he would need to call back to London for help. He began to wish he had never heard the name Rousinac.

The Locals (7)
Rousinac, Southwest France 2019

"Uncle, it's me."

"It's okay Laetitia. We know who they are."

"Are we in danger?"

"So far as we know, they know nothing. Remain calm. I know we are asking a lot of you."

"I will do anything you need."

"Of that, I am sure."

"Goodnight."

Pierre moaned as he lowered himself into an armchair.

He glanced up at a photograph on the wall.

An action that had become a habit whenever he sat in that particular chair. Black and white it showed a group of men, all bereted and brandishing guns. One of those faces was his father's.

Papa.

The war was never far from Pierre's mind. There was no relief.

He closed his eyes and began to whimper.

The Germans (1)
Rousinac castle, SW France, 1944

He looked like any other man as he went about the business of making coffee.

The grinding of beans by hand, the inhalation of their musky aroma and the careful patience he took to bring them to percolation was devotional.

It takes time but the wait is worthwhile.

He brought the cup to his desk and sat down.

French roast. Ethiopian beans.

He lovingly gazed into the cup before drawing it to his parted lips.

Wunderbar.

This man drinking coffee alone in a dark laboratory was Nazi doctor Klaus Moritz. It was a place where all manner of diabolical things occurred.

An overhead lamp cut a neat little circle over his desk. Animals stacked in cages, growled and squawked from a room down the hallway but Moritz didn't notice.

In this precious solitary moment, he simply sipped his coffee.

The work.

A thought broke in. There was no denying it for long.

The work.

It drew his eyes to a pile of papers.

A dossier of research he'd made a few months earlier, while based at Dachau Concentration Camp, Germany.

The work had truly begun then, he nodded in agreement with himself.

The Gestapo had transported fifty-three Romanian gypsies (all male) to the camp for forced labor, research or extermination. He had been given first selection. Per his instructions, the new arrivals had been stripped naked and retained in the main outdoor yard for hours.

On that bitterly-cold evening, Moritz had waited patiently for the temperature to drop.

He hadn't been disappointed.

The Germans (1a)
Dachau Concentration Camp, Germany, 1944

A few months previous …

It was the coldest night of the winter. Moritz methodically unbuttoned, buttoned his jacket as he walked down the corridor towards the holding yard. A scarf wound around his neck like a noose.

A savage gale rapped at the corridor's windows, rattling its fractured panes. The doctor's breath pulsated in front of him. Reminding him of the abattoir freezers he'd used to store the mangled bodies of his early animal experiments. So much work, so many years of dedication.

Tonight, he felt hopeful, perhaps even jubilant? New specimens meant his true work could continue, not the pointless tasks his superiors set him.

Recently, Dachau had been graced with a visit from his medical superior, Dr. Rascherat; a man connected directly to Heinrich Himmler. A sure sign that Berlin's favor was turning his way. Rascherat had been encouraging. His words still rang in Moritz's ears.

"I am pleased to hear that your request for a higher caliber of specimen has been positively received. This shows initiative and confidence in your work Klaus."

"Thank you, Herr Doctor. As you know, working with ghetto Jews deeply affects a definitive scientific outcome."

"And even the children, well, I would have thought them more resilient? You certainly had more consigned here at Dachau than anywhere else."

"Actually, they diminish more quickly than the adults, sir."

"Surprising, not like our own robust kinder?"

"Indeed not!"

"Still, the results were illuminating. Previous to your study, we did not know the full effects of seawater intake on the human body. It all helps."

"Yes. It was fascinating to watch them lick the floors after mopping, a universal behavior exhibited toward the end of the trial. I found that the most curious part. We implemented a double blind test to ensure accuracy."

"Perhaps like an animal, they could sense moisture on the floor?"

"Yes, very interesting."

"Yet, the outcome was ultimately disappointing?"

"Yes, a pilot downed in the ocean would die an agonizing and slow death within days, without access to fresh water."

"Oh, that's a pity."

The night's frozen air brought Moritz back into the present moment. Canvas cots had been placed outside. As he approached the holding yard, he saw lines of naked men flinching in the snow. Sounds of chattering teeth and clanking metal filled the air, but this came from the guards. In their midst, the inmates writhed, whimpered and groaned. Their bodies contorted in spasms.

Moritz briefly thought about his order from High Command. "Invent something to prevent death by hyperthermia."

He rolled his eyes. *What a meaningless exercise*, still, if his imbecilic superiors wanted potions, he would give them potions along with another useless pile of bodies.

The only good thing was that these were decent specimens, representative of our men on the Eastern Front, he observed. *I'll test the intravenous heated saline on the worst and keep the best for my real work.*

He knew that administering heated saline to men dying of hyperthermia would not work. If anything, it would hasten their deaths. Still, the idea had bought him a regular supply of good specimens and that's all that concerned the doctor.

Moritz began to move towards the exposed men. He walked along each aisle of human misery with astute observation. *They always stink*, he thought, holding a scented handkerchief to his nose. Each new arrival looked downwards, not daring to catch his eye. That is, with the exception of a few.

Moritz's eyes lit up. A tall, broad man forced himself to arch straight up as Moritz approached. A guard instinctively raised his rifle and pointed it at the prisoner. The man's entire body quaked with cold. His lips involuntarily emitted the same grunts of hyperthermia as the others. Yet, something in his eyes remained defiant.

Perfect.

Moritz smiled softly.

"There you are. The one I am looking for."

The man glared at Moritz.

"We will do such wonderful things together."

The Romanian spat on the ground. Enlivened by this, other men followed suit, cursing and spitting on the ground. The guards in the yard glanced at one another, puzzled, nervous.

"Good, this is all very good."

Moritz nodded back to them. Then, a selection process began. Any man that demonstrated a spirit of resistance was hauled away to one side: twenty in all.

"Feed them, clothe them, and let them rest. And no violence, not even a gruff word." Moritz pointed at the remaining men.

"These we will use for the saline experiments."

As the selected were dragged away, they howled with rage. Some had left behind sons, fathers and brothers in the yard. They knew that the cots and surgical equipment being wheeled out did not bode well for their loved ones. Strange names rang out like a siren. Moritz waved at the departing men.

"Get some sleep." Then he checked the tubes attached to thirty three large buckets.

"Let's begin." He said so quietly that no one heard him.

"Start!"

The remaining men in the yard were hosed with freezing water. Many folded on the spot. A few attempted to keep warm by jumping up and down but this behavior was met by savage beatings. When the buckets were finally emptied, Moritz noticed rivulets of icicles forming on the quivering bodies. He turned his head to one side.

Beautiful.

"Good. Good. Now tie them to the cots!"

Each prisoner was strapped to a cot and monitored. But the freezing temperature penetrated Moritz's thick coat. He hopped from one foot to another attempting to thwart the cold. In the rear of the yard, he spied an orange glow. A few of the night guards had kindled a fire in a metal drum and Moritz moved toward it.

"Any significant developments inform me." he called out to the guards by the cots. Occasionally, a soldier sprinted across the yard to give him news.

"Herr Doctor, three more have died."

"Are you pumping the saline?"

"Yes, Herr Doctor, but ..."

"Well, keep going."

Half an hour passed, and Moritz was eager for an update. Despite the fire's heat the cold was nipping at his bones and sucking feeling from his feet. He paced back toward the cots.

"How's it going?"

"There are just six left, Herr Doctor," a guard replied.

"Are you following my instructions exactly?"

"We are Herr Doctor."

"Good, then carry on."

One guard dithered.

"Herr Doctor, forgive me but we are to test the effectiveness of heated saline on hyperthermia, correct?"

"Yes."

"Well, it's just that ..."

"Go on."

"When we administer the saline, the men deteriorate immediately."

"What is your point?"

"We have determined that the prisoners die of shock, not of *hyperthermia*. It's the saline that finishes them off."

"Really?"

"Yes. Perhaps we need to stop the procedures before any more are lost?"

This one was a smart Alec; someone I'll have to watch out for, Moritz thought.

"It seems that you have some medical knowledge?"

The man stood erect.

"I do, Herr Doctor. I was in my third year at medical school when I was drafted and ..."

Damn.

"Yes, yes, I don't want your life history. Report to the lab tomorrow morning, six am sharp. I could use an informed assistant."

"I would rather …" The guard began.

"That's all. You're dismissed for the night. Get some sleep. We have plenty of work ahead of us tomorrow. The rest of you carry on with the procedures."

The guard nodded and walked away. But he stole a look back as the other guards continued administering the saline.

It was obvious. The doctor was insane. German soldiers were dying in their thousands on the Eastern Front, and this quack was wasting valuable time. Ludwig Roth determined.

Office of Strategic Services
Germany, 1945

Ludwig Roth's meticulous note-taking would prove invaluable when discovered during liberation and passed onto American High Command. It would never see the Nuremberg light of day, but the journal had identified a certain doctor. A German who would later be designated by the allies as an "asset of high interest."

The experiments performed on the twenty Romanian prisoners had been unusual even by Nazi standards, the Office of Strategic Services (O.S.S) had concluded. Ludwig would die before he could be questioned, but his journal spoke volumes.

Back in '44 twenty Romanian prisoners had been subjected to a rotation of torture, a cocktail of drugs and incessant hypnosis techniques. To what end, Roth and the O.S.S were unclear. Every prisoner had been driven insane, besides one.

That survivor had become Doctor Moritz's "pet" according to Roth. He was treated lavishly and allowed to roam the camp. That is, until the day he went berserk and tore Ludwig Roth and a few other guards to pieces.

The Germans (1b)
Dachau Concentration Camp, Germany, 1944

The murder of five armed German soldiers by one unarmed prisoner brought a swift reaction.

A telegram marked URGENT was delivered within hours.

It was as Moritz suspected. He was being summoned to appear before a select committee in Berlin, HQ.

A summons? A trial?

It had been a mistake to recruit that medical student Roth. He should have had him transferred out. Moritz's ego had gotten the better of him, he knew.

The guard's death along with four others had come about because he had lost his focus. It was such an inconvenience and had resulted in the loss of an exceptional specimen.

The work simply required more time, more patience, more data.

I have been careless and for that I should pay.

The Germans (2)
Berlin, Germany 1944

Sitting alone on a wooden bench, dwarfed within the huge marble mausoleum, Klaus Moritz' knees began to tremble. Perspiration seeped under his arms, leaking into his shirt and jacket. He adjusted his collar to let in cool air and studied the gigantic Nazi flag above him. It hung majestically still, fluttering only at its tips each time the revolving doors turned, two floors below.

"Thank you for your patience, Herr Doctor, you will be seen presently," a guard informed Moritz before disappearing back behind a steel door in the hallway.

Approaching footsteps echoed behind the same door. Moritz sat tall and steadied his nerves. The door jolted open as an imposing figure filled its frame. A heavily decorated general with wavy blond hair motioned for Moritz to follow.

By the time Moritz entered the room, the general had already taken his place behind a long, oak desk. His half smoked cigarette parked in an ashtray.

"*Please* have a seat, Herr Doctor."

Moritz stammered, "Thank you, forgive me but..."

"Schmidt, *General* Helmut Schmidt."

Schmidt indicated to a small chair to his left as he pulled out a stack of documents and began thumbing through them. Moritz fidgeted.

Will he decide if I'm shot?

The General looked up dispassionately from the pages of a thick blue folder. Over the past few days, he'd heard a great deal about this obscure Hamburg doctor.

Moritz's research in genetics had certainly earned him SS Heinrich Himmler's attention. Himmler had even described the doctor as "the consummate Nazi." Schmidt struggled to contain his amusement.

Closet Jew?

The doctor's deep-set eyes were as black as coal. His spectacles sat perched on a hooked nose like a Rabbi's. He had a fat fleshy mouth like a woman with hips to match. *Perhaps he should have started with his own genetics?*

Moritz saw the smirk.

He's playing with me.

The General glanced down at the dossier and noted Moritz's marital status at age forty-five: single. Then there was the imported Italian suit. It all added up in his books. *Moritz was another SS dandy.* It revolted this military man to see how low Germany's command had stooped.

There had been an embarrassing silence in the General's stare. Moritz squinted to focus on the man in front of him. Sunlight had illuminated the cigarette smoke around the General's head and formed a halo.

"You're probably wondering why you've been summoned to Berlin?"

Schmidt took a long drag from his cigarette.

"Yes, and to be frank," Moritz began, "my work is at a critical stage. It cannot endure interruptions."

General Schmidt exhaled a plume of smoke.

"I would agree that your work has reached a critical stage, Herr Doctor. Judging from its failures…that is."

Moritz stiffened in his chair. He struggled to recompose himself.

"I beg to differ, General. After all, your uninformed bias distorts an exact analysis of clinical data."

Schmidt leaned back and grinned.

"Relax… Klaus, isn't it?"

Moritz nodded 'yes.'

"If our SS leader is satisfied with your unorthodox and reckless methods, then who am I to judge?"

Moritz uncrossed his legs.

Satisfied?

"Then why am I here speaking to you? I presumed I would be meeting with …"

"I will be supervising your next project and our Fahnenjunker Reichsführer-SS, in his infinite wisdom, has deemed it important for us to become… acquainted."

General Schmidt closed the folder on his desk, smudged out his cigarette and made his way toward an old, dusty cabinet.

"Do you like wine Klaus?" he asked, retrieving a bottle from the top drawer.

"I do not drink General …"

"Call me Helmut, please."

"I do not drink Helmut … like our good Fuhrer."

"A noble disposition, I'm sure. I'm … how can I put it - a devotee of the vine myself, and of Bordeaux in particular."

The General poured himself a hefty glass of claret and swirled it. With each rhythmic lilt of his wrist the wine left a rim of purple. He drew it to his lips and took a long, relishing swallow.

"Ah…magnifique!" he purred. "This wine is a product of an ancient Roman vineyard in Southwest France. Are you familiar with the area?"

"I am not," Moritz bristled.

"It's a place called Rousinac. Home to an exceedingly rare red."

Nothing more was said, and the General drank his wine with deliberation.

When he had finished, General Schmidt slid the folder across his desk to Moritz.

"It seems that your work, your real work that is, has attracted some admirers."

He sauntered towards the door.

"Look over the dossier carefully. You have one hour to familiarize yourself. Then someone will escort you to France."

The general clicked his heels and saluted.

"Heil Hitler!"

Moritz reciprocated. General Schmidt left the room.

The office was left smoggy by the General's dying cigarette. Moritz felt himself gag. Clutching the dossier, he crossed the room, and opened a window. There was a strange insignia on the cover. He flipped open to the title page:

'Sanguis Regius' Rousinac, Southwest France

From its first page, Moritz was hooked. He was so absorbed with the dossier that when the guard returned to collect him exactly one hour later, he leapt out of his skin.

The Americans (13)
Rousinac, Southwest France 2019

Across the forest from Laetitia's restaurant, Didier Perodeau had just finished his lunch when he noticed the dog stirring. The agile retriever moved from under the table, its body tense as it padded suspiciously towards the door. Didier had lived with the dog long enough to know that someone or something was approaching the house.

Feeling uneasy he made his way to the hallway and peered through the window as a vehicle pulled into his driveway. Didier opened his large, green door. The dog shot past his legs and bolted towards the visitor's car.

"Can you take the dog inside Monsieur Perodeau? We need to speak to you."

David shouted from the safety of his car. Didier frowned.

"I don't have time. Get off my property!"

"Oh I think you do, especially when you hear what we've got to say."

There was something in the American's eyes that told Didier Perodeau he was not going away.

"Five minutes, that's all," he said, reaching for the dog's collar.

Panic rose in Perodeau's throat as he chained Pako to a rusted metal gate.

One email.

"Go on then." he asked, turning toward David.

The men got out of their car.

They're going to arrest me.

"Just get on with it," Perodeau muttered as his legs began to shake.

David turned to James, "Tell Monsieur Perodeau what you saw in the tunnels?"

Didier Perodeau felt a knot of hysteria unfurl in his stomach.

The tunnels?

"How dare you come onto my property without my permission! Who do you think you are?" Perodeau yelled at James.

"Shut your damn mouth!" David snapped.

James began.

"We know about your smuggling ring. And we know that the Graystons found out."

Perodeau looked from one man to the other then burst out laughing.

"You're both crazy! Smugglers!" He laughed so hard he had to cough.

"They might when we show them the blood sample the Graystons sent us you fat French fuck!" James blasted.

Perodeau's body jolted upright as though someone had driven a stake through his spine.

"What are you talking about?" he jabbered, flushing red.

"The Graystons sent us a blood sample taken from here. Now

they've disappeared. And that sample points directly to something that happened on your property,"

"Tell us what happened to the Graystons, Monsieur. Don't wait for my forensics team to pull your house apart." David looked purposely at his watch.

Perodeau began to stammer.

"Y-you leave me with very little c-choice. I will give you answers but I can't do it *now*."

It was not the response that either man expected.

"What?" David asked incredulously.

Perodeau shuffled on the spot.

"I have an appointment I'm already late for. It is urgent, my mother is very sick."

"Do you think we're stupid?" David asked, leaning towards him.

"No, I swear it's true," Didier Perodeau pleaded. "My mother has been very sick recently. She had to undergo a series of tests. I am her only child, so I am going back to the hospital today to find out the results. But I promise you if you come back later, I will tell you everything. I agree this is a terrible burden Messieurs, but I cannot do this in five minutes. I cannot do this now. There's too much to tell."

"But I saw you visit your mother yesterday. She seemed fine to me." James blurted.

Perodeau and David looked at James in disbelief.

"What do you mean, you saw me with my mother?"

"Yesterday, I was on the patio of the Fromblier hotel, and I saw you delivering groceries to some old lady."

"That was not my mother, I can assure you, as if it's any of your business."

"Man, tell me that wasn't your girlfriend, holy shit."

"You're going nowhere." David pressed.

Didier Perodeau shrugged.

"I have nowhere to run Messieurs. This is my home and besides, I have carried a terrible burden and it is time for it to end. Yes, I know what happened to the English."

James suspected that Didier Perodeau was simply stalling. He approached Perodeau until they were almost toe-to-toe.

"Then we'll come with you to visit mama." He said quietly.

"As you wish but if *they* see you following me. Well, I'm afraid *we will all be in the shit*. The whole town is in on this. You must trust me. I am sick of this terrible secret. I'm ready to talk. I want it to stop."

It was a convincing performance.

James nodded to David. *The whole town knows about this.*

"How long will you be at the hospital?" James probed.

"Oh, I don't know."

"Of course, you do. Just answer the God-damned question!" David rounded in on him.

Perodeau knew he was running out of options.

"A few hours."

"Then we'll wait here for you. And if you're not back here by then, we will call our guys in. Turn this place over until we find the evidence." David replied.

"That means no funny business, got it? We're cops. Police. Anything happens to us, and you're fingered. We let our people know where we are." James added firmly holding up his cell phone and mouthing the letters C.I.A.

"Yes, yes, fine, but I'm leaving my dog behind. Stay in the car. I don't want you trespassing any further."

Perodeau waited until the Americans had climbed back into their car before untying the dog. It barked uncontrollably at the visitors while Didier Perodeau locked up his house.

As he drove up the lane, Didier knew if he waited long enough, the Americans would be dealt with one way or another. The tunnels were open.

The Locals (8)
Rousinac, Southwest France 2019

Pierre Malraux had lived alone for seven years ever since his beloved wife Chantelle passed away. He missed her terribly and although his son, Christophe, was good to him, Pierre could never completely dispel his feelings of loneliness. Besides Christophe now lived permanently in Paris, miles away from this cursed place.

Chantelle had been unclouded in her approach to life. She had been his soul mate. He had been initiated into The Custodians many years ago but as any good local would do, Chantelle had accepted it as a part of their marriage.

As a young girl, like all the others, she had been forbidden from venturing into the woods after dusk at certain times of the year. But when one night Pierre had told her the full story of his initiation, she had simply wept.

Ma chérie, tu me manques tellement.

Pierre was in the kitchen making a coffee when the doorbell rang. It knocked him out of his memory.

"Ah the absolute last person I want to see," he spat.

Didier Perodeau stood sheepishly on the doorstep.

"Pierre it is much worse than we imagined," Perodeau said as he entered the house.

Pierre looked towards a crucifix on the wall and groaned, *please not more trouble.*

Didier Perodeau made his way to a familiar lounge where under different circumstances he'd enjoyed many a social evening. Today was different. With shoulders slumped and his head held low he looked every one of his sixty-nine years.

Pierre didn't offer him a seat.

"What's gone wrong now?"

Perodeau's eyes darted nervously about the room.

"Get on with it!"

"Please be patient Pierre, this is very difficult for me."

In a corner of the room Didier Perodeau spied an old photograph of his father Phillipe Perodeau, alongside the other Maquis members of the French resistance. He turned quickly away, filled with shame.

He told Pierre everything about the Americans' visit. As Pierre listened the acid in his stomach began to curdle. With every word that Perodeau uttered Pierre found himself fantasizing ways to end his useless life.

"You've been a thorn in my flesh for as long as I've known you."

"That's all you've got to say," Perodeau snapped. "Well, that is it then, we're all finished."

"No Didier, we aren't, *you are finished*," Pierre retorted sharply.

"If they take me down, I won't go alone Pierre, I swear it."

Pierre walked to a closet and pulled out a shotgun.

"You are such a stupid man, a disgrace to Rousinac," he said calmly.

Perodeau fell back into an armchair and flailed his arms.

"I didn't mean it Pierre. I wouldn't do anything to harm our way of life. You know that."

Pierre released the gun's safety catch, stepped back and took aim at Perodeau's trembling body with indifference.

As a younger man, Pierre had caught Didier many times stealing wine from his neighbors' cellars or cheating on his wife with the town's whores. Pierre should have run him out of Rousinac years ago.

"Please you must help me Pierre," Perodeau whined.

"I am going to call the others," Pierre said finally, lowering his gun.

"Then we will decide what to do about *you* and *the Americans.* You can go and sit in your car until they arrive. I don't want to see your face until then."

Didier Perodeau limped out of Pierre's house like an injured dog.

An hour later Patrick Clayburn and Laetitia Dupre arrived.

Pierre whistled for Didier to join them in the back room. The four gathered solemnly around a dining table. The three Custodians listened attentively to Perodeau's report, followed by a stunned silence.

"We cannot let them leave," Clayburn said reluctantly.

"Just listen to yourself! Talking about the murder of two more innocent people!" Pierre lamented.

"Are they at Didier's house now?" Laetitia interrupted.

"Yes. Waiting for me." Didier Perodeau offered bleakly. He didn't mention the open tunnels.

"We can't do anything there," Patrick Clayburn insisted.

"We need someone to lure them away," Didier said, turning to Laetitia.

"No, we can't put her life at risk because of you," Patrick snapped.

"She's just the bait." Didier countered ignoring Laetitia's glare.

"Tell me what you want me to do, I will …" Laetitia turned to Pierre.

"STOP!"

He had slapped the table.

"I don't want them harmed in any way. Do you understand? Just lure them away."

Pierre said in a low voice.

"We need to buy ourselves some time. We need to think. Perhaps we can bluff our way out of this."

"What about the blood sample? And what they saw on my land?" Didier jabbed.

"All roads lead back to your incompetence Perodeau." Pierre snarled.

"Hear me out uncle. They're not here on official police business. If they were, we would have been closed down days ago, Interpol crawling everywhere. I think they're bullshitting about everything. They knew Tom Grayston from somewhere and now they want to know where he's gone. Maybe he owes them money?" Laetitia said.

"He owes me money." Didier grumbled under his breath.

"All I know is that we need to get them away from his house somehow. God knows we can't trust this idiot."

Pierre looked at Didier.

"… But if they won't leave. We will just have to call their bluff. Hear what it is they think they know and deny everything." He added.

"They will leave. They have nothing. We can sort this out." Laetitia replied.

"Well, you'd better have a better plan than the last one." Didier sneered.

Laetitia bristled, "We are in this position because of you. And you can disappear as quickly as the British did."

Her words shut Didier Perodeau down, but they unnerved Pierre Malraux. Something was festering away inside of him, and it wasn't his ulcer.

The Americans (14)
Rousinac, Southwest France 2019

David flinched as Perodeau's dog lunged once again at the car window.

"Remind me again, why did we let Perodeau go?"

James was busy rummaging through a backpack.

"We want him gone. All part of the plan."

"Right, so we just sit here and wait for the locals to come back? That plan?" David returned.

"No…"

James pulled out a half-eaten ham baguette and held it up to show David.

"Picnic?"

James smirked.

"Ever since my back operation I've carried around this prescription shot… just in case. It's a strong sedative and works like a rhino tranquilizer. Enough punch to put anything out for at least an hour."

He produced a packaged syringe.

"You seriously carry that around?" David asked incredulously.

"Has your spinal disc ever popped?"

"No."

"Then you wouldn't understand. This shot is meant to block out the trauma of agonizing, piss your pants pain, long enough for you to get to a hospital."

"What are you doing?"

"Injecting the sandwich."

"To give to the dog?"

"Yes."

"That's genius."

"I know."

James cracked his window open and wedged out a morsel of the sandwich. Within seconds Perodeau's salivating dog had leapt up and gulped it down in one.

"Predictable creatures, dogs," James grinned.

Pako waddled off to sit in the sun. Three minutes later he was sprawled out and snoring.

"How long does that give us?" David asked.

"Not sure, it's a big dog, so we'd better be quick. Perodeau probably locked up the house. I'll check the outbuildings, the gardens and grounds. See if I can find any sign of those animals from the other night."

"Oh so, I break into the house?"

"You know the layout."

"What if Perodeau comes back with an armed posse?" David darted a nervous glance up the drive.

"I guess we bullshit about C.I.A. back up?"

"New Scotland Yard. I have my id badge on me."

David and James emerged from the car while keeping a close eye on Pako. The dog twitched under the heaviness of a chemical dream.

"He's out," James confirmed.

"Okay let's rendezvous in fifteen," David proposed.

Just as they were about to execute their plan, they were stopped in their tracks by a sound. Somebody was headed their way through the woods, whistling. Both men stood rigid.

"What the…?" David gasped.

"That can't be Perodeau. Too soon," James whispered.

"Get back in the car."

David and James sprinted back to their vehicle. A few seconds later, an elderly man came into view through a gap in the trees. He spied the car and its occupants and squinted against the sun to get a better look.

"Who the fuck is that?"

"Maybe a neighbor? He's alone so that's good." David noticed.

"He's coming over."

James slouched lower into his seat.

"He looks pretty friendly."

"Yeah, well he's probably the scout, sent to distract us."

"He looks as surprised as we do."

The man looked first at Perodeau's house and then to the dozing dog. He approached the driver's window and gestured for David to lower it.

"Open the window but make it real small," James advised as he nervously checked up and down the lane.

The man grinned.

"Bonsoir Messieurs," he bowed slightly.

"Ah bonsoir Monsieur," David chimed back.

The man babbled in French until David raised a hand.

"Pardon Monsieur, désolé, je ne parle pas Francais."

The stranger was taken aback. He paused and peered more closely at James.

"You English?"

"Americans." David replied.

"You stay here?" The man said.

"No – no …"

James leaned over and said loudly.

"We're looking for our friends. Man and woman. Have you seen them? L'anglais?"

David shot James a blank look and mouthed *what are you doing?* The man scratched his head and looked up at Perodeau's house again.

"Monsieur home?" he asked cautiously.

"No," David replied.

"You see, we were supposed to meet our English friends in Rousinac this week, but they never showed up," James continued. "They gave us this address."

The man looked around him on all sides.

"A man and a woman, you say?" he asked in a whisper.

Both men nodded enthusiastically.

"Oui, Tom and Catherine Grayston." David showed the man the photograph on his phone.

There was a pause, as the old man contemplated his response.

"Yes. They here a lot of week ago."

The Americans were stunned.

"Really? Are you sure?"

David stepped out of the car.

"I old, not blind." The man replied.

"They were staying here?" James pushed.

"Yes. The woman, blonde, very beautiful."

"Did you speak with them?"

"No. They not, see me. I am in woods. I see them go to house. It late. I not want to bother them."

"Are you sure they were ...?"

"Yes."

"Thank you ... merci beaucoup," David beamed.

James thrust his door open and stood up.

The man braced for further questioning while searching James for any identifying insignia.

"Do you live close by?" James inquired.

"I live far but I live in Rousinac when a boy. I come back I have sister here." The man answered.

"You did not see them again after that, the British couple?" David asked.

"No, I take taxi. It too late to be ... in these woods."

"What happened to them Monsieur? Tell us. I know you know." James drew closer.

The man began to inch away. "I old man," he said dismissively. "I go now."

He turned and started to walk away.

"Please, the truth is, no one has heard from them since they arrived in Rousinac," David implored. "We're afraid something bad has happened. If there is anything that you can tell us?"

Picking up speed, the old man took a small track that fingered to the side of Perodeau's lane. Within seconds the trees had completely hidden him.

The Americans leaned back onto their car, deflated.

"Can you believe that?" David gasped.

"They were definitely here. We just can't prove it."

"The old guy sure wasn't keen to talk." David offered.

"You can say that again. Something spooked him."

Their conversation was interrupted by David's phone ringing.

"It's Laetitia. Should I pick up?"

"Sure, just don't tell Snow White where we are."

"Laetitia." David beamed, putting her on speaker.

"David, I... I need your help. It's urgent."

"Why? What's going on?"

"I can't tell you over the phone."

"Okay but I can't come right now. James and I are looking at a property. It'll take about an hour or two. Can I come after that?"

"No, it will be too late. Goodbye." Her voice trailed off.

"WAIT, wait a minute. Look, maybe I can get James to drop me off somewhere, sooner?"

"Okay, please come to my cafe. You know where it is. *Both of you.*"

"Can you give me a hint as to what it's about?"

"It's about Didier Perodeau. It's about *that* house."

The phone went dead. David hesitated for a moment then he asked.

"Should we go?"

James shook his head.

"It's a fucking honey trap. And what about Perodeau?"

David shrugged.

"Yes, but it sounds like she knows something and wants to talk."

"That's a big *'if'*." James frowned.

"How about you wait for me in the car outside the cafe?" David offered.

"You've got to make it quick David. If Perodeau goes AWOL we've got nothing." James resolutely announced.

"I know."

Fifteen minutes later James and David had pulled up outside Cafe Napoleon. David entered the dining room. Sylvie, the waitress, darted out from the kitchen and spotted him. She approached and mumbled, "Upstairs," pointing towards a side door.

David quietly found his way to Laetitia's bedroom. He stopped for a moment to watch her from the open doorway. Her face was red from crying. Laetitia felt his presence and turned towards him. David closed the door and eased her into his arms.

"What's going on?"

She took a deep breath.

"I'm scared. I am scared for you and your friend. There are people here in Rousinac who will do anything to stop you from ..."

"From what?"

"What would it take for you to forget about all this and go home?"

"Just tell me who these people are and what this is about?"

Laetitia pulled from his embrace and sighed.

"This all started a long time ago. Just after the war there was nothing here, no work, just a heavily bombed ruin of a town. So many young people with no fathers, all desperate for money. And so, they began to use the sewers, the tunnels under the castle to run contraband. In the beginning it was cases of cognac or wine, but then, later on it turned to drugs. There were cartels from Marseilles who traded in heroin. They needed a place to store their drugs somewhere on the way to the Atlantic coast. They began to work with some of our men."

"Perodeau."

"Yes, he was one of the ring-leaders because one of the tunnels led directly onto his land, and deep into his woods. Didier Perodeau is a cousin through my mother's side."

"Okay, so I have a feeling that this has something to do with the missing British couple?" David asked.

"It has *everything* to do with them." Laetitia replied.

"What happened?"

"I think they found some money on the grounds. A huge sum and they disappeared with it."

"What?"

"Didier Perodeau has only just found out and now the smugglers are looking for your friends. He is furious because some of the smugglers damaged his house in revenge."

"In revenge for what?"

"For exposing the network to outsiders. So now, he's bringing the gang back to his house to deal with you. They think you and your friend will lead them to the British couple, to their money."

"Did the Graystons know about the smuggling ring?"

"I don't know. All I know is that they found the money and …"

"Oh Jesus, Tom." David rubbed his forehead. The couple's financial circumstances resurfaced. It was now obvious that Tom and Catherine had disappeared themselves with a shit load of money. They had sent him the blood sample to buy them some time. It probably belonged to some wild animal. He had been played like a fool.

James had been right all along.

Tom wasn't a good guy. Rousinac was the epicenter of a huge smuggling operation of drugs, women, and God knows what else. The entire town was in on it.

Laetitia walked toward her bedroom window. She looked out over the surrounding forest and spoke with deliberation.

"You must leave *immediately*. These men are all over town and now they know who you are. You must forget all about Rousinac."

"Would they?"

Laetitia nodded grimly.

"They would kill you in an instant."

"But this doesn't make any sense. Why would Perodeau place such a risk on his own enterprise?"

Mon Dieu, more questions. Why won't he take the bait and leave?

"He is both greedy and stupid, I'm afraid. The main haul each month went out of his woods through his tunnel. He took a fat cut from the profits of course but then he began to ask for more money. This angered his partners, so they cut his share in half."

"And this was his way of getting back? Renting out his property so that they couldn't access the tunnels? That explains why the Graystons complained about weird criminal activity." David said.

"What?" Laetitia's heart quickened.

His statement stumped her. *How much did he know?* She'd have to bluff it out of him.

"I know everything. They came here and told me." She said.

"What's everything?"

"That they heard things in the night. I told them it was the wild pigs. Did they tell you the same?"

David wasn't sure how much to reveal. *Did it matter at this point?* It seemed conclusive by now that the Brits took off with a booty, leaving him and James vulnerable. *What did he owe them?*

"Tom wrote me a letter and sent me a sample of something he'd found splattered on the side of Perodeau's house one night. It's why James and I are here…"

"What kind of sample?"

"A blood sample. Not sure from what, yet."

"Why would they send you a blood sample?"

"No idea. We thought it was weird."

"We? You and your companion?"

"James. Yes."

"Real estate guys?" *She knew this was a lie.*

"Yes."

"I know you're not in real estate."

David flushed. *Fuck.*

"I know all about you and that you lied to me."

"I'm sorry, I …"

"And that you slept with me to get information."

"It wasn't like that. At least not for me." She stared at him. He didn't know what to say.

"Who else knows?" She asked.

Can I let them go?

"Just me and James."

"You haven't told anyone else?"

David thought briefly of his lab assistant Michael Jones, Hannah his secretary and Graham Wells back at New Scotland Yard. But all they really knew was that he was chasing up an old friend on his own vacation time.

"No, just me and James."

"Your name is David Frankel."

"I'm sorry Laetitia."

"And you work for New Scotland Yard."

"Yes, but this isn't an official investigation."

"What do you mean?"

"I mean, James and I are on vacation. Tom is my friend and he's disappeared. We were just trying to find out what happened to him. To them. His wife. I mean, they both disappeared."

"You should have been honest from the start."

"We thought. We thought maybe you were involved somehow?" She searched his face.

Could she trust that he was telling her the truth – this time?

"You're the best thing to come out of all this for me." David moved closer. The embrace felt genuine. He attempted to kiss her.

"You don't have much time." She pushed back.

He stroked her cheek. "Come with us."

"I can't leave Rousinac, David, at least not now. Perhaps later." Laetitia struggled to hide the jubilant flicker in her eyes.

No, just me and James.

"Now, go!"

David ran to the car and told James everything. It took a few moments for the information to register.

"It doesn't add up."

"What do you mean?" David snapped.

"If the Brits got away with all that dough, why was Perodeau so jumpy? Why did he take off? Think about it. He has more to gain from us, than we, him."

"Laetitia said he went to get his gang partners."

"So why wouldn't he take us to them? Why take off?"

"Look, I think Laetitia is looking for a way out of *something really bad*. I think that she's been involved all along. Maybe she sees this as an opportunity to get rid of Perodeau?" David pressed.

"Okay, so what about the sample and the letter? Are you just going to buy this gangsters in the night story? That Tom and Catherine found some drug money and took off? Isn't that a bit convenient?"

"What do you mean?"

James scratched his stubble.

"I think something really bad went down here with the Graystons and Laetitia and Perodeau and fuck knows who else are covering it up."

"Look I trust my gut on this. And my gut tells me that Laetitia didn't sign up for murdering people. She wants out. Let's be honest we have next to nothing on Perodeau besides a hunch." David argued.

James groaned.

"Your dick's talking right now, buddy."

"No, it's not."

"So, why would the Brits go to the trouble of writing you just to disappear themselves with a shit stack of money?"

David chewed his nails.

"To put us off the trail? To buy themselves some time? I mean, there is evidence that Tom Grayston was facing bankruptcy. They never returned home. James admit it, we've got nothing."

Pause.

"Fuck, you're right. And now *maybe* we've got some drug cartel gunning for us. Okay, let's go."

"There's just one last thing." David said softly.

"What?"

"I want to thank Laetitia and ask her to leave with us."

"You sad fucker. She wants us gone. I'm sure our presence is holding up valuable contraband. Still, I wouldn't want to stand in the way of true love."

David entered the restaurant unseen. He could faintly hear Laetitia upstairs laughing. As he ascended her words became audible.

"He believed every word like an idiot. Yes, he thinks the English made off with the money. No, they won't be coming back. Can you let Perodeau know? We will deal with him later. Teach him a lesson. That will be fun." She punched the air then threw the phone on her bed.

David knew enough French to know that Laetitia had lied to him and was boasting about it. It took a few moments before she realized the American was standing behind her.

"How long?"

"Long enough."

"Your French is terrible."

"Good enough."

"What did you hear?"

"James had your mark."

"What?"

"You're involved."

"Involved? Involved in what exactly Mr. Detective?" She hardened.

"Drugs, murder."

"What?"

"Did they get too close to the truth?"

David watched the penny drop. *Merde!* Laetitia covered her eyes.

"Oh, David." She groaned.

"I don't know if the Graystons took your money but if they did, you all deserved it." He whispered.

"You have no idea."

"You're going to jail. All of you. This whole rotten town."

He watched her thinking.

I can't let them go.

"This is all on you." David made to leave.

"It was a tragic *accident*. You need to know that." Laetitia said slowly.

"What?"

"The English. They didn't take any money. They found out about the tunnels. They went into one of them. A fight broke out between a few of the smugglers and Tom."

"What happened?"

"They were taken."

"They? You mean Tom and his wife?"

"Yes."

"Taken where?" Before she had time to answer he blurted.

"W-wait, why did you lie to me?"

"Because it was too dangerous to tell you the truth! I needed you to go." She shrieked.

"Jesus Laetitia, where are they?" David grabbed her arms.

"Stop it, you're hurting me!"

"Just tell me where they are!" He shook her.

"The Graystons were in the wrong place at the wrong time. Perodeau should never have let them on his land. This is his fault."

"Why should I believe you now?"

"I'll prove it to you. I will take you to where they are. But we must be discreet. If we're caught, they will kill me too."

"You know where the Brits are?"

"Yes, but not for much longer. They'll be moved before long. It's now or never. Right now, there's only one guard with them. We can get them out."

"How do you know all this?"

"I took a cut. I won't deny it, but I have been arguing for the couple to be released for … look we don't have much time. If you want to help them. We have to go now."

"I won't go without James." David insisted.

"Yes, of course but I must ask you one question first."

"What."

"If I take you to them, will you promise to protect my identity with Interpol?"

He paused.

"Promise."

Back at the car David updated his friend. James shook his head in disbelief.

"How can you believe one word that lying bitch says?"

"She's telling the truth this time. I caught her out. She's obviously way more involved than we originally thought."

"You mean up to her neck in smuggler shit? And now you think she's going to just lead us to the Brits?"

"James, I think she wants out. This is her way out."

"Did she say WHERE the Brits were being held?"

"No, of course not. She doesn't want us showing up like cowboys. She told me to meet her at Rousinac's castle."

"Well, the castle is a big place, David. Where in the castle? Back, front, under, over?"

"She told me to meet her at the back entrance." David replied.

"Okay, so let's call your guys in London and hand this over."

"James, if we do that, we risk Tom and Catherine being killed."

"Yeah? Well, what if they're already dead and now it's our turn?"

"I believe her, James. I know she's telling me the truth. I'm going to go. You can leave." David held his friend's eyes.

"You're serious, aren't you?"

"Totally."

"Fuck it. I can't let you go alone." James conceded.

Five minutes later.

"It's David. Can you talk?"

"Yes."

"James is on board, and we can meet you at the back entrance of the Chateau in twenty. "

"Thank you, David." She whispered.

"Wait, one thing… we need to get some weapons."

"Weapons?" Laetitia's brow creased.

They can't have guns down there.

James leaned over and whispered loudly into David's ear.

"Rifles or handguns with ammo, knives, axes, pepper spray."

David repeated James' request but with some further explanation. There was a lengthy pause at the other end, but Laetitia finally agreed.

"Okay I'll see what I can do. But this will delay us a bit, you do understand?"

"Understood."

"Meet me at the back of the castle in thirty minutes."

Laetitia hung up and speed dialed Patrick. They had plans to make.

"What did she say?" James asked.

"She said that she'd need some time to get weapons. We're meeting in a half an hour." David answered.

"Good. That gives us some extra time to hit up a store in Rousinac."

"What store?"

"Local hunting store. Great knife collection."

"James!" David groaned.

"There are some situations you can't sweet talk your way out of pretty boy."

The Maquis (11)
The woods, Rousinac, Southwest France 1944
8:15pm, June 11th

The drone had come in heavy and strong. Maquis look out, Frederic Arriver, guessed it was an Allied air fleet. He was, in fact, witnessing thirty B-17s escorted by twenty P-51 and P-47 fighters.

It was still light.

As they approached his location, Frederic broke into a sweat. Everything below this metallic sky seemed damned.

Is this it? Is this the end of the war or the world?

The fleet made their drops through a canopy of cloud, peppering the sky with thousands of tiny parachutes. The fleet's size and sudden appearance had taken the German defenses by surprise. Many posts were picked off by the P-51s. From his vantage point, Frederic Arriver could see it all.

On first appearance, Operation Blitz appeared to be a bold ammunition drop for the region's hundreds of Maquis groups. But the entire operation was a distraction, intended to draw attention away from what was about to unfold at the Rousinac munitions depot.

The plan was working. Several key German units had been immediately dispatched from Rousinac into the surrounding countryside.

A skeleton staff now guarded the munitions depot. Panic had begun to set in, just as Jean Dubonnet had expected. The Germans huddled around a small radio, listening to Berlin Today, a Nazi propaganda station.

In the meantime, explosives had been positioned in three key sections of the mine. The first denotation would topple the support wall, creating confusion, during which time the two patriots would split up and ignite two smaller devices.

These were designed to start fires in highly flammable chambers, culminating into one giant inferno. The Maquis men had been instructed to sound an alarm once all three fires were well under way and then escape in the ensuing chaos.

It was all going to plan.

What nobody had anticipated was a sentry with a sixth sense. Wilhem Heigler hadn't trusted the young French men from the get-go. Something just hadn't felt right. So, he'd made it his business to surveille Alain and Jean-Baptist at all times.

This night was no different.

Heigler had trailed Alain to the first detonation point and from the shadows he had seen it all. Immediately, he yelled, "Sabotage, Bossuet!"

Heigler drew his gun and clicked.

It jammed.

There was nothing Alain could do but pull out his own pistol and shoot the German. The commotion alerted the other guards who came running. Alain was apprehended and the search was on for the other devices, and for his accomplice Jean-Baptist.

When the first blast went off, Alain managed to break free. He made straight for the exit.

Jean-Baptist would not be so lucky. His fuse had gone out three times. He had bolted the chamber's door to buy himself more time. It would take precious minutes for the advancing Germans to kick it down.

The guards had laid the mine's chambers out as German cities for easy navigation. He was in the largest chamber, marked "Anhalt." Inside, hundreds of crates of ammunition were stacked to the ceiling.

Once they had broken down the door, the guards split up and painstakingly crept in search of the saboteur. They discovered Jean-Baptist barricaded inside four walls of gunpowder. Any shots fired in his direction would risk blowing the mine sky high.

A desperate stale-mate ensued.

"Stop now Jean-Baptist, there's a good lad and your life will be spared."

The Germans pleaded.

Silence.

All the while Jean-Baptist was dealing with a damp fuse. With an unimaginable calm he cut the fuse short to its driest point, ending any possibility of his own escape.

He kindled the fuse for a fourth time. Finally, it took. The sound bought guards charging at him from every direction. But they would not reach him in time.

BOOM!

Alain had barely made it twenty yards when there was a terrific explosion. It rocked the Bar Chateau, throwing everyone to the floor. Whistles sounded everywhere. Germans spewed from every corner, and Rousinac's fire brigade charged into action from the base of the castle.

The Maquis men made for the bar's entrance. They watched the explosions like fireworks on the horizon. Debris was hurled everywhere, setting off mines that ringed the munitions depot.

BOOM! BOOM! BOOM! BOOM!

"Halt!" A German officer shouted as Gerard's men moved to leave the bar. They were arrested on the spot. *Betrayed.* Gerard thought bitterly as they got rough-handled into the castle.

Dubonnet Chateau was next. Everyone there was to be brought in for interrogation. But when the German troops had arrived, they discovered that Jean Dubonnet and his aunt had simply vanished.

The Germans (3)
Rousinac, Southwest France 1944

In the hours before the appearance of the Allied air fleet, and the destruction of Rousinac's munitions depot, General Helmut Schmidt had stood smoking on the castle's royal balcony.

It had been a beautiful afternoon. The sun exposing every feature in Rousinac's picturesque square.

"Intoxicating," Helmut murmured as he inhaled the warm air. A compatriot stepped into the room, a bottle of red swinging in his hand.

"I thought you could use a top up."

The man poured a drink for his superior, an old friend that he was visiting for a few days. He went to turn on a nearby radio, but Helmut gestured not to.

"I find the silence soothing," he whispered.

August Hussel gazed down upon the castle square and sighed.

"You wouldn't know there was a war on."

Helmut grunted in agreement. August stood beside his friend and lit a cigarette. Both men seemed lost in their own thoughts.

"That doctor's a queer fellow, wouldn't you say?" August suddenly said.

General Schmidt eyed the door behind them before replying, "I'm a decorated war general August. I fight armies with guns and tanks and whatever else our Furher will give me. But I do not enjoy these … experiments."

"They brought in some circus animals for him yesterday. A lion I think and a couple of snakes. What's that got to do with winning a war, do you suppose?"

"He's not the only one." Helmut muttered under his breath.

August eyed his friend warily, noticing the deep lines carved into a once carefree face.

"Beck?"

There was no response. Helmut's silence told him everything.

"I knew Moritz back in Hamburg when he first joined the party. I think his father was some village chemist. Do you know how he ended up here?"

No response.

"I heard he'd invented a fumigant? That's right! A gas to kill cockroaches. Can you believe it?"

"Fitting."

"Then somehow …. Moritz discovered that it worked on humans. The nasty shit even designed a shower head so children wouldn't be afraid." August's words turned the General's stomach.

They were surrounded by unnatural men with no values, August thought as he absent-mindedly toyed with one of the medals on his uniform. Helmet cast a weary eye at his friend.

"For now, August, let's just enjoy the sun."

The Germans (4)
Rousinac, Southwest France 1944

General Schmidt hadn't slept in days.

After the conversation with his friend he had stolen away to his office to grab a nap when a colossal explosion ripped through the chateau. His room lit up like a lightning-strike. He instinctively dived to the floor.

It was obvious what had happened.

The Allies had blown the munitions mine up, and right under his nose.

Finally ... it's over. He pulled out a photograph and kissed it tenderly.

Forgive me, meine liebste.

The explosions had rocked Klaus Moritz's lab, crashing crates with wild animals to the floor and fatally injuring many of them. Out on patrol, Officer Beck had headed straight back to the castle. Upon his arrival he was informed of General Schmidt's suicide.

An emergency meeting convened, with an immediate changing

of the guard. Officer Hans Beck was now the Kommandant Beck of Rousinac. Word got to Moritz, and he made for Beck's office.

He was enraged.

How could these idiots have let this happen?

Kommandant Beck stood with his men flicking through a pile of maps as Moritz barged into the room. None of them acknowledged his presence.

"I must be heard!" Moritz bellowed at the backs of the group.

Beck slowly shifted his gaze to the doctor.

"Is this urgent?"

"Is this urgent?" Moritz repeated.

The doctor found himself the object of violent stares.

"Oh, I should say Officer Beck."

"Kommandant if you don't mind."

"*Kommandant* Beck. This interruption in my work cannot be tolerated."

Beck stopped him,

"I have no time to discuss your circus tricks doctor. I am here to win a war."

Moritz fell silent. He examined the circle of gray faces.

The penny dropped. Germany's impending defeat was upon them. His mouth slackened.

"What is it? Speak!" Beck barked.

It was over.

There was one thing left to do.

Moritz had to find a way out. His work must be preserved at all costs. His manner unnerved Kommandant Beck. Without a word, Moritz turned and left the room.

The Maquis (12)
Rousinac, Southwest France 1944

While the destruction of the ammunition mine had been a huge success for the Allies it had proven disastrous to Rousinac's Maquis men.

During the first few days of capture, Gerard Dupre, Daniel
Malraux, Charles and Phillipe Perodeau, and Alain Boussuet had
been taken deep inside the castle.

They had all expected to be interrogated, tortured and shot.

Instead, they were detained in a room, in a make-shift hospital.

Medical staff busied around them, administering drugs, taking
blood samples.

Two guards were posted in a corner of their room at all times.
No communication was allowed. Days passed as the men were subjected to the same routine.

Isolation. Sedation.

Through the drug cloud each man struggled to find the faces
of his loved ones. Certain memories surfaced over and over again.

For Gerard Dupre it was the smell of his wife's hair as it tousled over her pillow. In the darkness of the early morning before their children woke, he would breathe that scent in deeply. It was her - unsullied by soap or perfume or the hands of children.

That alone was his to enjoy. Only now, as the hours crept by, he struggled to find her. Where she lay in the bed was now a thick blackness and the faint odor of death.

Daniel Malraux found himself in his kitchen, approaching Cecile from behind. The sweet smell of cake was in the air, another pudding being made by her slender hands. No doubt a gift for a family in need, he smiled to himself. *I married an angel.* The back of her neck shone like marble; a soft hum crooned in her throat. His hands reached out, to enfold her. But as soon as his fingers touched her body, she fell into ashes.

The Perodeau brothers too, found the eyes and bodies and lips of their wives before the faces of their children, or mother. The smallest glances, the simplest of touches – fluttered back into their drugged minds like butterflies. And as sheer as butterfly wings these memories were quickly torn and scattered.

For the boy Alain Boussuet a few people came and went, girls mostly but then, one memory patiently lingered at the doorway.

He was around two years of age and riding high upon his father's broad shoulders. He'd gripped his mother's hand to steady him. The other made to grab at the balloons bobbing about him. So long as he had her hand, he could take the height, the roughness, the pace …

He was terrified and elated. *Mama.* But each time he looked down he saw a gray shadow where his mother's face should be. The ride grew more monstrous. The sky turned black. And the balloons transformed into ravens that attacked him, pecking at his eyes.

Dark dreams plundered each man's mind.

Then, one night around 3am, both guards began to doze. Gerard Dupre had resurfaced at the sound of their snores. He turned to Alain Boussuet, strapped adjacent.

"Alain," Gerard whispered. "Alain? Wake up boy."

He did not respond. His movements were fitful, and his body soaked in sweat.

"You can't sleep either?" Daniel Malraux murmured from across the room.

"No. How do you feel?"

"Like I drank some bad cognac. They are testing something new on us, I think."

Gerard agreed.

"A British agent told me once about experiments that the Germans perform on prisoners of war. They have drugs and methods to make a man talk. I think that's what's going on here."

Daniel remained quiet.

"With the munitions mine destroyed the war will soon be over."

Pause.

"I just hope you're right." He finally replied.

"All we need to do now is pray – pray that we can hold out until then. France will prevail. You'll see." Gerard encouraged.

A nurse entered the room. Her footsteps roused the sleeping guards. Approaching the beds, one by one, she injected each Maquis man with a brown substance. Within seconds Gerard and Daniel were rendered unconscious as the others slept on; but all were plagued by the same strange nightmare.

They found themselves in a forest. It was night and the air was still. Thoughts dissolved. Hunger surged, and everything was revealed to them. It was as if the forest had been illuminated by a neon light.

Hunt! Go and hunt.

It was time to chase. It was time to devour. All the animals of the forest were to be hunted and eaten. The night never seemed to end, and the hunger was never satisfied. A terrible fire dissolving them from within.

One morning the German doctor entered their cell pushing a trolley laden with steel utensils. He examined each surgical piece against the window's meager light. The sounds woke the Maquis leader.

Gerard Dupre noted levers, cutting forceps, vascular probes, spine instruments and bone files. The German caught his eye.

"Ah, you're awake." He said gently, approaching Gerard's cot.

"Shhh-shhh, there now. Don't fret. I have some very big plans for you."

He noticed that the blond boy was also awake, with eyes wide and white, like a trapped animal. It was the effect he had wished for.

Metal objects clanked in on a second trolley: saws, surgical knives and a set of abattoir pliers. The noise stirred the other men.

"This kraut is a butcher!" Charles Perodeau yelled out. The outraged Maquis thrashed against their cots and hurled a barrage of insults at the doctor and his staff. He held up his hands.

"Now gentlemen, please." He said in perfect French.

"Allow me to explain. My name is Doctor Klaus Moritz, and together we will do extraordinary things."

The German passed by Alain's bed and stroked his hair. The boy shivered. Omnipotence pulsed through the doctor's body.

"There-there. If you don't fight it, it will go easier."

The Maquis men battled with their restraints. Their eyes ablaze with defiance; their hatred made clear.

That is, until armed guards dragged a large cage into the room containing wolves. The men were stunned.

"You filthy bastards! Gerard thrashed. "Treat us like prisoners of war!" His bed rocked so violently that it threatened to tip
over. Additional guards filed in followed by a nurse. They slammed
Gerard's cot against the wall and held him in place while the other
Maquis men writhed and cursed.

"Sedate them," the doctor instructed.

Everything melted away.

Hours passed ...

When the blackness of unconsciousness eventually lifted from
each of Gerard's men, a new darkness awaited them.

"Daniel? Are you awake?"

"I am. How do you feel?"

"Like I have the flu."

"Me too. They've moved us. It's so cold and dark here."

"I can smell those animals," Phillipe Perodeau whispered.
"Nearby."

"Why would they move us?" Daniel asked.

"To frighten and disorientate us." Gerard added.

"And no covers, no lights?" Charles Perodeau griped.

"Are you all still chained to a bed?" Gerard asked.

"Yes!" came the chorus of voices.

"S-shhh! I can hear them coming!" Gerard warned.

"Pretend you're asleep."

"It sounds like a bolt lock. I think we're in the castle dungeons."
Daniel noted. His words sent shivers through the men. As locals,
they knew the history of the dungeons all too well. Diabolical things
had been done here before and by the hands of their own kin.

Someone labored to unlock the door. It was the doctor.

"I think you might enjoy this part." He said to a companion, obscured by the door frame. Guards burst in with rifles cocked. One flicked on a flashlight drowning the room in light.

"The men appear to be sedated, Herr Doctor," one of the guards reported.

"Good."

But Alain's eyes flinched open as the guards approached.

Daniel was right. We are in the dungeons.

The walls around them were decayed and furred with mold. There were no windows, and the air was so cold his breath made clouds. He looked down at his ankles and toward the other men. An intravenous tube ran from each man's arm into a suspended bottle containing a thick red liquid.

"Enter Kommandant Beck. As you can see, everything is going to plan."

"Yes, yes. But it's taking too long!" The other man shouted.

"We are close to Phase Two."

"You will turn this wolf into a werewolf?" The Kommandant chuckled.

"Not exactly but something close."

"You'd better live up to your claims. My patience is wearing thin." Gerard interrupted.

"We blew it sky high. Pfff! Right under your nose you dumb kraut."

Beck made towards Gerard; his fist raised but the doctor restrained him.

"I must respectfully ask Herr Kommandant that you do not allow these men to antagonize you. It weakens our authority not to mention damages the specimens."

Beck turned on the doctor.

"You'd better make your fighting men soon Moritz, or you'll be joining them I swear." He shoved the doctor to one side and stormed out of the room.

Moritz, a name I vow never to forget. Daniel Malraux promised himself.

"Gag each subject and be sure to gently pull the tongue over the leather bite." The doctor said.

Daniel struggled to understand the medical instruments stacked around them. In the background he could hear the sounds of distressed animals.

It was surreal, like a circus act, *hilarious.*

"What's that?" A soldier looked down at Daniel.

"Pay no attention to him, it's a side effect of the drugs we're administering." The doctor offered.

Daniel giggled, and then the others joined in. Before long all of the Maquis men were howling in laughter.

"It sounds like they've lost their minds, Herr Doctor." A guard muttered.

"That's what we're hoping for."

The doctor's words stabbed at the Frenchmens' hearts, and they all fell quiet. So quiet, the staff checked their pulses.

The Maquis (13)
Rousinac, Southwest France 1944

The butterflies had turned into giant moths.

They'd hatched from the cocoons that nested about the cave. Somewhere, far away, there were floods of pain. Lightning bolts that tightened the ropes around his body.

The moths slowly unfurled and descended upon him. They padded gently on his skin, then stuck their fangs into his chest drawing up heart blood. And with each suck the cave grew darker.

This was Alain's recurring nightmare.

The boy's screams were disturbing the staff and they were now being rotated on shorter cycles, Daniel noted.

Elsewhere, in the chamber his compatriots writhed and called out, to one another, to their wives, and finally, to their mothers.

After a while, Daniel could not hear them. Pain fed by the electrodes tied to his feet simply knocked him out. It was the same every time.

Boom! Out.

Then he would fall and fall and fall through a layer of cloud as thick as wool. Each bolt sent him further, deeper. He floated down like a paper bag.

Cecile, Cecile, Cecile? Oh, my love, help me!

Then.

He would see a small white dove in the distance, surrounded by a halo.

Ah, clever my love. I see you pretty one.

Behind Daniel, angry, gray clouds raged and rose like tidal waves. They threatened to devour the clouds, but the single white dove kept them at bay.

Oh, brave little dove.

She held the heavens together. A white light shone out around her and blasted away the blackness. Each time, Daniel would feel the grass of home under his feet, and he would fall to his knees and thank God.

Thank you, Father. I am not forsaken.

A universe away, the Perodeau brothers had quickly surrendered to the darkness of repeated torture. It was a relief. No longer burdened by the soft faces and distant calls of children, they gave themselves to the night.

Each thrust of pain electrified their shadows until they were the masters of this dominion. Soon, no devil would dare to challenge, no diabolical creature to attack. They alone tormented the creatures in these nightmares. Just one voice, one tender voice, pierced the black swamp.

And to this one, they rendered fealty.

Were they nightmares? Or was this real?

They could no longer tell.

The Maquis leader walked another path. Unlike Daniel, Gerard had no faith to anchor him. Unlike the Perodeau brothers, his will was strong.

"You are powerful my friend but why fight so hard?"

He would hear.

"You are loyal. You are valiant. You are worth one hundred men."

In his tormented mind, Gerard raged and fought every beast sent to devour him. Even as the ground raised up a legion of skeletons, he smashed and shattered them one by one. When the waters swallowed him whole, and he couldn't breathe he railed. Each charge of blinding pain through his feet, drove him further into resistance.

"Surrender my son. Let go, let go, now."

Over and over the voice spoke.

It flowed and flowed and anything in its way got smoothed over.

"That's right. That's right."

Eventually Gerard grew weary. His body ached.

Then, one day he simply laid down his arms and drowned.

"That's right my son."

The voice silenced him. His heart dissolved.

Grand-père? Is that you?

"Yes, my brave boy. I am here."

Blackness overcame him, then became him.

Métamorphose complète.

The Germans (5)
Rousinac, Southwest France 1944

As Moritz had anticipated, the Maquis men were strong and had taken far longer to break than previous specimens. But a methodical routine of torture: electrocution, suffocation, sedation followed by powerful stimulants had made significant inroads.

The men now howled and snarled at his staff like wild animals, calming only to his voice. Each man had succumbed, besides one.

Daniel Malraux had become a fascination of the softly-spoken doctor.

What kept him unreachable?

Moritz decided to stop Daniel's regime of torture and drugs. There were many ways to torture a man. Perhaps he would crumble watching his compatriots' demise? Daniel Malraux was an educated man and not some brute animal to be trained, the Doctor determined.

But the French man had kept his eyes closed, refusing to engage in his surroundings or the fate of his country-men. His mouth repeated the Lord's prayer, over and over.

Moritz grew agitated.

"I think it's time for something new my friend."

He said, tapping Daniel's arm.

"Today, we begin Phase 2. I think this might be what works with someone like you."

Daniel heard the doctor announce in French and for a few seconds, he felt utterly afraid.

The Maquis (14)
Rousinac, Southwest France 1944

"Sedate them, strip them naked and move them into their separate holding cages." The German doctor barked at the guards.

"Besides this one."

Daniel's stomach lurched.

"Restrain him in that chair and make him comfortable, no sedations."

"I want you to experience *everything* Daniel."

He gestured with some papers.

"Everything I need to know is here, Daniel Eduard Malraux. You're quite accomplished I see. A university education, well, well. I've made the appropriate notes. It's these kinds of details that will help me fine-tune my work."

Daniel did not react. The doctor took his pulse.

"I've asked the Gestapo to be lenient with your wife."

Cecile! His heart thumped. *There was no way she would have been captured. This monster was bluffing, surely.*

"Of course, between you and I these types are animals. And....
well, your wife is very uhm ..." The doctor's voice trailed off.

Daniel felt a rush of calm. It was as though someone had whispered, "he's lying to you". A soft smile lifted his mouth.

Cecile.

Moritz threw Daniel's hand down.

The other prisoners were brought into the room, one by one. They shuffled behind a guard, pale and lifeless.

Here then, were his band of brothers.

Animals. Daniel thought.

They look like broken animals.

Extra guards filed in. They stood by the entrances of this huge chamber deep in the castle dungeons.

The M aquis m en w ere p laced i nto i ndividual c ages. A round 6ft x 4 ft, Daniel noted. There was another noise, the rumbling of a trolley in an adjoining tunnel. A gate was levered open, and a large cage was rolled in.

Wolves! Mon Dieu!

Daniel watched as the strange doctor moved from cage to cage whispering to the men. He strained to listen but couldn't quite make out his words.

When the wolf cage was hinged onto Gerard Dupre's cage, the two wolves fell silent. The Alpha peered cautiously ahead, the second cowered in a corner. There had been no reaction from Gerard at all. He sat quietly with his eyes closed.

A lever slowly raised the partition that separated Gerard from the wolves.

Silence. Nothing.

"Attack!" The German doctor ordered.

The Maquis leader sprang up and charged into the wolves head first. It was over in seconds. Gasps echoed around the chamber. Daniel was speechless. Someone began to clap. The others cheered.

How could Gerard have done that and at the command of his sworn enemy?

Daniel retched.

"He is quite something isn't …"The doctor's words were shortened.

"Gerard! No! No, my friend!" Daniel called out.

The Maquis leader was now devouring the two slain animals. The hoopla had activated Alain the blond boy and the two Perodeau brothers who thrashed about in their cages.

"Fear not my boys, you're next!"

The doctor called out.

They were moved to another chamber with a hole at its center. Daniel knew that it was the castle's bear baiting pit. He felt the dark-ness of that place, a thousand years of misery.

As a Rousinac native, his father had told him about the castle's history. For his eighth birthday Daniel had been taken into the castle's deepest caves where he had gawked in horror at an eerie hole gauged from the very earth.

"Rousinac has a terrible past." Daniel's father had murmured as he held his son's hand tightly. "For centuries, this pit was used to torment all manner of beasts and men."

"By whom Papa?" The child had asked.

"By those who called themselves the Merovingians. They were the Dukes and even the Kings who ruled many lands. But Rousinac was their home, and their blood still flows through our veins." Daniel's father explained.

"How Papa?"

"You are too young to understand such things, however we must never forget the brutality of men Daniel. You must always fight evil."

Here he was back again … so many years later.

Daniel watched as his comrades were lowered into the pit. Then barrels of rats were poured over them. At first the men instinctively drew back from the vermin that swarmed and attacked their feet. But soon a more dominant trait emerged.

The captives turned on the rats with a pathological vengeance, swiping, snatching and tearing them apart. When Gerard tore a piece from a rat's under-belly with his teeth and savored the liquid that pumped into his mouth, the others followed suit.

Within minutes, the bottom of the crate was littered with disemboweled rodents and gore. The spectacle had impacted some of the soldiers. They'd backed away, a few had vomited. But the German doctor stood back in awe. His eyes wide and gleaming.

"I will admit. I am most impressed, Herr Doctor. These men are nothing like their former selves." A man said emerging from the shadows. Daniel recognized him as the one who had beaten them unconscious when they'd first been arrested.

"Yes, Kommandant Beck, you will soon feel pity for the animals we pit against them."

Beck. I will remember your name and avenge my brothers.

"When can we use them in battle?"

"Soon enough but first we must replicate this process, test others."

"Why?"

"At the moment they only obey my voice."

"What about this one?" He pointed at Daniel.

"A very special case."

"Well, time is running out, Herr Doctor. And while your displays are certainly impressive, I need fighting men now." He eyed the Maquis men.

"You have a week. After that, I'm closing this entire operation down and putting these men to work."

"But I ..."

"One week Herr Doctor. If these apes are not ready for battle by then I will shoot them all myself."

There was no reaction from the doctor, Daniel saw, besides irritation, disdain even. He watched as the soldiers followed the Kommandant out of the chamber along with the medical staff, and the Maquis men.

They were alone.

The doctor sneered and mumbled something under his breath.

Daniel avoided the man's eyes.

"Oh, I must tell someone."

The doctor sat down beside Daniel.

"There is a vital stage in these experiments that I left out with Kommandant Beck. My orders were simple, childish to be honest with you. I was tasked with turning prisoners of war into soldiers for the *Third Reich*. But that order seemed lack-luster by comparison with what could be achieved. And do you know what that is, Daniel Malraux?"

Silence.

"Nothing less than the complete wiping of a man's mind and the implantation of a new personality."

Daniel closed his eyes.

"You see, creating fighters is relatively easy. You beat a dog long enough it will become a predictable monster. Creating an entirely new individual with autonomy requires dedication, patience. Such individuals would be a blank slate but not without intelligence. Think about the possibilities Daniel? They could be mobilized as spies or assassins. Imagine the wider applications? What if it were possible to engineer an entire society?"

Silence.

He tapped Daniel's hand. Daniel flinched but his eyes stayed shut.

"I think it is. I think it's possible. I have something that no one else knows about. Just me and now you. I've been saving it. I'm going to use it on you and your friends."

No reaction.

"It's called DGH 39. DGH for its chemical composition. Thirty-nine, for the year of discovery. You see Daniel, I've always had a fascination for radiation and DNA. Human DNA in particular. I was inspired by Dr. Martin Ecker's studies demonstrating time and again that ionized radiation can trigger chemical changes at an atomic and molecular level, causing biological genetic mutations."

"We're all Jews." Daniel found himself blurting. It stumped the doctor for a moment.

"Really? But only two of you are circumcised." He was referring to the two Perodeau brothers.

"We're all Jews. So your breakthrough would be wasted on us."

The doctor sighed and fell silent.

That's it then. I've signed our death warrants. Daniel thought. The doctor began to chuckle.

"Oh, very good, really, you almost had me there." He touched Daniel's knee. His hand lingered. Daniel pulled away.

"We are more alike than you would like to admit Daniel."

"I am nothing like you." He instantly regretted answering this devil.

"I'm going to burden you with something terrible and yet, truly liberating."

It was an odd statement to make.

Daniel peered sideways at the German, then to his rolled up sleeves. He glanced down at the doctor's slacks, thickly hemmed. Then to his collar, which sat slack like a schoolboy's around his stick neck.

There was nothing to this man. What a joke? He was a marionette. No, *Pinocchio!* That was it. He was *Pinocchio* with his long nose. Daniel began to belly laugh.

The doctor jumped up and slapped him hard across the face. His palm caught Daniel's nose and it began to bleed.

"The noise had drawn the nearby guards. They charged into the room. Daniel made to get up, but his chair toppled over. The fall dashed his head and he passed out.

Half an hour later, he lay unconscious in a new room, along with the other Maquis men: Gerard Dupre, the boy Alain Boussuet, the brothers Charles and Phillipe Perodeau.

The room had beautiful tall windows and bright paneled walls. Had the men been able to open their eyes they would have known they were in the former Duke of Rousinac's private wing on the first floor of the castle.

The impressive suite overlooked the royal gardens and faced South West. As a consequence, it was filled with sun from morning to dusk. The tall trees housed all manner of birds, and their songs could be heard when the windows were open.

The German doctor appreciated none of this of course. The room's light and impressive space made it perfect for medical procedures.

That was all he cared about.

The Maquis (15)
Rousinac, Southwest France 1944

For Daniel Malraux and the other Maquis men, DGH 39 was like being thrown into Hell itself. The war had gone into the very fabric of their souls.

In the beginning, in the first few hours, there was just a fog. A void with no sense of time, or order, of light and darkness. Into this artificial haze diabolical figures arose. They were bestial chimeras, devilish abominations.

In one brief moment of consciousness, Daniel raised his head from his cage. He could see that the boy Alain was curled up in the next bed. He looked like a child, baby white and soft chinned. His large blue eyes still.

"Alain -Alain. My sweet boy."

The boy lay silent. A nurse checked his pulse.

"Specimen 5 has terminated Herr Doctor," she announced.

"Damn!" The doctor cursed. The blond boy had been his favorite. Youth had so much potential.

"And sedate that one. No one should be awake."

Daniel watched as the boy's body was slung into a waste cart and wheeled away. With it went the symbol of France's future. He fell into a deeper despair.

With every passing moment, the Maquis men were being transformed by DGH 39. Animal imagery flooded their dormant minds. Surges of instinct that needed no words. Replacing resistance came a persistent need to hunt, to reproduce, to fight. Hunger had given way to brute appetites.

Eventually, all thought-forms ceased. Their minds offered only a primordial landscape. In it echoed a distant voice. It spoke to them softly, like a mother's whisper.

Go to the forest. Let it go. Follow the darkness. Follow the night.

With every word Daniel Malraux felt what was left of him ebbing away. He withdrew into the furthest corner of his mind. Only the power of love could push away the evil that called to him endlessly.

Cecile. Cecile.

He would summon her. She would come.

Cecile – my sweetheart, my darling one.

"Remember the day Daniel. Hold onto that day."

A day like none other.

The day they had met.

A summer evening that had been brutally hot. The annual Rousinac festival was in full swing. The war had begun some place far away. Germany's military machine hadn't yet drilled down inside of France. Groups of French soldiers sat in outdoor cafes, smoking and discussing the fall of Poland.

The night was colored with the smell of sausages grilling. Fragrant local cheeses glistened on wooden slabs. Carts of fresh vegetables shone as brightly as birthday balloons. A Spanish band played.

Cecile had taken her brother's arm and together they wormed their way through the crowds as they hurried to catch the Russian circus. That was where he was.

Daniel Malraux had seen Cecile as soon as she had arrived in the audience, and he was immediately captivated. He knew that she must be from another place. He could not have lived alongside such loveliness in ignorance.

He watched the performance entirely through her eyes as she laughed at the clowns, gasped at the high wire acts and cheered at the antics of the elephants. Daniel could not take his eyes off of her.

Entranced by her raven hair, which was cropped fashionably short against a long porcelain neck, she had Coco Channel red lips and fluttering blue eyes. When the show ended, the boisterous crowd spewed out of the large striped tent and into the streets.

But then, she was gone. Battling against the blast of revelers, he painfully eyed each face. *I cannot lose her, the face I have known since the beginning of time.*

He scouted the cramped streets that night, but the labyrinth of feasters would not yield her. He finally gave up. Despondently, Daniel leaned against a smoking chestnut cart stationed in front of the village church and rolled a cigarette. He gazed up gloomily at the worn gargoyles hanging above him in the Norman arch. A couple giggled as they emerged from the church's archway. Their arms were linked.

It was *her.*

"Go on," the chestnut seller chuckled, handing him a warm paper bag.

"Offer her one."

Daniel couldn't move so the man let out a shrill whistle.

"Over here darling," he chirped. "A bag just for you courtesy of this handsome fellow!" He indicated toward Daniel and winked.

Cecile's gaze jumped from the chestnut seller to Daniel. Everything grounded to a slow, muffled dance. She didn't remember walking toward him, she would tell him later. All she noticed were his beautiful almond shaped eyes framed behind fashionable American spectacles.

A thin brown mustache outlined Daniel's soft sensual lips. His dimpled chin and slicked back hair shone under the lamplight. She walked over to him and took the bag. Then she introduced her brother, much to Daniel's relief.

That evening they had sat on the church stairs, talking almost until sunrise. They embraced one another's words as though they had invented language at that very moment. At some point Daniel took Cecile's hands in his.

"Would you ever think of living somewhere else other than Bordeaux?" He had asked.

"Yes Daniel. And I think Rousinac may do very well."

Three months later on their honeymoon Daniel had confessed to her.

"It was the longest circus performance of my life, mon cherie. I wondered who the boy was at your side. I had to know, or I thought my heart would burst."

That boy, Cecile's brother Henri, would die in the second year of the war.

Pfff...!

Gone ....a black tar poured into the memory.

"This one is awake, over here!"

He heard someone shout. Clammy hands grabbed his arm.

He felt the plunge of a needle. Heat, burning liquid, pain pushing further and deeper.

Cec....

What was her name?

Darkness devoured everything. The terrible, soft voice returned, only louder and closer. Then came animal dreams. Scenes flashed in and out, of flight, of stalking, of breeding. Heightened sensations, exhilarating instincts.

Go to the forest. Follow the darkness. Let go ...

The Germans (6)
Rousinac, Southwest France 1944

Heavy droning from the overhead Allied planes was now a daily occurrence. But the bombers posed no threat to the Germans in Rousinac. With the munitions mine destroyed they were flying undisturbed to Paris, to Munich, and on to Berlin where the end of World War II was finally unfolding.

The writing was on the wall.

Germany had lost.

Bordeaux's Maquis had taken over from their Rousinac brothers and had begun attacking checkpoints in broad daylight. No German felt safe in Rousinac anymore. Kommandant Beck was consumed with deserters and countering resistance fighters.

But none of this concerned Klaus Moritz.

Only Kommandant Beck's threat against his work had registered. There could be no interruption of this final and crucial stage. Something had to be done about Beck.

But what? Poison?

The Kommandant was not to be under-estimated. Moritz had watched in quiet admiration as Beck out-maneuvered General Schmidt.

The clock was ticking.

There was no time.

It was now or never.

There was only one option.

The Maquis (16)
Rousinac, Southwest France 1944

The remaining Maquis men were moved again, down through the castle toward its dungeon pit. As they moved, they grew animated.

Soon my brave sons, you will show the world that you are superior.

Each man heard the same voice in his head, beating like a drum. Even the quiet one felt the sway of the illuminated figure who now stood high above them at the pit. Bright lights obscured his form but there could be no denying who he was.

Father.

"We have gathered here my brave sons to watch you fight. To watch you honor us. To watch you bring glory to your people. To show these lesser mortals that you are the master race!"

The voice thundered.

The quiet one felt a shiver down his spine. His leader stood erect and saluted the shadows huddled above them. He would go first.

"Release him!"

The Maquis leader thundered into the pit as soldiers shot at

him from above. Small wooden darts plunged into his body causing multiple lacerations. Although he had no weapons, the leader
rejoiced in fighting the wolves discharged through a gate.

There was no separation between them. He was a wolf. They
were wolves. He would protect his brothers. He had no thoughts
of fear. In fact, there were no thoughts at all. His body moved like a
machine, fierce and quick.

Crack!

He ripped and slaughtered until he had torn out the last wolf's
throat. It hung in his bloodied jaw like a macabre ribbon.

He had proven victorious. Loud cheers resonated around the pit.

Ger…

What was it?

Ger…

No name now.

Alpha.

He let out a bellowing roar and the other Maquis men followed
suit. As news of their feats spread many soldiers came down to watch.

More fights were organized, more adversaries proposed: dogs,
boar, whatever they could get their hands on. Bets were made. The
guards had favorites. Kommandant Beck encouraged it.

Good for morale.

The Maquis men were learning to feel a sense of pride in their
accomplishments. Like gnarled gladiators, they stood tall in their
filth, and blood and nakedness. Even the quiet one.

In this unending darkness they only had one another.

All other faces were gone.

Brothers, brothers, brothers.

The Germans (7)
Rousinac, Southwest France 1944

"Your work is extraordinary, Herr Doctor." The young man who brought his afternoon coffee said as he put down the cup. He got no response.

"None of us can believe that these men now obey your every command. They meekly move back into their holding crates and wait to be locked up like dogs."

"They're not dogs!" Moritz snapped, waving him away. He was a new posting, young and another know-it-all. Perhaps a spy for Beck? He'd have to watch this one.

But he did make exceptional coffee.

Hmmm....

"An authentic ground roast Herr Doctor. It makes all the difference."

Moritz leaned back in his chair and savored.

The young man lingered.

"Do you not wonder if they are fooling you, Herr Doctor? Simply biding their time …"

"If I asked them, they would tear one another apart." Moritz shot back with pride.

"But that would be a waste." The young man added, as quick as a flash. Almost as though he had rehearsed the entire conversation. Moritz sipped his coffee and kept silent.

"What about if we tested their loyalty on a comrade? On someone they knew? We have dozens of locals in custody. You could pit them against their own terrorists, then share the findings. It would demoralize the enemy and would be good sport for our men?"

Moritz hadn't thought of that.

His idea had been to sabotage a guard and see if the Maquis men would obey on cue. There were plenty of opportunities to leave a door unlocked. But this was even better. Failproof.

Would a patriot turn on a brother?

"Arrange it."

The Maquis (17)
Rousinac, Southwest France 1944

In the silence of their separate holding rooms, the Maquis men: Gerard Dupre, Daniel Malraux, Charles and Phillipe Perodeau, discovered that they could hear one another's thoughts.

At first, each man assumed it was a literal sound, as in a heightened sense of hearing. But the walls that divided them were cut from solid bedrock and these words lacked a distinctive signature.

They were also finding it difficult to determine where one man's thoughts began, and another's ended. It felt like one continuous thought stream.

My bones are aching.

Am I dead?

I think I can see in the dark.

Me too.

Can anyone hear me?

Who is this?

I can hear you.

I hear you, but I can't see you…
Close your eyes and you will see me.
All of us.
We are apart but close.
I feel you all.
Yes – yes – me too. We feel …
Different.
We look …
…different.
Who are we again?
Brothers.
We are all brothers…
Brothers, brothers, brothers.

The Germans (8)
Rousinac, Southwest France 1944

Several floors above the dungeon pit, Klaus Moritz inked a white paper. It was a secret document that accompanied an official dossier filled with data.

Two sets of records.

One real one fake.

One for Berlin.

One for the Allies.

The atrocity had to be accounted for somehow.

How could three unarmed men kill that many and in just minutes?

There had been no question that the Maquis men hadn't recognized their own people. It had been decisive. One order and the other prisoners were dispatched like boys picking apart insects.

But then something unpredictable happened.

As fast as a spider the leader had leapt up from the pit and snatched down his prize.

Wolf.

Moritz thought he had heard the Maquis leader murmur.

The others followed his lead, managing to drag down which ever stunned German stood gaping at the pit's rim.

"Stop! Stop!" Moritz had desperately commanded. He hadn't been afraid, just frustrated. *Why had they disobeyed him?*

Eventually the Maquis men obeyed.

But the delay had cost lives. Eight dead in total.

Kommandant Beck's death had been a severe loss to the Rousinac battalion. Even a decapitated Nazi HQ was demanding an explanation. Moritz knew he could face a hasty firing squad if he wasn't careful.

He checked his watch. Where was his coffee?

Damn. That's right.

The young man was dead. Moritz doubted any of the other imbeciles would remember to bring him a cup up. He would have to go back to making his own.

How could this have happened? What could I say? He tapped his pen on the desk and peered out of the window. A bird had landed on the sill with a worm wriggling in its mouth.

Electrodes!

He would make something up about the men's brains being damaged. *Electrodes applied to the frontal lobe, too much voltage? Human error.*

He knew who he could blame. The dumpy woman with the bad teeth. She was always making mistakes.

Human error. That should do it.

He stopped writing and swooned.

His Maquis men were sublime killing machines, lean and agile; they had executed their skills effortlessly. There could be no end to the application of such fighters: personal guards, special operations.

Magnificent.

They had performed beyond his expectations. Moritz cheerily reflected.

Besides ... oh yes.

His smile dropped.

There was that.

Staff had begun reporting a toughening of the mens' skin and a discoloration. They'd noticed that the prisoners' eyes were changing too. Their eyes were now adapted to seeing in the dark, and completely black even the corneas. A solid liquid black like a beetle's.

And there was a peculiar smell like, *what was it?* A decomposing body, rotting flesh. No matter how much the men were hosed down they stunk foul. It was causing problems. His staff were growing superstitious, refusing to be alone near the prisoners. They complained about hearing the men's voices in their heads.

Rubbish!

Insubordination was common. Discipline was breaking down. He made some notes.

Test on future specimens using lesser quantities of bat, spider and wolf DNA. Repeat tests to decrease unpredictable side-effects.

Climbing walls would be an advantage in war situations, but what if it produced other arachnoid behaviors, less controllable, less palatable?

There was another disappointment.

Moritz frowned.

One of the prisoners hadn't obeyed, hadn't attacked his fellow French prisoners.

Daniel Malraux.

What made him unreachable?

He was an enigma.

It was over. No more work to be done. Not here anyway. Every-thing was over. Soldiers were throwing themselves off the castle walls.

Not good.

The test specimens had killed Germans.

Failure.

But they hadn't killed him either.

Data.

What was the switch, the trap door into Daniel Malraux's mind? It had eluded him.

Failure.

For a moment the face of his father appeared, bright red and swollen with rage.

"You're a failure!"

No!

He had failed because there hadn't been enough time.

That's it.

The science was good. The conditions were not good. It would work if there was enough time given.

Furthermore …

A guard interrupted his thoughts.

"Herr Doctor!"

"What is it!"

"Herr Doctor, you must leave now. It is a direct order from our supreme commander in La Rochelle. We are to withdraw immediately …"

"But the …" Moritz barked.

"You must report to the Kommandant at La Rochelle. That is a direct order! We have all of the samples in our possession, and they are ready for transport. Do as you're fucking told!"

The guard ordered, his hands trembling, his eyes red.

Liberation
Rousinac, Southwest France, September 4th, 1944

Rousinac's freedom came like a thief in the night.

In conquest the Germans had thundered in, in broad daylight. In defeat they had stolen away in darkness. Allied soldiers would not set foot in Rousinac for weeks.

When they did, they found that the Bordeaux Maquis and the Free French Army had already secured a decisive victory. The straggling German platoons that had been trapped between Bordeaux and Normandy were now frantically charging toward a last stronghold at La Rochelle.

But in defeat they were particularly dangerous. The RAF and U.S air forces were picking off their convoys on a daily basis. Emboldened locals were also taking revenge pot shots.

As a consequence, the German soldiers were now mostly paranoid, sleep-deprived drunks who were trigger-happy and quick to execute anyone that they feared was an enemy combatant. It was considered too risky to take the main roads until these retreating invaders had been properly dealt with.

The town of Rousinac had witnessed a partial German withdrawal back in August, however, a reserve platoon of around 130 soldiers had been left behind to protect a valuable quarry close-by. They were sitting ducks.

Nobody knew exactly when the attack was launched but on September 4th the Bordeaux Maquis and the Free French Army sent word to Rousinac's Maire (mayor) that the quarry had been retaken. A victory parade through Rousinac's main promenade was planned for the following day.

In the surrounding villages, liberation was a different experience. An urgent murmur traveled from house to house, village to village. *Have they finally gone?* Nobody could be sure. It was still too dangerous to venture out onto the highways.

Once the declaration notice had reached every village Maire (mayor) the locals wanted to head to the castle. They were in desperate search of their loved ones, prisoners, and their captive Maquis men.

But they were held back.

Armed compatriots advanced upon the castle from other Resistance units, fearing that the occupiers had left it booby-trapped.

They discovered a castle completely devoid of life. In its chambers, surgical instruments strewn in twisted piles as if spun by a tornado. Nazi offices and makeshift laboratories had been destroyed. A terrible stench permeated the castle's interior pointing to a massacre.

Forty-eight men and boys were later found dead, mutilated, deep in the castle's dungeons. Locals. Husbands. Fathers. Brothers. Sons. They discovered cages large enough to fit a man. Then there were the rotting carcasses of wild animals, piled ceiling-high in the castle's cellars.

It had been enough to make the battle-hardened puke.

What evil unfolded here?

The whispers began.

Where are our Maquis men?

Operation Paperclip
Normandy, Northern France 1944

The holding place in Normandy was comfortable enough but with the British breathing down his neck General Huey Macmillan knew that he didn't have long to ship one more Nazi butcher back home to the States.

On his desk was a brief. His next directive.

Operation Paperclip what kind of shit show name was that? Macmillan thought as he chain-smoked over an empty whiskey glass in his command room. Irritated, he used the brief to swat a fly.

"Shit!" The insect left a blotch.

This new type of operation with a kooky name was not what he had signed up for. He was a fourth-generation military man who got to kill the bad guys.

Smashing out his cigarette Macmillan held up his assignment. An inconspicuous fishing boat would dock at 2am tomorrow morning off a Normandy beach. He would hand over his Nazi prisoner along with all his medical samples to the crew aboard.

It made no sense. This fruit and nut, Klaus Moritz, belonged in the dock along with his Nazi comrades. The kraut doc hadn't given a crap about the war. Gunfire had raged all around him, but his beef was whether "his work would continue."

It turned Macmillan's gut just talking to the creep. And yet, his orders had been clear. Keep the Nazi doctor safe and get him to the States. It nagged the General that this operation had taken precedence over routing the last remaining German forces from Royan and La Rochelle.

Macmillan wasn't sure where the boat was going, only that it was someplace in the U.S. – *Montauk*? He'd heard from a buddy that a military base was being set up there to pursue a bunch of top secret programs.

All Macmillan knew as he'd glanced over a stack of papers taken from the doctor was that some French Resistance guys had gone through some *god-damned unnatural shit* in a place called Rousinac. Their wretched faces, in the black and white photographs, would haunt him for the rest of his life.

The Americans (14)
Rousinac, Southwest France 2019

After purchasing a hunting knife in the town's sporting store, David and James drove into a lot adjacent to the entrance of Rousinac castle, and parked.

"One thing's been bugging me from the get-go, James said, pointing up to a lamp post."

"What?"

"See the lights?"

"Yeah."

"Wonder why they're pink."

"Mauve."

"Whatever, notice that they're not standard municipal lights?"

"No."

"Well they're not."

"What are they then?"

"They're full-spectrum UV lights. We had some on tour, they kept certain critters away from the camp. Nocturnal predators. The lights act like sunlight."

"So."

"So, why does Rousinac have UV lights everywhere?"

"Maybe it's energy efficient?"

"Or maybe ..."

"They want to keep things away at night?"

David was about to answer when Laetitia's red Citroen came into view.

"Does she know about me?"

"About you?"

"Jesus! Does she know I was a marine?"

"It didn't come up."

"Ha-ha, well don't mention it. I want her to underestimate us."

"I'm sure she does."

"Okay, so let's talk strategies."

James grew animated, waving his arms as he talked about different scenarios and responses. But as James plotted, David felt his nerves begin to jangle.

When they finally emerged from the car, the castle's shadow loomed over them. And although the sun had baked the afternoon dry, a shiver ran through him. James glanced at his friend.

"Sure, you want to go through with this?"

"I'm sure. Tom's a good guy. If he's in trouble, I want to help him."

"You know what David? I think you'd actually make a good marine."

James' comment stopped David in his tracks.

"You'd never leave a man behind."

"Guess I learned that from you."

"No, that's all you. Look, for what it's worth, should anything go down here. You've been a good friend and ..."

"James, stop."

"No, it's important. You're like a brother to me man." James pulled David into a tight bear hug. It turned him into a neck lock.

"You're so much better when you're on your meds." David gasped.

"Who says I'm on my meds?"

They both cracked up. It was nervous laughter. James lit a cigarette up and power smoked.

"Fucking nerves." He mumbled. David saw his hands trembling.

Laetitia pulled into a vacant bay, got out of her car and looked cautiously around before walking toward the castle.

The rear entrance was a part of the castle's most ancient section, dating back to the 12th century. The walls and turrets stood chiseled but resolute, weathered blocks nibbled by battles and the elements. Tucked into the stone was a small door. The men waited beside it in silence.

"Okay, here she comes," David said anxiously.

"Finally," James sighed.

Avoiding James' eye Laetitia kissed David tenderly on the cheek. Her perfume wafted in the surrounding air. It masked the stale odor coming from behind the door.

"They're in here," she said looking at James for the first time.

"What do you mean, they're in there?" James shot back.

"James please ..." David began.

"No, wait a minute. Do you expect us to believe the Brits are tied up someplace in this castle? What do you take us for?"

"It's the perfect place. No one would think to look there. Plus, they can be moved easily. The tunnels lead from here to many parts of Rousinac."

"And the security guards?" James pushed.

"There are no guards." She laughed.

"You'll understand once we go down, believe me. The castle is as deep as it is high. It's like an under-ground city." She pushed open the door.

"Come on."

The door led into a narrow, dusty corridor. At the end was a second door that opened into a descending spiral staircase.

James hesitated.

"I'd like to see the firearms before we go any further."

Without speaking, Laetitia pulled out two small pistols from her backpack. James checked both barrels. They were loaded.

"I thought you'd bring at least one rifle," he added as he handed a gun to David.

"You can't use a rifle that far down in the rock. It's too danger-ous." Laetitia replied.

"You can if you aim straight sweetheart," James cackled.

Scores of steps took the party down two levels into the castle's basement. It was an unpleasant descent. At times entire steps were missing or the ceiling above had bowed, causing the men to stoop. Eventually the staircase led out into a gloomy internal courtyard lit by a few light bulbs.

Laetitia headed to an ivy-matted corner and touched a small metal door.

"This is where they are." she whispered, jamming a key into its lock.

"Wait! How come you've got a key?" James barked.

She ignored his question.

"I must warn you; the smell is bad. This is the oldest sewer in Rousinac."

James grabbed her arm. Laetitia held his stare.

"Because I'm a part of this *obviously*." She said through clenched teeth. James released his grip.

As she levered the door open both men gagged and swore.

"That's not sewage. You've got dead people down there." James stepped back. David recognized the odor too. His stomach lurched.

"How do you think they get rid of the bodies? The bad guys? Think about it." She tapped her temple.

"Know a lot about that, huh?" James pressed.

"Unfortunately. Yes. Look, do you want to get the English people out or have an ethical debate?" She eyeballed him. Her answer took James by surprise.

Sociopath. Tick.

"James, she's right. We don't have much time." David interrupted their gaze.

"Afraid of monsters?" She mocked.

James broke into a giggle and leaned close into Laetitia's face.

"The only thing I'm afraid of is myself."

David saw the first sign of fear in Laetitia's face since they had entered the castle.

"Time is running out." She finally said.

As she pushed open the door a spider's web as heavy as a shawl dropped. A wolf spider sprang out from beneath it and scurried into a crack in the wall.

David had experienced every type of murder scene imaginable, but nothing had prepared him for this. He peered ahead of them. The caves beyond were dark and dank. A spongy black mold carpeted the walls.

Laetitia pulled out three flashlights. James hesitated at the group's rear, reluctant to step away from what little light bled into the cave from above. The French woman walked swiftly ahead as David struggled to keep up. James didn't budge.

"Wait up. How do we know these things work?"

"Would you like to go back outside and test them on the pigeons?"

James glared at her.

"These are fucking antiques. I know about guns."

"They work. I promise you."

"James, leave if you want," David said. "The upstairs door is still open. Just go wait in the car."

"How come you don't have a gun?" James asked Laetitia.

"These are the only guns I own."

"James, I'm not kidding, go if you want. I need to see this thing through." David pleaded.

"How much farther are we going down into this hell hole?" James pushed.

Laetitia realized that James would be a major problem.

"Not far now." She softened.

"Yeah, well maybe I'll wait right here." James indicated back to the open door.

Merde!

Laetitia suddenly spun around.

"You can't! If the smugglers discover you, they'll kill us all. Please! Hurry while we still have time to find them." She begged.

He'd spooked her. *Good.*

"How often are they here? The smugglers?" James nodded up to the ceiling.

"I don't know. That's the truth of it." She tried to sound vulnerable.

"Fine, give me the key then." He answered.

That was the last thing she could do.

"W-why?"

"Insurance."

Laetitia had to think quickly. If she gave this G.I. Joe the key, she wouldn't be able to lock them in. But refusing would arouse David's suspicion. There was only one choice. She would need to take them deeper. She handed the key over.

"Trust me now?"

"Nope."

"Let's go."

James searched David's eyes for a sign to abandon, but his companion returned a vacant stare.

Reaching down James felt for the small sharp blade tucked discreetly into his left boot. Then he patted David's back for the hunting knife they'd previously purchased from the sports store.

Ammo. Tick.

"Okay let's get this shit-show over with." He growled.

Laetitia shone her flashlight ahead of them into the dirt. The men kept their flashlights at the ready. Though sandwiched between James and Laetitia, David was growing more afraid.

"Thought you said they were here." He found himself asking.

"They are."

"Like here, fucking where?" James chimed in.

"Like here in this cave but there are many chambers."

Within a few yards, the first cave had spread out into a large, cavernous room. Laetitia's flashlight spilled all over it. Both men turned on their flashlights in unison. The space appeared much bigger under this penetrating triple light.

James and David gasped.

The Locals (9a)
Rousinac, Southwest France 2019

A small white van driven by Patrick Clayburn passed the château castle. In the passenger seat was Didier Perodeau.

"You're sure they're all down there now?" Perodeau asked.

"Yes of course, don't worry. She knows what to do." Clayburn snapped.

"Are you ready?" He glared at Didier.

"Yes, yes. Let's just get this over with."

The Locals (9b)
Rousinac, Southwest France 2019

Pierre Malraux mopped his brow, as the vines crackled in the heat. He was looking for a hedgerow bush that had grown over an old sewer, long fallen into disuse. The shade from a nearby tree brought Pierre some light relief and he leaned against it.

Mon Dieu!

He would never forget the night ....that night.

His mother Cecile had decided that the time was right. Pierre was eleven years old. The drive into the old quarter of Rousinac was a quiet affair. Even by the mid '50's half of the town remained dark after sunset. Street lights would not be implemented until '78.

The castle tunnels were situated at the back of the old Templar hospital, which was now completely in ruins. Cecile had left the car's engine running and the headlamps on as she whispered, "over there."

Ahead was a gigantic black hole clawed from a side of rock. Pierre peered back at his mother. *Surely, she did not expect him to enter it alone?* Her expression was resolute. She didn't even blink. It was a wordless command.

Alone.

The smell had been the worst part. It was far worse than the suffocating darkness of the tunnel. Why hadn't his mother warned him? He immediately threw up over and over again until his stomach ached.

"It's okay son," a faint yet familiar voice issued from within the tunnel.

"Come closer."

The boy had simply obeyed. A shadow carefully approached him. Pierre felt his knees buckle. The odor was by now over-powering. In what meager light bled into the tunnel, Pierre could make out the form of a man.

He seemed completely black, even his eyes – but they were soft and recognizable. They were the same shape as his own. The boy's heart began to slow. The tension lifted.

"Papa?"

"My son."

Papa.

A squabble between a group of sparrows in the bush behind, pulled Pierre Malraux into the present.

Mon Dieu.

His gut throbbed.

At this very moment, a critical situation was unfolding. His directions had been clear, the Americans must somehow be persuaded to leave. Laetitia's idea about drug smugglers and a hidden vault of money was a good one. He was sure the two men would believe such a thing about Perodeau. He wouldn't be surprised if it were true himself.

And yet, Pierre Malraux continued to be plagued with guilt. He had been toying with the idea of confession. The need to get the death of the English couple off his conscience. After all, the situation had been forced upon them by Perodeau. It was not his fault. Surely, there would be forgiveness for that?

In the meantime, he would pray for everyone's souls.

"Son …"

A husky voice called from the tunnel. Pierre scurried over to its entrance and crouched down low.

"Papa."

"Is that you Pierre?" The voice asked again. But Pierre had stepped back, doubled over and almost vomited. The smell never got easy to bear.

"Yes, Papa. It's Pierre!" He called out loudly.

"Have you found a Padre?" The voice quivered.

"Not yet, Papa. There are many sympathetic but none that will risk their soul to give you the sacraments. I will keep searching."

"I am growing weaker."

There was a pause.

"I don't know how much longer I can live."

Pierre had heard this statement before, many times. The sad fact was that his father would probably out-live him. What Daniel Malraux meant was that it was his soul that was dying – a little more, day by day.

He heard a pitiful sound. It wasn't exactly the sound of someone crying. It was more like a low, animal groan.

"I promise Papa. I promise to find a Padre."

Thank you.

The body inside of the tunnel loped away. The heat of the afternoon evaporated the moisture in Pierre's throat, and he struggled

to swallow. He looked up at the beautiful blue sky and wondered
whether God could see the sins of Rousinac.

The Americans (15)
Rousinac, Southwest France 2019

"Before you ask, those are recently excavated tombs. Hundreds of years ago prisoners were buried in these quarters." Laetitia announced.

She's playing mind games.

"What about the German girls?" He blurted.

"W-what?"

"You heard me. What's the real fucking story?" James pushed.

"I don't know what you mean."

How could they know about the women?

James went to respond, but David dashed him a look.

Then, something caught James' eye. To their left was an archway as tall as a man. It had been blocked up with clean red bricks. *Recently,* James noted.

"What's on the other side of that wall?"

"Don't worry about that now. There's not much time."

"These bones don't seem that old to me." David said.

"They are probably from the war." Laetitia countered.

"Yes, but …"

Laetitia felt panicked. She pulled away from the two men and moved quickly toward an opposite corner. James chased after her.

"Going someplace?" He herded her back to David.

"How old are those bones?" James asked him.

"It's hard to tell in this light and without my equipment but they don't seem old. Maybe thirty years or less?"

"Quiet," Laetitia said, holding up her hand. "Did you hear that?"

"What?" James whispered.

"Listen!" Laetitia pointed to the back of the cave.

"I don't hear anything." David said.

"I heard a woman's voice."

"I didn't hear anything either." James added.

Everyone paused. It grew weirdly silent. Laetitia's mind raced. There was no Plan B. The men had to be left here alone. Soon Patrick and Didier would arrive, and the Americans would hear them.

Suddenly, a noise from the darkest part of the chamber startled them all.

"What the actual fuck was that?" James trained his flashlight toward the sound. Everyone strained to listen.

"Sounded like a cat."

"Or a woman crying." Laetitia added. As the two men focused their attention on the back end of the chamber, she moved to the side.

The sound came again, only louder. It was clearly a woman whimpering. David leapt up and headed toward the noise.

"Hold up David!" James cautioned.

He didn't feel good about this at all. He pointed his flashlight to where Laetitia had been standing."

"Laetitia?"

The two men heard another sound. Faint footsteps scurrying away from them.

"She's bolted David!" James yelled.

"W-what are you talking about?" David stuttered.

"SHE'S FUCKING GONE! Let's go! Now!" James blasted. David didn't move.

James dragged him in the direction that Laetitia had taken. As yet, there was no definitive distance between the men and Laetitia.

But, in the dim light of their flashlights, the cave became a labyrinth of never-ending corridors. The men quickly became disoriented. From a level above, Laetitia could hear their muffled voices as they tumbled around the bone-strewn chamber.

She had to get to that first gate. James had the key for the first door but there was a bolt the other side. Once shut the key would be useless.

"Laetitia! Laetitia!"

It sounded like the Americans were closing in. Laetitia charged up the narrow stairs, on and up, until light loomed around the open door. As she raced towards it, Didier Perodeau's face appeared. For one horrible instant, Laetitia doubted her escape. The look in Didier Perodeau's eyes was odd.

Had he come to kill her?

When Patrick Clayburn leaned forward and yanked Laetitia free, she collapsed into his arms gasping. Didier levered the door's bolt shut and added a padlock. He could faintly hear the Americans shouting below him.

"Come on, let's go. It's done."

The locals ran frantically toward the castle's first floor.

James and David stopped still. They heard the bolt shut a level above them.

"She's fucking locked that door somehow," James shouted. David began to call her name.

James motioned for him to stop.

"Don't give our position away ... I think I can locate it by sound. It's in that direction." He pointed.

Kneeling down James picked up a thick nugget of stone. It crumbled upon touch.

"Great. Chalk-based. Okay David, mark that wall right there with an arrow pointing this way."

James broke the rock in half and tossed one piece to David.

"I'll draw arrows on the floor. We can map our way back. I'm pretty confident I can carve out the soft rock around the gate's hinges with this hunting knife."

As the men marked their positions, they realized that the chamber they were in was larger than originally thought. When they swung their flashlights wide an enormous interior graveyard was revealed. They saw piles of bones in every corner.

"What the fuck happened here?" James winced as he chalked along the floor.

David moved carefully toward the bones.

"Looks like a mass grave."

"Yeah, whatever. I ain't joining them. Come on!"

Outside in the fresh air, Patrick hugged Laetitia.

"You are a Dupre," he whispered.

Didier, Patrick and Laetitia, made their way back to the castle's car park in silence. Laetitia glanced over at the Americans' rental car. Patrick took her arm.

"Don't worry, someone's coming to take it. Follow us on the back roads. You probably need a stiff drink, eh?" he winked. Laetitia could not reply.

Deep inside the castle David had noticed something.

"James stop!"

James pointed his torch over to where David was standing.

"It's water. Look over there." He indicated.

A small, rusted tap poked from a hulk of rock. It was dripping. Underneath stood a large glass bottle.

This has got to be where they're keeping the Brits. James primed his pistol. David clumsily followed suit.

"We're not getting out of here, are we?" David whispered.

James ignored him. "Use your flashlight like a lighthouse. Like this. If we stand back to back no one can creep up on us."

"Shouldn't we try to find them?"

"Plan's aborted. We're on exit. Got it?"

"Got it."

Methodically, they began to creep back along a crude path of chalked arrows.

"Shit!" David gasped.

"What?"

"S-something just ran behind that rock, I think!"

"What kind of something? Describe it!" James yelled.

David shot his flashlight toward the base of the rock.

"I don't know. They were too q-quick."

"David, get a grip, remember we've got guns," James said.

He felt a tremor in David's back.

"It was probably just a rat. Come on!" He offered, but it was cold comfort. James knew they were not in this chamber alone.

The cave grew silent besides the Americans' labored breathing.

"Whatever happens, whatever you see, just shoot."

James' words produced a flashback.

Their orders had been simple. The Taliban in retreat were

torching everything in their path. James' unit had been sent in to flush them out of a small bomb-wrecked town. On its outskirts was an abandoned chemical factory. Advancing forces had intel there was a suicide band dug in.

"Flush'em out. Give'em fire."

Those were the orders. Sweep. Flush. Secure.

James and three others got the shortest straw: the basement. They had followed a twitchy bomb disposal officer. The basement was pitch black, ice cold. Seconds passed like hours.

Then all of a sudden, a man came out yelling. There had been no time to think. It was instant. Then others ran out of the shadows. One after another screaming.

Clap-clap-clap-clap.

Then silence. A pile of bodies.

A family.

They were nomadic shepherds, caught up in a dirty war. The Islamic terrorists had taken everything. Including the family's tents and slaughtered their flock.

So, they had taken shelter in the bombed out factory. A father, a mother, a baby, five children. Somehow the baby survived, and James had been tasked to drop it to a *Red Cross* hospital.

No therapy, just some tough advice.

Shoot, don't think. If you think, you're dead. Got it?

He had never dealt with that day. It festered inside of him like cancer. Truth was, he had killed innocent people in the call of duty. The only thing that had made sense to James since then, was his job. He profiled and hunted psychopathic serial killers for a paycheck. He didn't have time to contemplate what it all meant.

Fuck it.

Back in the caves, the two Americans moved backwards again with painful apprehension. Every step echoed.

James whispered, "I can see the corridor. We're good."

"There's another opening w-way back over there. I – I think that they… came from there," David stuttered.

"Just keep moving."

Their joint shuffle was like an awkward dance.

David stopped still.

"They're here," he panted. Panic thinned his voice. "We just can't see them."

"Keep moving."

A wail sounded from the back of the chamber. The sound froze both men.

"What the f-fuck!" James said.

"Sounds like a woman crying,"

"Move!"

"What if it's the British woman?"

"We can't help her."

James pulled away with determination.

"J-James?"

David turned his flashlight back towards the source of the crying.

"Tom? Catherine?" He called louder.

Just then, without warning, movement sprang from all corners of the chamber. Black shapes darted, scurried behind rocks and crept along the ground. David's torch dangled, haphazardly spraying rays of light onto the floors and walls. James called back.

"MOVE IT!"

From where he was positioned, James could hear David's hysteria mounting. The swirling light indicated that his companion was frantically trying to track something.

"They're everywhere James. Oh, sweet Jesus, they're all around me!" David cried.

James desperately tried to recompose himself.

"How many?" he thundered back. "Fire a shot, frighten them off!"

"They're like fucking lizards … no, spiders!"

"What?!" James thought he hadn't heard right.

Everything around David stopped as quickly as it had begun. Nothing stirred.

"W-what do you see now?" James yelled, sweat dripping down his neck.

He turned in David's direction. He was welded to the spot. *Shock, he's in shock is all. I need to keep him moving.*

A soft whimper came from the back of the cavern.

"Help! Someone help me, please!"

A woman. English.

"They're here. James, the Graystons are still alive."

James raised his firearm and took aim past David. He knew something was about to happen. More sweat saturated his torso, leaking into his pants. He attempted to find the words, *aim your gun David get ready* but he couldn't even speak.

In Iraq, James had waded through a flooded sewage tunnel. The water was murky and stunk like shit and blood. With infinite patience he and a small group of men had advanced in almost complete silence. Above them an unaware sleeper cell was busily building bombs.

At one point a bloated body floated toward him. Any sound would have alerted the enemy. It harbored against his moving form. The smell was overwhelming. It's head stiffened by death, tilted up directly at him. A face with no eyes.

He had stifled a scream at the cost of emptying his bowels. A cloud of warm stink mushroomed around him as the body bumped, then moved away. The sewer's tide had washed away his fear that day.

That fear was back.

All at once the chamber exploded into a circus of movement. James swung his gun and clicked. Nothing happened.

Click – click – click!

The pistol permanently jammed. James bent down to retrieve his knife. He looked up at David. The gun sat idle in his shaking hand.

"Laetitia?" David called out.

"You came back?"

James spun his torch in the line of David's vision.

A naked female figure had emerged out of the darkness. She recoiled from the glare of James' flashlight.

What-the-fuck? What-the-fuck? Fucking naked? What-the-fuck-Laetitia?

"Move the light away from her face," David countered. James pulled his light slightly away.

The emerging form mesmerized both men.

It was female. She straightened to an erect posture and David could see that her skin, unlike Laetitia's, was luminescent. In contrast, her eyes were as black and shiny as a bugs'.

"W-who are you?" James heard David ask.

No reply.

"Just keep moving David, back to me. Come on buddy!" James called out.

Why would Laetitia come back naked?

"That ain't Laetitia. C'mon David... come back toward me," James implored. Everything told him to bolt but he wouldn't leave David.

He couldn't.

David did not move. He was transfixed by the figure in front of him. The woman looked like a corpse. A black tongue flickered over her lips, jolting him out of his trance. He jumped back.

"Oh, fuck no!"

James seized the opportunity to charge forward and seize David's gun.

Click-click-click!

He sprayed the room with imaginary bullets. The pistol was another dud. In a frenzy James had dropped his flashlight. In the seconds it took for him to pick it up, the female had crossed the cave. Her speed paralyzed both men. Her motion was virtually soundless, like a hummingbird's wings.

Had she levitated?

She was now just six feet away. David watched her lips part into a twisted canine smile.

Stink.

There it was again. The stink from Perodeau's land.

A fruity odor like rotting apples. David had smelled it a thousand times at crime scenes. It marked the first stage of death. A body is sometimes still warm but dead.

Death.

Blossoming death.

David's bladder emptied noisily onto his shoes. James lurched forward pointing his flashlight trying to draw the female's attention away.

Glaring at James, she released a high-pitched scream. It summoned movement from every quarter. David could hear James uttering a Catholic prayer. The names of saints punctured the sinister noises that now flooded the chamber.

The female moved toward David. Her stench was unbearable. He let out a futile cry. With lightning speed she snatched his hair and knocked him off his feet. He hit the cave floor hard, knocked out.

James stood impotent.

"Oh God - oh Jesus - oh please J-Jesus Mary Joseph help us," he stammered.

He didn't notice the shapes unfurling from the ceiling above.

Colony (1)
Rousinac, Southwest France 2019

Gerard Dupre had picked up the scent of the intruders long before they had entered his territory. His eyes, perfectly adapted to the dark, had taken in their forms when they'd first entered the grand chamber. Their voices spoke a language he had long forgotten.

Dropping from the cave's ceiling like a spider, he had crashed on top of the second invader. The man's neck broke like a twig, his warm carcass torn apart by the hungry.

The other one had been claimed by the female. She'd dragged him along the ground towards the back tunnel. It was good that she had taken him. It was her time. She was fertile. Gerard searched the chamber for his brother.

Brother?

Daniel Malraux always held back at these kinds of events. It never got any easier for him. The abandoned flashlights tossed to the floor shed two shafts of light. The light picked up Daniel's contorted face. Gerard spat on the floor of their grand chamber.

Still tormented – Mon Dieu!

The Locals (10)
Rousinac, Southwest France 2019

"I hope this has been a lesson for you Perodeau," Patrick Clayburn growled from the head of his kitchen table. Laetitia sat to his left. A bottle of cognac, now empty, stood at the table's center.

"Yes, I keep saying I'm sorry, what more can I do?" Didier Perodeau blubbered.

"You do realize these were important men?" Clayburn glared at him.

"They will most certainly be missed."

"So, what do we do now?" Perodeau threw the question at Laetitia.

"The Americans' car is going to be p-parked s-somewhere on your land," She slurred.

"Why my land?" Didier whined.

"Because we couldn't fucking leave it at the castle, could we?" Patrick Clayburn railed as he drained his glass of liquor.

"And what am I supposed to do with it?" Didier blasted as he leapt up from the table.

"You'll soon find out." Laetitia Dupre muttered into her glass.

Didier Perodeau fell into an armchair like a pouting child.

"*Oh, yet another* plan?" he added sarcastically.

"YOU UNGRATEFUL BASTARD!"

Patrick hurled the empty cognac bottle at Didier. He ducked.

SMASH!

It hit the wall.

"This has all been your fault!"

Didier simply shrugged.

"We are all in this together, remember?" He shot a look in Laetitia's direction.

"Just wait until Pierre finds out."

HER (2)
Rousinac, Southwest France 2019

Catherine Grayston fell back into the darkness. This Hell had become all too familiar. The never-ending darkness, being dragged along tunnels, the violence. Even the stench had become tolerable.

But this recent turn of events had cruelly summoned her from total despair. *Had it been recent?* She didn't even know if it had been real at all.

Catherine had heard voices, men's voices, and in English. They had been so close she could have crawled towards them if there had been just a little more light.

There had been two of them - two distinct voices. She could tell that much. *Were they looking for her? Was it the police? Would more people follow them? Oh, please dear God. Had they heard her?*

And then ….the screams had come.

The first man had clearly met the same fate as her husband. The second man had been dragged away alive into the tunnels. He had called out her name. *Was he the American her husband had talked about? What was his name?* She couldn't remember.

But it was clear that Tom's letter had drawn two more innocent people to this abyss. The thought tortured her. It meant that there were people above ground protecting these devils. It meant that more could be lured down.

She had called out to him, "American, American, I know you are here!" but his voice had grown fainter. He had been moved further away. Sometimes, she thought she could hear him crying.

In the never-ending darkness Catherine would relive the night they had come for her at Perodeau's house.

Once the bathroom had been stormed, she had closed her eyes and listened as Tom was torn limb from limb. Then it went blank. She must have passed out. When she came to, she screamed and fought like an animal. At first, her captors had been fascinated by her wildness. For days they'd snuck around her like lions.

In the very beginning, Catherine had thought that her abductor was some homeless kingpin. The necessity to live underground, the savagery and the stench certainly lent to that opinion.

It would take time, but she would soon begin to understand that such an idea would have been a blessing … by comparison …

Occasionally, there were weak and fleeting flashes of light, breaks in the incessant blackness. Some of them evidently carried lamps to navigate the tunnels. This light would finger its way to her dungeon. In those pockets of sight, she would be able to see *them*.

Them …

They were in human form, but they were not human.

They looked like something out of a *Marvel* comic: dark and covered in some type of skin, like snake scales. Their eyes were black, and their mouths filled with fangs. *Was she in a nightmare? What was this place? Why had they taken her?* The horror of what she saw each time reduced her to hysteria.

Eventually the true purpose of her abduction became clear when the dominant one came and defiled her. This male was clearly the leader. The others seemed deathly afraid of him. It took time to recover, to stabilize again after each violation.

In order to study them. She knew that she must in order to plot her escape. There would be something in their habits that would be a weakness. There had to be some way out of this black hole of despair. A way back to the light.

There were males, females. Some appeared more human, besides their eyes, which were completely black. They wore hoodies pulled down low over their faces. Sometimes she even thought that she heard children. She guessed as many as twenty comprised this group, maybe more. It was hard to tell.

Nest.

That's what they were.

A nest.

Once in a while Catherine could make out whispers in French. She had tried many times to speak to them in English, in French, but it made no difference. They kept her in one place, but it was evident that they occupied a network of underground caves.

One of the leaders did not defile her. He would loiter outside of her chamber and stare at her. Sometimes, he brought wild berries and animal skins to sleep on. She sensed a profound sadness in his eyes. Out of all of them he appeared to be the most human. But in this dark, foul hole it was difficult to determine if anything could be truly good.

Catherine's hope had been to persuade this one to help her. She had also intended to win over some of the younger ones. They were ghoulish looking, like zombies, but when they brought her food, they seemed genuinely curious. So, she endeavored to win their trust.

Her plan would work too if only a certain female wasn't around.

Freakish like the others, with the same black eyes, dead skin, and strange way of moving. But she seemed to be in charge when the dominant male wasn't around. And she watched Catherine like a hawk. Nothing got past her.

She can read my mind.

Catherine had so many questions. Why had she been kept alive? What was their agenda? Where did they come from? Where were they headed? If they had snatched her, whom else would they take? Why would they keep a man down here too?

Then it hit her.

Breeding.

Nest ...

Yet even that thought was a cruel irony. How long would it take for them to figure out that she was infertile? What would happen to her once they found out?

Colony (2)
Rousinac, Southwest France 2019

She was so sad and pure in her innocence, the fair one. It was an abomination. The Anglaise were their allies in the war. They should never have killed the man and taken his woman. But there was something else, something in the woman's blue eyes that spoke to him of Cecile, his beloved.

There were so many questions.

Who were the intruders? Had they come to rescue the woman? The man taken, certainly knew the woman's name.

Catherine.

It was a shame. The man would not last long. Gerard would eventually silence him. Only fertile females survived a year or more.

Daniel Malraux longed to lead these innocents up through the tunnels to a hilltop vineyard. Where, among the vines, he would lead them to a weather-beaten cottage. And in the shadows of the grapevines, he would call out to the blood of his blood above ground.

He would beg his forgiveness and speak in a low, heart-wrenching cadence. He would give the innocents over even though it would seal his fate. But Gerard Dupre could read his thoughts and he guarded the innocents closely. There could be no end to this misery so long as Gerard was alive.

This torment must end ...

Daniel had asked his son to find a priest, to receive an absolution for the darkness that festered. But now ... after this latest butchery could there be any forgiveness left? Should he tell his boy Pierre to seal up the tunnels and flood them.

Would it end there?

Daniel loped along the tunnels until he reached an entrance where the moon shone brightest. He came to this spot often, to remember his wife, Cecile and his son.

Daniel had stroked Cecile's swollen belly as the child inside turned.

"It's a boy, I just know it," she purred.

"Then we shall call him Pierre after your father."

Daniel Malraux closed his tired eyes in the moonlight and ran the story over in his mind. He needed to remember what he once was and what he had become.

He must never forget.

Colony (3)
Rousinac, Southwest France 1945

It had been several weeks since the Second World War was officially declared over and yet people were still dying. Landmines continued to harvest. German soldiers disorientated and now hunted were capable of desperate acts when cornered.

Reclaiming freedom was a painful slow step. Everyone's nerves had been shattered, and a terrible sense of loss hung in the air. Prisoners of war returned home tattered and half-dead. The dead were buried, barbed wire taken down.

Only the animals and children knew no better. Their innocent sounds rhythmically called for the people to heal, and they began to, in sharp bursts and heaving agonies. People grew used to men weeping and silent women. So much had happened. So much had been done.

Where were our men? People whispered.

And then, one crisp Fall day.

Frederic Arriver had found them in the woods.

He had somehow known where to go. The four Maquis men: Gerard Dupre, Pierre Malraux, Charles and Philip Perodeau were covered in blood and voiceless. How they'd gotten there from the castle, nobody knew nor dared to ask.

The people came and took them home.

At first, exhaustion had overwhelmed the newly liberated men. They slept for weeks, for hours on end *like newborns*. People joked.

But their nights were plagued with nightmares, their waking hours by horrific hallucinations. And then there was the odor.

Other issues quickly surfaced.

The men would grow quick to anger, to uncontrollable violence. When Phillipe Perodeau discovered that his nephew had drunk a bottle of his best cognac, he had beaten the teen half to death.

Sunlight burned their eyes. Their skin was darker, tougher. They kept themselves covered up. The noise and bustle of daily life agitated them. But the nights brought a preternatural alertness and peace.

The black heart of Rousinac's forest called to them.

Individually, they would escape and head there. They could smell prey. They would track and hunt, naked, barefoot. Each man connected to an emergent nature.

In the beginning, they felt ashamed of the savagery that lurked just beneath the surface. Then, one cold winter's night just before dawn, every Maquis man found his other.

Brothers ...

The men soon began to hunt as a pack, and they rejoiced in their wildness. As those nocturnal activities grew in importance, homelife became less so.

Although their men were back where they belonged, the women knew that something was gravely wrong. They naively believed that love could close the gaping black void, the strangeness.

It took time, in agonizing realizations, to chip away at that hope.

A coldness slowly crept into Rousinac, home by home. Elation ebbed away and was replaced by secrecy. A fear firmly kept behind closed doors. A secret kept within certain families.

Nicole Dupre had noticed it first: the family dogs avoided her husband. In fact, all of the animals seemed wary around him. *The men who had returned were not the fathers, husbands or sons that they had once been*, the families quietly confided in one another.

The chattering began in earnest once the men universally refused to attend church. The Maquis women huddled together at the back of the chapel and whispered. They desperately needed answers.

The Padre had none.

Nicole knew that Gerard now followed her everywhere. *He is paranoid*, she told Cecile, *he thinks we are secretly meeting with the Germans!* Cecile had advised patience, even though her sweet Daniel was becoming more distant.

Daniel, like the other Maquis men, now spent his days asleep, apart from Cecile in a separate room. He would no longer undress in front of her or take a bath. Their sporadic lovemaking, which had always been deep and passionate, was now a mechanical function. It left her feeling violated, like an animal. He avoided his newborn son.

There can be no secrets for long in a town like Rousinac.

And so, it began like this.

A relative of Nicole Dupre's who worked at the Maire's (mayor's) town hall discovered that Rousinac's top officials were receiving money wires directly from Paris each month.

New buildings, businesses were popping up everywhere - *all paid for by someone and for what?* Certain people were lining their pockets. The rumor was that the government was wiring the officials money that was meant as a pension for the Maquis men.

It was the trigger everyone needed. Nicole Dupre, Cecile Malraux, and some of the other women stormed the Maire's (mayor's) office one morning to find out if this was true.

"I understand how difficult it is for you ladies and I am personally working on getting a pension for each and every one of our brave heroes," explained Monsieur Ribault under a barrage of accusations.

"Forget it! We already know that you take money from the government, you shameless shit. My husband would kill you with one hand were he capable of understanding how you and your family capitulated with the enemy during occupation!" Nicole spat on the Maire's floor.

He languidly rolled his eyes.

"The money is for reconstruction Madame. Every region is getting these payments. But while we are on the subject, what are we going to do about your men?"

'What are you talking about?" Nicole yelled back.

"Don't you think I have been lenient with the complaints from your neighbors and the strange goings on in the woods? People are afraid to go out at night even the *chasse* (hunting group) refuses to hunt. And then there are the unexplained thefts of sheep, pigs, cows and even horses now. Everyone in Rousinac sympathizes but if this carries on, I will have no choice but to send in the Gendarme."

"You have a short memory," Cecile sneered.

"Look, the war is over. People just want to rebuild their lives. Your men were casualties of the war but we all were. And this simply can't go on."

The women stood, unable to speak.

"How dare you!" Nicole launched herself at the Maire. Cecile pulled her off.

His face clouded.

"They're not normal!" He shouted.

"They frighten people. What are we going to do? Huh? Tell me that? Maybe we should take them back to the dungeons." He sat back in his chair and lit a cigarette.

The women understood. Nicole's eyes flashed at Cecile. *Let's go.* Satisfied his threat had worked, the Maire dismissed them from his office.

A few months later, that Maire vanished. Nobody knew how or why. Although it was whispered, he was embezzling the town to support a mistress. One of the Perodeau cousins became the new Maire, and a Dupre the head of police.

The Maquis families now had Rousinac in their control. They closed ranks in the small, secluded town. A few bad apples were warned off, old debts got settled in alleyways, neighbors turned a blind eye.

Underneath it all their sympathy pulsed for the Maquis families. Rousinac's inhabitants had endured a thousand years of revolution, wars and plagues. They'd stuck together through good times, through bad times. They honored their heroes.

Blood was blood.

Still, certain villagers kept their children in at night during the summer months. Women didn't walk home alone past a certain hour. Farmers and hunters kept clear of the deepest parts of the forest.

No one talked about it.

The town's priest arranged for a special mass to bring about healing. Out of respect for the Maquis men they held it in the woods at midnight. One clandestine meeting led to another, and a core group formed, mostly of relatives. Their bitterness and pain twisted into a Cause.

But nothing could close the chasm between the Maquis men

and their families. One day they simply failed to return home. What occurred between then and now belongs to another book.

The fact is, back in 1945 a secret became a Cause, and with the passing of time, a Cause became an Order to protect the Maquis men..

Blood is blood, after all.

That had been it.

That had been the beginning of The Custodians.

The Locals (11)
Rousinac, Southwest France 2019

It was market day in Rousinac. The town thronged with locals keen to get the freshest produce and best deals.

Laetitia Dupre was loading groceries into the back of her Citroen when Claude Dubonnet, the new Deputy Police Chief, pulled up alongside her.

"Bonjour Laetitia."

"Ah, bonjour Claude."

"Welcome home. You just got back?"

"Yes, just getting stocked up as you can see."

"How was Paris?"

"Wonderful as always but the weeks flew by."

"And how's Christopher Malraux?"

"Good. My cousin sends his regards."

Pause.

"Did you hear about Didier Perodeau?"

"No, what?"

She slammed the trunk shut and approached the police vehicle. Claude gestured *drinking alcohol* with his hand.

"Not good."

Laetitia shrugged.

"He's a rotten drunk. What's he done this time?"

"Well, it would have been justice if he'd just hit a tree and died."

"What?"

"He's dead but unfortunately he hit two other cars head on." Claude clapped his hands together.

"Pfff! Killed four other people just like that."

"Who?"

"Oh, you wouldn't have known them. Outsiders. An English couple and two Americans." He studied her face as the news registered.

"I see."

"At any rate, the crash was so bad ....the metal was like liquid. No bodies."

Pause.

"It took three hours to put out the fire."

Pause.

"Perodeau just happened to be carrying six full gas cylinders back from town. Whoosh! They all went up. You could see the smoke for miles."

Bodies.

Her mind clicked back into focus.

"So how could you identify the ..."

"*Some of our locals* saw the whole thing. So, from their descriptions we were able to tell who the victims were."

"And the British police were satisfied?"

"Yes. We notified all the relevant authorities. It was an open and shut case. A tragic accident."

"When did this happen?"

"Just after you left for Paris."

"How awful."

"Yes, Laetitia, just *awful*." A faint smile erupted.

"Ce la vie."

Laetitia leaned against the police car and groaned. An enormous burden had been lifted from her shoulders.

"It's over." He leaned over and gently tapped her hand.

"It was kept out of the papers, just so you know. We didn't want to scare any tourists away because of one bad fly in the ointment, eh?"

"Of course."

"Anyway, I just wanted you to know."

"Thanks. How's my uncle doing?"

"Not good. Patrick Clayburn's in charge now."

"Patrick?"

Laetitia held Claude's eye. Claude was the nephew of Rousinac's former Police Commissioner. A man now retired. Claude's deep connections would likely land him in his uncle's shoes. More importantly, three generations ago their families had been joined in marriage.

Blood.

"It's a temporary position. We all know what you did for Rousinac. You're the leader now."

Claude put his car into gear.

"Let's have a drink soon, okay? I can fill you in."

"I look forward to it. Take care."

As the police car rolled away, Laetitia looked back at Rousinac's castle and sighed.

"Finally... Finally, it's over."

The Locals (12)
Rousinac, Southwest France 2019

News of Laetitia's return had reached her uncle's ears.

But Pierre Malraux had no intention of seeing her. Her transgressions had surpassed his ability to forgive.

Because of her more innocent lives had been taken. A fellow Custodian had been murdered. Didier was bad news, but he was *blood*. Patrick Clayburn had seized power and surrounded himself with cronies. He was sure Patrick was drugging him.

None of that mattered anymore.

More importantly, his prayers had been answered. He had found a priest just outside of Rousinac's principality.

Perhaps now his father's torment could end.

Padre Alain Boussuet (named after his uncle, a Maquis man, who had died while still a boy) was from Rousinac originally. He would surely understand what needed to happen next.

Pierre's 1986 Renault drew little attention mid-morning as it growled to a halt in a tidy village square. He quickly spied his destination. The chapel maison was a humble affair, small and made of tumbled stone. Its battered wooden door was always left open an inch or two. The priest had a reputation for sympathy even toward those cast outside of the Catholic holy family.

Pierre Malraux was expected. A phone-call from his cousin Teresa had seen to that. And although it was only 11am in the morning two small glasses of Pineau de Charentes had been poured and were set on a small table. As he entered the priest's lounge Pierre observed that the Padre was sitting quietly with his hands pursed together as if in prayer.

In his lap lay a leather bound book filled with a handwritten code of honor known simply as *The Plan*. Padre Boussuet had read its contents from cover to cover several times, over the past two weeks, when Teresa had slipped it to him after mass.

The Maquis families knew about *The Plan*, but few were ordained to read it let alone administrate its rules. It had jarred the Priest how little of *The Plan's* decree involving Germans had disturbed him.

Every fiber in his body felt a natural sympathy for the justice that called for *an eye for an eye, the sins of an entire generation to be visited upon the next*. The moral authority cited for revenge came from the Old Testament. The language used sounded biblical in tone. The argument was simple:

A great crime had been perpetrated against the people of Rousinac by another nation. This was not the sin of war. This crime was spiritual. It had demanded human compensation.

They had burned women and children inside of churches. They had altered men's natures perhaps even snatched their souls. Yes – yes, this was an abomination. There must be a sacrifice and atonement.

German blood in return for Rousinac blood until the seventh generation.

But now, after hours of prayerful meditation the Padre understood that *The Plan* was simply a warped system of revenge fomented out of a terrible pain. It was evil and it must be stopped.

He would have to tell this small, broken man from Rousinac that redemption for his crimes and those of his Custodian brethren were out of the Padre's hands, and that no absolution whatsoever could be offered to the monsters underground.

"Bonjour Padre," Pierre bowed, eyeing the book in the priest's lap. The priest smiled although he did not rise. He was younger than Pierre, but his back was playing up. He indicated as much, and Pierre groaned in sympathy.

Pierre took a chair opposite and for a few minutes the two men simply sipped at their liqueur.

"You must know why I am here Padre," Pierre finally broke the silence. His companion arched his eyebrows and sighed.

"I wondered when this day would come." He replied.

"Is it possible?" Pierre leaned forward penitently.

"Possible?"

"For absolution to be given?"

"To be given, perhaps, to be obtained, I am not so sure." The Priest dashed a look to his front door. It had been left ajar. Threading his glance Pierre jumped up and closed it with a thud.

"Does not the mercy and grace of our Holy Father extend to those who were violated by those Nazi monsters?" He said breathlessly as he crossed back to his seat.

"Of those mysteries I do not know. But I do know what has occurred since and two wrongs do not make a right." The priest's tone was neutral. He solemnly passed *The Plan* back to Pierre.

"The abomination was not ours, Padre. It was committed by *them*! Their blood must be shed. Blood for blood!" Pierre remonstrated.

The Padre raised his hand, but he did not speak. Pierre bit his tongue although it suddenly occurred to him for the first time in his life that the old Rousinac priest back in 1945 might have got things wrong. Perhaps the entire town of Rousinac was now damned to eternal judgment?

"Will you offer my father the sacraments? Will you give him hope so that he can die in peace?" Pierre heard his voice twist into a plea. The men locked eyes, but no words were spoken.

There followed a horrible, heavy silence. Pierre glossed over some framed prints behind the priest's head. The clock ticked. A donkey brayed in the distance.

The Padre's chin began to tremble. Suddenly he felt the conflict surge up in him again. His blood was at war with his conscience. In the presence of his kin this battle between flesh and spirit was fiercest.

Alain had grown up knowing about the Maquis men. He understood what they had become. His mother's own brother - a mere boy - had been experimented upon like some lab rat. Mercifully, God had taken his soul before the Germans.

No, if the Maquis had been robbed of their humanity it wasn't their fault. The abomination had sprung from Germany, from the Devil himself. It was not his place to judge anyone. Christ had died for all. If not him, then who else could lead them back to the Holy family?

He nodded. *Yes.*

"Oh, mercy upon mercy, father." Pierre Malraux fell into a child-like sob. He kissed the Padre's hand with a force that was painful.

"But your father must come to the light, no matter the consequences to his mortal body, do you understand?" The priest spoke in a hushed tone. Pierre nodded.

His father would need to free the innocent ones, leave the tunnels and face the consequences. He knew that Gerard Dupre would come after his father, hunt him down.

"It would be a death sentence for my father, but one that he now willingly embraces," Pierre tearfully told the priest. They clasped one another tightly.

"To the mercy of God's judgment and eternal grace we will give the soul of Daniel Malraux, my cousin. The Lord's yoke is kind." The Padre gently offered.

Together they made the necessary arrangements.

The Custodians (1)
Rousinac, Southwest France 2019

It had been an exhausting day at Cafe Napoleon. As Laetitia locked up, she contemplated a long bath and a glass of wine. Through the front window she watched Sylvie dive into a car to kiss her fiancé.

"Young love …"

She suddenly felt old. Claude was buzzing around her these days. But it would take time to remove David Frankel completely from her conscience. She poured a hefty glass of merlot and made her way up the stairs.

Her cell rang.

"Hello?"

"This is an abomination," Pierre Malraux groaned. "The Order will not go on. I forbid it. …!"

It wasn't the first drunken phone call. There had been many in recent months. He often ranted about vineyard meetings with his father and absolution. He was becoming a liability. She tried to calm him down.

"Uncle you need to rest …"

"They're coming."

"Who?"

"Them?"

"Them."

"Yes, *them*. They're coming above ground."

"Get some sleep."

"Laetitia, this must end. We must seal up the tunnels."

She hung up.

Laetitia tapped speed dial.

"I was just about to call you I swear." Claude Dubonnet gasped.

"Why?"

"You're not going to believe it."

"Go on."

Colony (4)
Rousinac, Southwest France 2019

The Deputy Police Chief informed Laetitia that Rousinac police station was now dealing with numerous incidents, trespassing, and multiple break ins involving odd-looking intruders.

People are getting jumpy.

Locals.

Incident 1: afternoon, the day before.

Outside her cottage, Madame Gullet was customarily sweeping her back step. After this sweep she would sit in her grandmother's chair and take in the view. Just beyond her garden a thick green line of trees advanced. Every year they came closer to the house, at a sapling's step.

She didn't have the strength to uproot them.

Once this had been a valley of vines. Rolling hills of green tilled by generations of her kin. Now, just one vine-field remained, although it was overgrown. The vine leaves indistinguishable from the weeds.

Such a pity the young live in boxes when they could grow their own wine …

She clucked her tongue at an imaginary guest.

But then ….

As the setting sun toyed with the foliage, the woman noticed two shadows heading in her direction. The only inhabited house for miles around.

Madame Gullet backed up onto her step, fumbling for the doorknob behind her. There had been whispers of strange goings on, gangs of kids roaming the countryside and even some break-ins. Derelict houses seemed to be their target.

She bolted the sturdy oak door shut and leaned her back against it. Luckily all the shutters were closed, windows locked. She hurried inside.

BANG! BANG! BANG!

They were at the door.

With every thud the door buckled, but she made no sound. Someone fiddled with the latch. *They were trying to break in.* Madame Gullet wanted to call out to her husband, to her children, to her neighbors but they had all long gone. She would be the last bird to fly.

Silence.

Her hearing wasn't good, but she could vaguely make out - *panting*, was it? Yes it was the sound of panting.

"You must help us madame, please!"

Was that English?

She couldn't understand a word. But a stink worse than a tramp seeped under the door. *Anyone who smelled that bad couldn't be up to much good.*

She stifled a gag.

"Please we just need water!"

What were they saying? Probably a trick. Vagabonds. Thieves. There must be others, hiding in the bushes.

Her son had warned her about these types. No matter, she would grab her husband's air gun, then creep down the hallway and call the police.

Outside, two naked figures snaked their way back toward an outside tap. The old lady heard them turn it on and drink. Gasps of relief followed.

The voices were muffled but she had definitely heard Anglais.

Incident 2: dusk, same day.

A bungalow set in a large well-kept garden on the outskirts of Rousinac.

Stefan Delahaye, a retired captain in the Foreign Legion, was putting away his lawn mower when he sensed someone approaching. Widowed, childless, Delahaye now lived alone.

He preferred his own company and rarely engaged with his neighbors, who lived a mile away behind a wall of woodlands. His hearing was bad, impacted through active service, abroad in Africa and elsewhere. Explosions, chaos, war, human misery, he had seen and heard it all.

All he wanted was a few short years of peace before he died. Nowhere was quieter than Rousinac, the home of his ancestors. Now, as the day drew to a close, he began to feel uneasy. He made for the backdoor of his home.

Click!

Lock!

Double locked.

He'd had no time to close the door shutters and the door itself was glass, shatterproof and reinforced, but nevertheless - glass. A sledgehammer would be able to penetrate it.

Merde.

Thud, thud, thud!

They were running up to the door now. At least two of them.

They're quick, probably kids.

He hadn't been able to move away from the door in time.

W-w-what the ....?

He stood transfixed, inches away from two hooded figures on the other side of the door. They were teens no older than fourteen, fifteen, he estimated. He could barely make out their faces, but they were pointing to their mouths.

Were they hungry?

That's when Delahaye noticed their nails, long and black, curled at the ends into sharp points.

Claws?

Putain-putain-putain!

Chest pain spasmed up his right arm. Then his military training kicked in and he found himself running to the pantry to grab a rifle. It was the distance of a long corridor, but when he reached the room, they were already there, looking at him through the pantry window. It was unnatural how fast they'd moved.

Delahaye had toured the world's shit holes with his unit, but he'd never encountered anything like this. He just stood there staring at them..

Slowly, they pulled back their hoodies. They were as pale as corpses, with eyes as black as *black, black as fucking night!*

N-not possible.

They looked past him, spotting a row of sausages strung up

behind. The taller one pointed toward it then to its mouth. But Delahaye couldn't move and that's when they screamed.

W-what the …? Canines? Holy … Jesus ….!!

He yanked at the emergency cord that ran directly to Rousinac's police station. They'd be here within the hour he knew.

Can I hold that long?

Could I shoot them?

The questions didn't even surface. They were obliterated by what came next.

More of them.

Everywhere.

BANG! BANG! BANG!

Every door, every window was under attack.

Delahaye crashed to the floor, a fatal cardiac arrest and fractured skull took him out instantly. It was a small mercy. Moments later the back door was smashed and the intruders were in.

Incident 3: late evening, same day.

A young married couple in their twenties, Mabelle and Laurent Gauthier, were driving home from a family dinner. It had been a boozy affair. They were both over the alcohol limit and as a way to avoid the Gendarmerie they'd taken the back-roads home from Rousinac to their village.

Most of the journey had been in silence. They were both fixated on the road ahead as though they were driving through a war zone with checkpoints.

"We shouldn't have come this way." Mabelle finally said.

"The street lights are still on. We've got time."

"We should have left sooner."

"No one forced you to keep drinking."

"We could have stayed over. My mother ..."

"Mabelle! Stop, please! We're doing this. We're almost home ..."

They fell into silence until they saw the steeple tip of their village church. Mabelle let out a long sigh and settled back into her chair.

Finally.

The country road thinned into a tree lined lane. Branches arched over and touched, forming a green tunnel. But then, Laurent sensed movement to his right. Mabelle sat forward.

"W-what was that?"

"Don't know"

"Slow down Laurent!"

Two hooded figures emerged from the side and stood in the middle of the road. One of them was bare-foot.

"I'm not stopping." He honked the horn and slowed down.

"They're just kids!"

"No they're not."

Click! Click!

The car locks clicked off and back on.

"Just checking."

The figures did not move even when Laurent flashed his full beams. The car ground to a stop. The figures split up and stood either side of the car. One indicated for Mabelle to lower her window. She couldn't move.

Laurent switched on the interior lights revealing the strangers' faces.

"W-what the ...!?"

The hooded figures looked like the walking dead. Eyes as black as hell, mouths filled with canines. Monsters. Zombies. Aliens. Fucking whatevers unnatural. Then a stink filled the car like rotten game hung up to cure. Laurent gagged.

The couple screamed in unison when one of the figures tried to open Mabelle's door. Laurent scrambled to get the car into gear but it had stalled. He frantically tried to start it. Metal ground against metal and the air filled with the smell of burning rubber.

One of the figures jumped onto the car bonnet and attempted to open it. The other began pulling and kicking at the back doors, then the trunk. Then it thumped at the windows.

Thwack!

Thwack!

A single crack splintered up one side of Mabelle's door window. Encouraged by this, the other joined in.

Thwack-thwack-thwack!

"LAURENT!"

Laurent closed his eyes and took a deep breath, then slowly he turned the ignition and put the car into first gear. He lowered the handbrake with an excruciating care, and tapped the accelerator with his heel.

Vroom!

They pulled away at the same time as Mabelle's window shattered. Thousands of square shards flew everywhere blown by the speed of the car. Laurent looked in his rear view mirror just the once. When they'd pulled into their drive.

The Custodians (2)
Rousinac, Southwest France 2019

Claude had stopped talking.

There was a significant pause.

He could hear the static on their line.

What would she say?

"You know how the local kids get high and wear those weird contact lenses. And there have been so many raves in derelict houses. The music is crazy at all hours. They sound like junkies to me. Look, I've heard of this kind of thing before, but you did the right thing, reassuring people."

Claude Dubonnet groaned, "Jesus, Laetitia, don't treat me like an idiot."

She knew what he was saying. The lights were no longer a deterrent. A code had been violated. They were encroaching into people's lives.

"Well we have bigger problems right now. My uncle has lost the plot. We'll need to watch him closely and his lackeys."

"We need to call a meeting."

"No. He needs to be put into residential care. A place we can control."

Her coldness bothered him.

"Okay."

"I will talk with Clayburn about that." Laetitia fingered around in her bedside cabinet for a packet of cigarettes.

"And what about …" Claude added.

The phone was dead.

Claude Dubonnet turned the cell over in his hand as he thought about the last few months. There was some weird stuff going on. He could feel it, *but what?* Were the senior Custodians keeping him out of the loop even now? He had more than proven himself with Didier Perodeau and the foreigners.

Well, he wouldn't take it lying down.

The Custodians (3)
Rousinac, Southwest France 2019

Laetitia had arrived at Patrick Clayburn's house without remembering the route she'd taken. So intense were her thoughts.

He looked shattered.

Calming Pierre Malraux down with sedatives had become a full-time job. As he led her into his study, he reached up for a vintage port and poured them both a generous measure.

She told him everything.

Silence.

Laetitia knew Patrick well enough to recognize that when he reached for his pipe and began a ritual for smoking, that he was ruminating.

The situation was dire.

It wasn't just the cops that were hearing about encounters. Many others had too. People were beginning to talk. The street lights were no longer working it seemed. Things were going missing. No one felt safe anymore.

Patrick didn't want to bring that up, not now. Laetitia was clearly agitated.

The reality was that there were too many sightings, too many intrusions.

It was becoming impossible to keep a lid on things. Once the holidays began the villages surrounding Rousinac would be filled with visiting families. How could they prevent more trouble? There would be parties, walks in the woods with children.

They leave us no choice.

"We have to do something Laetitia."

"Yes, yes, I know." She raised her hand.

He felt dismissed, subordinate.

"They must be stopped!" He shouted.

He searched Laetitia's face for agreement. Instead, she turned away. He furiously smoked for a while.

It was a fucking ticking time bomb. How long would it be before someone made a phone call, took a photograph?

Didier Perodeau's face flashed up in his mind. His gut tightened.

What about the Brits, the Americans? Murder. Putain!

Clayburn fixed his eyes on Laetitia. She knew he wanted a response. None came. His pipe clacked against his teeth, a sign that his hand was trembling.

A sudden call on Laetitia's cell phone broke the silence and made them both jump. Laetitia saw Claude's number flash.

"Answer it. It's probably important." Patrick Clayburn urged.

"Hello."

"Are you with Clayburn?"

"Yes, why?"

"There's no easy way to say it."

"Say what?"

"Someone sealed and flooded the tunnels."

"WHAT!?"

"You heard me."

Patrick Clayburn had heard it too.

Click!

She took out a cigarette and began to smoke. Six drags in, she spun around and snarled.

"You look relieved Patrick."

"I am."

"Is this your handiwork? First Perodeau, and now …"

"No! Absolutely not, what do you take me for?" He stood up, eyeballed her. She backed off.

There was an uncomfortably long pause.

It was likely someone loyal to Pierre Malraux, as the old man was now largely confined to his bed. They independently concluded.

"So, Laetitia … what now?"

She slugged her drink and turned to Patrick Clayburn with cold, black eyes.

"There's only one thing we can do."

Resistance (1)
Rousinac, Southwest France 2019

At the same time as Laetitia Dupre was at Patrick Clayburn's, and somewhere on the outskirts of Rousinac, there was another break in.

Two naked figures lay huddled together in the far corner of the rafter they'd climbed into. A stand-to ladder had been pulled up to prevent anyone following them. Dogs had kept them from approaching the farmhouse. It was freezing in the barn but at least it was safe, the woman thought.

A siren sounded in the distance.

"Gendarme?" The man said.

"No, sounds like a fire truck. Anyway, it's moving away from us."

"We've got to try to get some clothes, some food. We need to keep moving."

"No. It's not safe."

Pause.

"They come out at night."

"Do you think they can track us?"

"How?"

"Through our minds?"

Silence.

Suddenly, they heard a rustle in the bushes outside the barn.

Neither of them spoke. They lay as still as corpses, hardly daring to breathe.

Then.

A fox barked at its companion.

"Just an animal." The man whispered. They dug further into the coarse hay that surrounded them, and shared the same thought.

If they find us, they will take us back …

Neither David Frankel or Catherine Grayston slept a wink that night.

About the Author

Jacalyn S. Burke, a British-American writer, entrepreneur and artist, moved to the US in 2002 to document the emerging Street Art scene in New York City. For the next fifteen years she worked as a tutor, a governess/nanny, an artist, a tech start up founder and a commercial artist.

In 2015, Praeger (now Bloomsbury) published Jacalyn's non-fiction work, *The Nanny Time Bomb – Navigating the Crisis in Child Care.* The book was based upon Jacalyn's experiences working for Manhattan's 1% and was reviewed by *The New York Times*, in the 'Wealth Matters' weekly column.

Through her work as an artist Jacalyn self-sponsored an immigration path, becoming a US citizen in 2017, as "an alien of extraordinary ability."

In 2018 Jacalyn relocated to SW France to realize a long-held dream of writing fulltime. Along with her partner Kate, she began to renovate an 18th Century farmhouse and the land about it. During this time she began two novels: *The Custodians* and *Wall Street Diva* as well as non-fiction projects. During the pandemic and subsequent lockdowns, Jacalyn continued to write and all book projects were completed in the Fall of 2022.

Jacalyn is a graduate of Middlesex University, the Morris School of Journalism and the School of Visual Arts.